COLD CRASH

JENNIFER YOUNG

INDEPENDENT INNOVATIVE INTERNATIONAL

Published by Cinnamon Press
Meirion House,
Tanygrisiau,
Blaenau Ffestiniog
Gwynedd LL41 3SU
www.cinnamonpress.com

The right of Jennifer Young to be identified as author of this work has been asserted by her in accordance with the Copyright, Designs and Patent Act, 1988. © 2017 Jennifer Young. ISBN 978-1-910836-77-4
British Library Cataloguing in Publication Data. A CIP record for this book can be obtained from the British Library.

Designed and typeset in Garamond by Cinnamon Press. Cover design by Adam Craig © Adam Craig.

Cinnamon Press is represented by Inpress and by the Welsh Books Council in Wales. Printed in Poland.

The publisher gratefully acknowledges the support of the Welsh Books Council.

Acknowledgements

This novel wouldn't be possible without my wonderful husband Joe Flatman. We dreamed up Max together over drinks at our local pub one rainy Saturday. Joe has endlessly listened, given advice and supported me throughout every stage of the novel's development. He's also been a fantastic archaeological and historical consultant! Thanks are owed to Cathy Young for being a superb reader, to Martin Flatman for steam train advice and to Bela, Simon, Bertie and JLD Hughes and Kyra Larkin for moral support (and babysitting). Thanks also to Frances Flatman and Dave Young for their encouragement.

Jan Fortune has been the most amazing mentor I could ever imagine. She brings such warmth to the process of editing and writing, and even allowed a two-year-old Zoe and Joe to come with me to a writing retreat in Wales. Thanks to everyone at Cinnamon Press, particularly the Debut Novel Prize judges, and to Adam Craig for the cover design. The School of Humanities at the University of Hertfordshire, especially Jeremy Ridgman, supported the writing of the novel as well as my mentorship with Cinnamon Press.

Finally, this work owes an enormous debt to my grandparents JW McCombs, Jr (1925-2015) and Rebecca Ann Towell McCombs (1927-2009) and their teaching across my life.

Information about Honor Frost's first dive was drawn from her book *Under the Mediterranean: Marine Antiquities* (London: Routledge, 1963).
Dedication quote from Ellie Stoneley, 2015.

To my daughter Zoe Anne Young Flatman

'…this time's our time, just me and you'.

COLD CRASH

Prologue

The blade nestled on the seabed beneath the crushed kelp. Had anyone else seen it in the thousand years since a storm washed it overboard from its Viking ship? Or had it slid out of a man's dying grip as the vessel tipped into the water? Max tilted her neck, fighting the constriction of her suit, and a finger of icy water cascaded down her spine. She yelped against her mouthpiece, but the sound simply absorbed into her bubbling expiration. Her crayon floated away on its string. She reached out to recapture it, the slow movement of her arm, encased in black rubber, still baffling her. She had rendered the sword fragment as accurately as she could in thick gloves. On land, her drawing would have been precise.

She let the current drift her away from the area of bruised kelp. Half an hour in this murkiness. Time to surface, wrap herself in a blanket and consume as much coffee as the thermos contained. The damage to the kelp looked recent. Whatever caused it had to be bigger than her plane, and unlike the Viking ship, it had not remained on the seabed long. Her fin brushed over the waving fronds, and another dull glint emerged. Max forced herself lower and parted the long leaves. A blade, yes, but one not forged by Viking hands.

It matched the one strapped to her right thigh, but instead of being shiny and new this knife's handle bore dents and scrapes of long use. The water gave a startling crispness to the shape imprinted on its side. Worn, partial, but a letter. And not a Roman letter.

A tiny space remained on her tablet, and she made a rougher, faster sketch of the knife. The half letter she drew enlarged, positioning it beside the knife, and then she hooked the tablet on her weight belt. Thirty-five minutes underwater, but still she hesitated. The Viking sword needed to stay in situ. But this? This couldn't be more than ten years old.

The knife slid easily into the sheath on her leg, and she kicked her way towards the surface. The shadow of her boat broke, shuddered and reformed. Max floated, staring at the silhouette above. Maybe it always shifted like that. The down line she held stayed constant. She blinked. One mass. She continued to ascend, tracing her hand along the rope.

On the surface, Max spat out her mouthpiece and gulped air. Air that didn't taste like rubber, that she could inhale and exhale without the cacophony of noise underwater. How could Victor prefer diving to land archaeology? The grey clouds overhead matched the dark water breaking around her as she treaded water.

'Shame we missed each other in London, Dr Falkland.'

Max shuddered. His conversational voice couldn't reach the half-mile from shore. She could dive back down, escape —hide—but for how long? Maybe fifteen minutes of air remained. Pale sunlight glinted against her mask, and then she saw him. John Knox leaned against the wheelhouse of her boat.

'How did you find me?' she asked. If her voice wavered, well, the wind blowing against her wet hood and making her teeth chatter, would make anyone's teeth chatter. Her tablet knocked against her leg, tapping the blade. He would see the sketches. More to the point, he'd see the knife's Cyrillic letter.

'Guess how many pretty American women rent boats on the Isle of Mull in April.'

'I'm not American.' She peeled off her mask, the chill assaulting her eyes. Smoke curled from his cigarette. The narrow shape disrupting the left side of his blue jumper had to be a gun. She detached her tablet and kept it under the shadowy water.

'You sound it.'

His own accent had blurred into neutrality, a generic American that couldn't be pinpointed to a single state or region. Was anything about this man honest?

'I'd appreciate it if you kindly got the hell off my boat.' Her cold fingers worked to tie the tablet by its crayon's string to the line, but she had to bite off one glove to manage it.

'What are you doing?' He stepped towards the ladder and flicked his cigarette overboard, towards the small sailboat moored to her boat.

Her tablet plummeted, but at least he wouldn't reach it. She unfastened her weight belt quickly and heaved it over the side of the boat. He jerked his boot out of the way just in time.

'Not nice, Dr Falkland.'

'Bad aim.'

He reached his hand towards her. No sign of the gun. With a deep breath, she put her ungloved hand into the heat of his.

Chapter 1

Max touched the pad of her white-gloved thumb to her index finger. White. Six months of black, and now one day of white.

Tudor portraits with flat, serious faces lined the walls of the meeting room. Had wars been more straightforward in the Tudor period? Max specialised in Vikings, but surely the Tudors had called their wars wars, not police actions.

The President of the Society of Antiquaries cleared his throat. 'And now the primary business of the meeting, a paper entitled "Viking Age Settlement Patterns in the North Sea Region: Cardigan, Newport and Fishguard", given by fellow Professor Stephen Seaborn.'

As the lights dimmed and the slide projector whirred to life, Max fixed her gaze on the blur of Professor Seaborn's glasses. She would not think of George. This related to her work, her professional life. She folded her hands precisely, as the first slide clunked into place. By the third, she dug in her handbag uselessly for paper as she disagreed with every statement Professor Seaborn made. How had he made professor with this pitiable level of interpretation of Viking artefacts? She shouldn't have packed her bag for the theatre. Her father silently passed her a handkerchief, so she forced herself to sit still for the rest of the talk, knotting her fingers around the crisp linen.

The lecture ended, with coughs and rustlings, and the lights rose. Max shot her hand up, but the President called on every ungloved male hand rather than hers.

'As we are running a bit late, I believe this should be the last question.' He indicated an academic from Cambridge. That professor didn't ask a question at all—he droned about his own work, neither Viking nor Welsh. The speaker got away with no challenges. She handed her father his handkerchief.

'Sherry?' her father asked. 'What was your question?'

'Questions.' They stepped into the marbled entry hall from the formal meeting room. 'Specifically about methodology, to begin with, and then his interpretation of...'

'Max!'

They both turned, but the elderly gentleman bearing down on them clearly wanted her father. She let her hand slide from her father's sleeve and crossed the brass lamp embedded in the floor. She threaded her way through fellows whose suits smelled of stale wool. Professor Seaborn eventually would make his way into the other room. George would tell her how boring the whole thing was and demand they leave to find alcohol other than sherry.

The books here languished behind glass doors. She hadn't had the nerve to try them, but they must be locked. She had visited the library upstairs, to check a few things for her PhD, but tonight was the first meeting she'd attended. Observed. She did not take part. The Society did admit female fellows, but she was too young, too junior. The steward, resplendent in a blue and red coat, pointed out the sweet, medium and dry sherries, deepening from straw to dark honey in the small stemware. She stripped off her gloves and selected a glass of dry.

'I believe you wanted to ask Professor Seaborn something, Miss...?'

'Doctor,' she corrected, almost before she registered the slow cadence of his Southern accent. The way the question didn't lilt up as high as it would from a British man. 'Max Falkland.'

'John Knox.' He picked up a glass, sweet. His lips pursed as he sipped.

She hid a smile. 'Mister or doctor?' His erect posture suggested he'd seen military service, but that encompassed the vast majority of men in their late twenties she met. The grey suit implied that his service had finished.

'Mister.'

'Are you a fellow?' Beyond Mr Knox's elbow, Max saw Professor Seaborn come into the room, surrounded by other fellows. 'Mr Knox...' She glanced back as he replaced his glass, his hands tan against the white tablecloth. Did she have to carry every bit of the conversation? If she could ease away from the table... but his fingers closed around a silver cigarette lighter. Thick fingers, with clean, broad fingernails.

'He said you always had questions.' A small smile cracked his serious face.

'I beg your pardon?'

'Maxine.' Very few people called her Maxine, and only one would be here. Edward, her PhD supervisor, reached between them to pick up a medium sherry. 'What did you want to ask? Seaborn could have been your external examiner, you know. Have you met him? Did your father bring you?'

'Excuse me,' Mr Knox said. His fingers brushed her arm so lightly she thought she imagined it, and then Mr John Knox was gone.

Edward did not fall into the unwashed archaeologist category. His suits were as neat as Mortimer Wheeler's, and his reputation for far better manners with his female students had certainly been borne out across the three years of her PhD.

'Now, have you sent out your thesis to publishers yet?' Edward asked.

The crowd around her seemed entirely made up of men in their fifties or over, and not one stood as tall as Mr Knox.

'Job applications?'

'I don't need a job. I need...' She bowed her head, but fought to keep her shoulders straight. She could be looking down at the table, the crisp white cloth.

'Everyone goes down a bit after they finish their PhD. And you have had a difficult time.'

'No more than lots of people in the war.' She blinked at the dampness that was not tears. 'Do you know that man I was just speaking to?'

'You need to do something. Apply for a job. Establish a routine.'

'I wonder who he came with.' Guests could attend a Society meeting only with an introduction from a fellow. And introductions were minuted. She'd written her own name in the book next to her father's, her sloping M so similar to his. But the book had been taken into the meeting.

'Maxine, you've been a very promising PhD student. Are you really just going to subside into your parents' home and eventually marry some worthy man who won't be able to talk to you properly?'

Max looked up. He'd never said so much about her. 'I'm promising?'

'That's what you took away from that? Look, I'm sure it's your duty to carry on the line or something, but you could have a real academic's life. I'm going to Denmark for fieldwork next month. Victor Westfield may be there too—come with us. It'd do you good to get out of the library.'

'I can't carry on the line.' The clap of Professor Seaborn's hand landing on Edward's shoulder obscured her voice. Max concentrated on the sherry pooled in the bottom point of her glass as Edward and Professor Seaborn exchanged pleasantries and compliments. A grey sleeve joggled into view behind Professor Seaborn, but the suit adorned a man who had to be nearly ninety.

'Stephen, may I present Dr Falkland? Newly minted, no corrections,' Edward said.

Max finally got to raise her issue with his methodology, but before she and Professor Seaborn could progress to a dispute over interpretation, someone tapped her arm. A definite tap, not a brush.

'Your mother will be cross if we're late for the curtain,' her father said. 'Hallo, Edward.'

'You must be very proud, Lord Bartlemas.' They both smiled, and for once, the smile went all the way to her father's eyes. That hadn't even happened when she came home after her successful viva.

'Now, we must go.' A coat hung over her father's arm. He'd taken some other woman's coat, and now he'd have to put it... but the champagne coloured coat was hers. Not the black one she'd worn all winter long. This grosgrain silk suited late spring, with its freshness of air. And her mother had insisted. Max forced her own polite smile, even for the man who knew nothing about interpreting Viking archaeology, and then she crossed the brass lamp again. Her father pulled the heavy wooden door open, and they stepped out into the cool evening air.

'You disagreed with everything he said.'

'I believe his name is his name. And the title wasn't too bad.' Her father held the pale coat out for her, and the fabric settled over her arms. 'We could walk.' Sitting in the meeting, sitting in the taxi, sitting in the theatre.

'Don't be ridiculous. Besides, we'll be late.'

'And Mother would fuss.'

She stayed silent as they walked over the paving stones of the courtyard of Burlington House and out onto Piccadilly. The lights of Fortnum and Mason blazed. Bottles stacked in the window promoted new liquid shampoos, ones her mother no doubt already owned. Something had turned up in her bathroom, but she hadn't read the package yet. Only her shoes remained black. Max had tried to refuse wearing mourning in the first place. But now...

'Max?' Her father stood next to an open taxi door. 'Coming, darling?'

She slid into the taxi and her father climbed in beside her. 'Theatre Royal, Drury Lane, please.'

'Off to that *South Pacific*, are you? My missus wants me to take her,' the taxi driver said.

'We're meeting mine there.'

Even the thought of Nancy Falkland being called anyone's 'missus' couldn't raise a smile.

'Max, there were other questions that couldn't be asked. And someday you'll give a paper, and not long after that you'll be made a fellow.'

Max nodded. They sat in silence. 'It's not that. I, I didn't recognise my coat.'

Her father gave her hand three slow pats and a squeeze. 'Hmm. I wonder, would we be the first father-daughter pair of fellows in the history of the Society? No, surely Frederic Kenyon and Kathleen have beaten us.'

She let him talk about taking on the obligations of being a fellow of the Society of Antiquaries of London, while she leaned into the taxi's upholstery and stared at the lights of Shaftesbury Avenue.

'Do you know anyone named John Knox?' she asked. 'American. Southern.'

'The tall chap you were talking to over sherry?'

'Was he tall?'

'You noticed the accent but not his height? Nothing wrong with fancying an American. Worked for me.' Her father laughed, a real laugh that eased some of the stress out of her shoulders, far more than his squeeze of her hand had.

The taxi pulled up outside the theatre next to the full-sized posters of Mary Martin washing her hair. Vivian had brought the Broadway recording to London, so Max already knew all the songs. She had heard them over and over again in Vivian's flat while Max tried to coax the first words out of the sticky-fingered Bobby. She had ambitions for her godson to start speaking with basic archaeology terms, or at the very least 'Max', rather than the chorus of 'Nothing Like a Dame'.

Her mother she had no trouble recognising, despite her periwinkle blue coat. With her blonde hair coiled high, Nancy Falkland had managed to make mourning look stylish. Back in colour, she looked beautiful.

'You're late,' Mother said. Her grip on her husband's hand mollified the slight scold.

Dad consulted his wrist. 'Eight minutes to the curtain. Plenty of time.'

'Oh Max, all those lovely new clothes and you wear grey.'

'Your magazines say grey is in this season,' Max said.

'I thought you'd want to wear colour again.'

Max followed her parents into the theatre and up the stairs.

Why had they picked a wartime piece set in a hot country for their first outing? She laughed along with the audience at the dancing, but the chorus boy soldiers' fake New York accents grated. Nothing like... John Knox. Mr John Knox. Her parents both went to the lavatories at the interval, and she went to the bar to order drinks. In the queue, with 'Some Enchanted Evening' soaring in her mind, she idly listened to the chatter around her.

She reached the bar and opened her patent handbag, but a male hand placed a tumbler in front of her. An inch of smooth brown liquid filled the glass.

'I'm sorry...'

'It's already ordered, miss.' The barman turned to the couple behind her.

Her handbag's snap resonated too loudly. She closed her numbed fingers around the glass. Maybe her father... but he always ordered her champagne at the interval.

'My apologies that it isn't Oban.' John Knox placed just the correct amount of pressure on her elbow to steer her away from the bar, then immediately withdrew his hand. 'Still, better than sherry.'

'You chose your sherry poorly.' She sipped the whiskey. 'Thank you.' Without touching her, he guided them—shepherded her—through the crush of people to a small gap against the far wall. People simply shifted out of his way. He placed his own glass, also whiskey, on the narrow ledge next to them.

Max clenched her glass. 'Who are you, Mr John Knox?' Handsome, in his way, if you liked square-jawed, blue-eyed men with perfectly done dark hair. Max had seen—had danced with—too many of them in New York to find them attractive.

'Just an American in London.'

'Who knows my preferred whiskey.' Nor did he judge her for drinking it.

'And that your plane is a Beechcraft Bonanza, and you have a strong line in asking questions.'

'Yet I know nothing about you except that you are Southern. Virginia?'

'North Carolina.' The small smile emerged again. 'I can share, see? You should drink your whiskey. The intermission won't last much longer. Still driving the DB2?' He reached into his coat pocket. 'Cigarette?'

'Your sources didn't tell you I don't smoke?' The case went back in his pocket. 'You should, however, if you wish.'

'Darling, your father is at the bar.' Her mother's perfume announced her presence a half-second before her soft touch landed on Max's shoulder. 'Oh, I beg your pardon,' she said smoothly, although Max knew not a modicum of a chance existed that Nancy Falkland had not noticed that her daughter was speaking to a man.

'Mother, John Knox. Mr Knox, my mother, Lady Bartlemas.'

'It's very nice to meet you, ma'am.' He reached towards her hand, but her mother turned it into a shake.

'I like to shake hands with fellow Americans. How do...'

'I, ah, encountered Mr Knox at the Society of Antiquaries this evening.' And now he was here. Buying her a drink.

'I knew your son, ma'am. I was very sorry to hear about your loss.'

Max's glass froze at her lips. Her car, her plane, her whiskey. He knew George.

'Thank you,' her mother said, pitch perfect as always. Her father arrived, carrying only two glasses of champagne. He'd noticed too.

'Darling, this is John Knox. He served with George.' Nancy managed it without a hitch in her voice. Max could not have. The lights dipped for the end of the interval.

Dad shook his hand too. 'Very nice to meet you. You must join us for supper afterwards. It would be nice...' Her father trailed off for only a second. 'It would be good to talk.'

'Yes, sir.'

Max stared at John Knox's shoes. Tie shoes, not those new slip ons, and highly polished. The way 'sir' left his lips so sharply, he certainly had served. But he was old enough to have served in the real war, not the police action her brother had gone off to.

Her mother sipped her wine. 'Are you enjoying the play?'

The lights dipped again, and people pressed towards the theatre doors.

'Shall we meet in the lobby?' her father asked.

It was settled around her, in a quick blur. Did he smile a goodbye? He certainly murmured good evening, his Southern accent dripping over the soft, barely pronounced g.

When her back was finally towards him, she tossed back a huge swallow of the whiskey. Its burn soothed her.

18

'He seems charming,' Mother said.

'You think most Americans are charming.' Her father corralled her mother's drink and returned it to the bar. Max placed her tumbler beside their flutes.

How did they not rage? Shout? How did they just move on? Her friends did too, the other pilots in the Air Transport Auxiliary. Six of them had lost their husbands and kept on flying. But that was a proper war, not like... She took a deep breath and climbed the stairs behind her mother's swaying skirt. Maybe her mother gripped her father's hand a little too tightly as they proceeded along the narrow walkway towards the theatre doors. Max glanced over the railing, as always. The first time she flew, she'd felt this same frisson from her childhood, looking down the three storeys to the lobby floor below. The smallness of the enormous adults. Tonight she saw perfectly sculpted hair above broad grey shoulders. A slight pause to light a cigarette, to place a hat on black hair, and then polished shoes walked out the front door.

Max rose while the audience still applauded. George had no one to rescue him in Korea. No Emile. How much better to have him come home with some Korean woman? Max shook herself, the tiny silver tips on the shoestring bows on her bodice tinkling almost imperceptibly. She slid into her coat as her father held her mother's blue one.

'He's quite handsome,' Mother said. 'Polite.'

'Emile?' Max asked.

'Mr Knox, silly.'

'Your mother will have you engaged before the evening is out, Max.'

'I'm not interested in him!' Her mother's quick glance told her she'd spoken too sharply. 'He didn't tell me. About knowing George. He just kept talking...'

'Very few young men bring up deceased relatives when paying court.' Her father held the door of the box for her, and his hand trembled against the frame.

The last thing she needed was an evening of stories about George, about war, perhaps even about the day he died. Or worse, those questions not being answered, while her mother watched every flicker of eyelashes, every turn of her wrist for signs.

'I have a dreadful headache,' she said as they descended to the lobby. 'I'll take a taxi home.'

'You need food. Of course you get headaches when you drink whiskey and sherry and don't eat the cakes at the Society,' Dad said.

'I'll have something at home.'

'Max, it will be rude.' Her mother gripped her forearm.

'I'm going home.' She kissed her mother's cheek to soften it. 'Enjoy the evening.'

'Well, we'll wait here. Mr Knox will be disappointed.'

Max let a tight smile move her cheeks, and then she stepped out into blessedly cool air. She closed her eyes, the shadow of a headache beginning to form.

'Dr Falkland.'

Did the man follow her everywhere? 'My parents are inside. I'm afraid I have a headache, so...'

'I was just coming to apologise. I've been called away on an unavoidable matter, and I'm afraid I won't be able to join you for supper.'

'Is that why you skipped the second act?' He blinked. 'Or did you see the play at all? No matter what my parents may think, you aren't flirting with me. But you are following me. Now, if you'll excuse me.'

'What makes you think I'm not flirting with you?' He lit a cigarette with thick fingers.

'Everything about you, what you say—I don't know what you want from me.'

He exhaled, the thin stream of smoke floating away under the yellow street lights. 'If I were following you, wouldn't I take up the offer of supper?'

'There is no offer of supper from me. Good evening.' She turned away from him. A taxi. She needed a taxi.

'Aren't you bored staying in London, Dr Falkland?'

'Finishing my thesis was hardly boring.' It had been though; those awful days of retyping, editing, the frustration of finding a mistake halfway through a page and the way it knocked on to the pages beyond. She stepped towards the curb, but too many people waited for taxis. The street stayed empty.

'I doubt your brother would have wanted you to do this.'

Max started walking. Mr Knox kept pace with her, slowing his stride to allow for her high heels. 'I don't want to talk about George.' No one did. 'Mr Knox from North Carolina, please leave me alone.'

'Certainly. Excuse me.'

Her heels clicked ahead, and his heavier tread stopped. Max continued around the corner. A lit taxi. She waved, and it pulled over. At least he didn't rush to open her door. The taxi turned by the theatre, and Mr Knox lifted his hand in a wave as she passed.

Max readied her keys in the taxi. No one would expect her home so early, and she slipped in the front door unnoticed. She climbed the stairs to her room and flung the damned champagne coat on the floor. Her heels followed. She paced, trying her best to ignore the family photos on her dresser. The summer stretched before her, endless parties and theatre trips with her mother parading suitors past her.

The carpet felt soft against her stockinged knees as she reached under the bed, then stretched to grasp the edge of a box. Dust adorned its surface, despite the regular cleaning her room received. She hoisted it onto the counterpane. Once this box had held only items from her own war days.

Her Air Transport Auxiliary uniform, letters, a napkin that that pilot—Peter—had doodled on in a club. The day she came home to the news of George, she'd added all his letters and crushed the leather of her flight jacket over them. She hadn't touched her plane since.

The rational voice of Edward sounded in her ears, reminding her that digs needed plans, funding, survey. She dropped the jacket on the bed and dug under the mass of letters with George's scrawl, until she found a scrap of paper, the back pebbled with tiny bumps. A two by three-inch map of the British Isles, one she'd carried in her wallet throughout the war. She'd pricked a pin in the location of each RAF base where she'd landed a plane while in the ATA. Her nail traced over Norfolk, but discarded it. Too close to her parents' country house, to memories of George. Northwards. Somewhere isolated. If she wanted loads of people, she could stay in London. Scotland. The Hebrides. Maybe Mull, too small to see properly on this map. Something had been done there in '49 or '50, but wasn't it only a dive expedition? And for a Spanish ship, not anything Viking.

The shearling lining of her flight jacket over her dinner dress felt like an embrace. She'd fly to Mull.

Chapter 2

Max parked her car a block away from Bar Italia on Greek Street. She tilted the rear-view mirror to reapply red lipstick. She had liberated it from her make up case this morning, tossing back in the pastel pink she'd worn all winter. She settled her sunglasses and locked the door.

Her heels clicked along the pavement with purpose. Victor whistled as she rounded the corner of Old Compton Street.

'Snappy. Kiddo, you haven't looked like this...' he trailed off, looking down at his shoe.

She brushed the red skirt of her dress and smiled. 'A while.' She would not dwell on it. Victor wore pale trousers, slacks, she'd read in her mother's magazine, and a pink plaid shirt. 'Very springy, this.' Max touched his sleeve.

'So you ring me saying "come to Scotland" and now you turn up in splendour. When did you decide this?'

'Last night.' Based on Edward's promptings, not Mr Knox's. 'I bet Emma would rather go home to Scotland than Denmark with Edward's lot.'

Victor grinned. 'Mull is hardly home to a Glasgow lass. Come on, I'll get the coffees; you get seats.' He held the door and the heady aroma washed over her.

She wriggled past the crowd at the bar. All the seats were taken. But the chatter and the sharp, jagged laughter —how she'd missed this. Nowhere she went with her parents got this loud just from talking.

A couple near the back pushed their cups and saucers away, and Max manoeuvred past three women wearing too much perfume, heavy even in the smoke, a man in a dark suit and a couple of teenagers. Nearly George's age, but Max didn't slow. She arrived as the couple rose, perched on the still warm red leather stool and plonked her handbag on the other, the one closer to the bar.

She opened her notebook and extracted a pen from her bag. She'd ring the airfield about her plane this afternoon. They'd need a place to stay. Proper clothes. The low mirror that ran along the counter reflected the white collar on her red dress. It had arrived in her grandmother's last parcel from New York, along with tinned meats, sugar and chocolate. She'd talk her mother into letting her raid the food before Monday.

Fuel. Film, and the kit to process it. Boots. Victor's diving gear, if Emma had agreed he could come along.

She glanced towards the counter to see Victor deep in conversation with a man wearing even paler slacks. Victor, without Emma, came across as a wildly flamboyant man consistently dressed in the latest styles. She'd seen a lot of people rapidly reassess him when he was with his solid Scottish wife, including her own father.

What else did they need? Her pen tapped its reflection in the mirror, and then she doodled a plane in the margin of the paper. The opening strains of 'Unforgettable' sounded loud over the conversation, and yet she didn't wince. When she heard the soft drop of a Southern accent, she did. Ridiculous. Lots of Americans came to get coffee at Bar Italia, and London surely hosted more than one Southerner. She leaned over her notebook to draw another plane. She would not look up into the mirror. Neither to check her lipstick nor the men around her. A blue suited man brushed past her, and she resisted glancing up. Her record player, and any albums other than *South Pacific*, for the end of the day.

'One might suggest you are following me.' His drawl preceded his finger landing on the wing of the first plane she had drawn. 'I got here first. You don't even have a drink.'

'I've been coming here since they opened.' She nudged his finger away with the nib of her pen, imprinting a small black mark on his tanned skin.

'Hey.' He took out a handkerchief from his inside pocket.

'Stay out of my notebook.' She smiled as she tilted her head up towards him. He stopped rubbing the ink mark, and his eyes traced from her face to her dress and back up to her lips. Maybe her mother was right—he was flirting.

Until he frowned at his inky finger. 'Flying off somewhere?'

'Possibly.'

'You took my advice.'

'My supervisor's advice.' Max rested her chin on her palm. A piece of paper lay against the red Formica bar. As he saw her looking, he smoothly slid his saucer over to cover it. 'Are you ready to admit you followed me?'

'I would call it living in London.'

She opened her mouth, but Victor placed a coffee in front of her. She moved her handbag off his seat.

'Sorry, the queue was horrific.'

'The queue was shorter before you started talking to that man.'

'Fashion, kiddo. Introduce me?'

'John Knox, Victor Westfield.' They shook hands over her notebook. Mr Knox's face didn't register any change, and she grudgingly let him rise a notch in her estimation. 'Victor's an archaeologist, and I have simply no idea what Mr Knox does. But he is interested in archaeology, or else he wouldn't have gone to the lecture at the Society of Antiquaries.'

'A well-rounded gentleman should have many interests,' Mr Knox said.

He dropped his handkerchief to cover the small scrap of the paper not hidden by the saucer. His left hand rested on the crease in his grey trousers. No wedding band. She would not think about that.

'But in my working life, I sit in a dull office in Fleet Street. Ah.' The same blue suited man brought two cups towards Mr Knox. 'My colleague, Mark Fuller. Mark, meet archaeologists Dr Maxine Falkland and Victor Westfield.' Max felt a tremor of pleasure at the title. Mark Fuller nodded and put the coffees down. 'Excuse me.' Mr Knox swivelled away from them, tugging the paper far out of Max's sightline. They whispered too low for her to hear.

'Handsome,' Victor mouthed to her. She poked him and pushed the notebook in front of him.

'What else do we need to buy?' She put her pen down. 'You are going, right?'

'Emma's back tonight. I'm sure she'll agree, as long as she can come along.' He grinned. 'Her cooking is better than ours anyway.'

'True.'

'You're coming to her welcome home party tomorrow night, right?' He touched her sleeve. 'I'm assuming this means you can go out again?'

Max nodded. 'She's been away nearly two months, right?' Emma's departure date would have played a bigger part in her life before she locked herself away in the townhouse.

'Just over nine weeks—I'll spare you the precise number of days. But it was a big restoration. Good money too.'

'Oh. I'm paying for all this, by the way. And a salary.' Edward would have paid him in Denmark.

'Yeah, I figured.' He lit a cigarette and examined her list again.

Victor, of all her archaeologist friends, had never seemed bothered by her money. 'Good. Fuel and film, I can do. What about your diving stuff? Shall I fly it up?'

'You're going to fly all the way to Scotland?'

'I'll need the plane to do surveys.' Victor pulled out his own notebook and pen, and they divvied up her list quickly. What Max couldn't fit in the plane, Emma and Victor would drive up.

'You know you're going to want to dive too,' Victor said. 'I'll teach you. Good archaeology up there. How are you at sewing, beyond samplers extolling aristocratic virtues?'

Max laughed. 'Really? Samplers?'

Victor waved his hand towards her. 'You aren't shaped like the average military diver. Buy some rubber, heavy thread, some glue—I'll make a list—and sew away. Emma made herself a dive suit, easy.'

'I'll think about it.' She stood. 'Another coffee?'

He nodded, turning a page in his notebook, and wrote rapidly in blue ink.

Mark Fuller walked past her as she rocked on her heels in the queue. He didn't speak to her, but they'd barely been introduced. She listened to the hum of the espresso machine. John Knox would go past her any minute, and... he didn't. She ordered two espressos and watched the white shirted man wrest the small metal tubs out by the handles and dump them hard against a bin. The tap, tap of filling it with ground beans. She would not look, but she did. John Knox and Victor spoke rapidly, Victor without his usual effusive hand gestures. He pushed a sheet of paper towards John Knox, which Mr Knox slid into his jacket pocket.

And then, as if they had just met, they shook hands and John Knox walked towards the bar. Towards her. As he came closer, she smiled and let the crush of people push her a bit closer to him. 'Where will you follow me to next?' she asked.

'Depends. Where are you headed?'

Her fingers skimmed the smooth wool of his coat. She tugged gently and saw a smidgen of blue ink.

'It's good that you have a PhD to fall back on.' His hand closed around her wrist, and she released the paper. 'You'd make a terrible thief.' He pushed a card into her other hand. 'If you wanted my number, you merely needed to ask.'

'I wasn't... it's very crowded here.'

He leaned down, until she smelled smoke and coffee. His smoke, his coffee, distinct from what filled the room. His breath touched her ear, as hot as his grasp on her wrist. 'Wear red more often.' She stared at his grey lapels, the black tie. Not at his face. He dropped her hand, and she watched him walk out of the cafe.

'Miss, miss.' The man in the white shirt motioned to the cups in front of her. 'Your coffees.'

'Thank you.' The card's left corner had crumpled. She smoothed it. John Knox, *Universal Dispatch*, London. Foreign Manager. The printed phone number had been scratched through, and another scrawled under it in black.

She knew Victor's handwriting well enough to know that the loops she'd seen could easily form a double L. Mull? She slid the card into her pocket, and carried the two cups and saucers to the table.

'You looked quite cosy,' Victor said.

'Leave it. Please.' He'd hound forever if he suspected even a hint of interest. And how could she ask what he gave Mr Knox and it not sound like interest? 'When did you leave the Navy again?' Max stared at Victor's fountain pen, the blue ink smeared on the nib. What had he written?

'Why do you ask?' Victor fumbled in his pocket and lit another cigarette.

He rarely smoked two so quickly. 'I just wondered if you did the Tobermory dive in '50. The article I read last night said it was Navy frogmen. But I didn't remember you going up to Scotland.'

'They let a reservist come play too. I was only there for a couple of weeks.' He unfolded an Ordnance Survey map on the counter. 'So if we plan on staying here, where will you want to fly? I'd like to have a look in this bay…'

Max took a deep breath. She'd known Victor for four years. How could one strange American make her doubt one of her best friends?

Chapter 3

Max walked down the stairs, her pink skirt flouncing around her. She'd say a quick goodbye and then drive to Victor and Emma's house. She'd have to tell her parents about Mull, certainly before she flew out on Monday. Maybe tomorrow after church, at lunch. When her parents relaxed with spoons poised over some delicate creation made with the latest parcel of sugar from her American grandmother.

Light spilled from the open drawing room into the hallway. Her British grandmother sat next to Mother on the sofa, while Dad stood by the mantel reading a letter.

'I didn't realise you were coming to dinner, Granny,' Max said. 'I'm sorry I'm going out.'

'Surely a dinner dress would be more appropriate for a party?' Mother asked. 'That new green one would be nice.'

'It's not that type of party. Mostly it'll be lecturers, PhD students—they simply don't dress up like that.' They couldn't afford it. This cotton dress, with a low v-neck and wide skirt, hit the right level.

'Have a drink with us before you leave,' Granny said.

Her father folded the letter. 'Charlie's doing well at school this term. He'll come stay for the summer.' He passed the letter to Granny.

'Is he still talking about joining the RAF?' Mother asked. 'Why he feels the need to fly after... well, it's ridiculous. Surely the war will be over before he's eighteen.'

Mother's fingers tightened on the stem of her champagne coupe. Max's cousin Charlie often spent the summer with them, but this would be the first summer since George had died, since Charlie carried the official title of heir.

29

'There's always National Service to consider, darling,' Dad said. 'Max, that reminds me, the airfield rang me this morning. Is there a particular reason you need your plane ready?'

Why did her face flush? Her plane, her choice.

'And when were you going to tells us?' Her mother's accusatory face needed no interpretation, but her father's stayed the bland expanse of a government minister.

'I just decided—I mean, well, now.' She uncurled her fists until her fingertips rested against the smooth cotton of her skirt. The controls of her plane would feel right under her hands. 'I'm going up to Scotland. To get back to work. Flying survey over Mull and Iona.' She took a glass of champagne from a tray on the table and sat in the closest armchair.

Her mother's voice reached a shrill pitch, and her father's basso punctuated it. She didn't try to listen to the words. Before George, lively family discussions had been far more common. Before George, no one would have cared if she wanted to fly somewhere.

'You've never gone on a dig alone,' her mother said.

'I won't be digging. And Victor Westfield and his wife Emma are coming with me.'

'Not sure how I feel about Mr Westfield,' her mother said. 'He's a bit odd.'

Homosexual, Max translated her mother's 'odd'. Although Victor wasn't.

'Oh, Westfield's all right. At least you aren't going alone,' her father said.

'I really will be fine.' She kept her fingers relaxed on the stem of her glass.

'Edward's going to Denmark, isn't he? He said he asked you.'

'I've had enough of lots of people. I want to do this.'

'You look so fragile still, my love.' Her grandmother, who never looked ill at ease, twisted her bracelet. 'Pale.'

'We can discuss it later,' Mother said. 'It's not like you're going immediately after all. It's your birthday so soon, and...'

'I'm flying up on Monday, Mother. I'm not changing my mind. I'm definitely flying. Scotland will have a distinct shortage of Communists shooting planes down, I'm sure I'll be fine.'

Her mother's ragged intake of breath stabbed at her.

'I'm sorry. I'm very sorry.' She spoke to the bubbles in her glass. Since making a decision, she'd felt brighter. The facade now pricked, she deflated.

'Maxine is quite right,' her grandmother said. 'We all move on, and this is what our Maxine does. I never liked it when you went flying as a young man, Maximilian. But I coped. And you were fine.'

Max forced her fingers to stay relaxed around the stem of her glass. 'I'll come home for my birthday.' It would take at least two days away from the survey, but she could manage. 'And I'll ring you.'

Her grandmother followed her to the hallway and folded her into a tight hug, rocking her gently.

'I'm sorry. I didn't mean to say it.'

'You can't stop being Max—and you've mostly done that lately. Your mother was even talking of marrying you off to some American she met the other day.'

'Not that man.' Max pulled out of her grandmother's arms.

'So you noticed him?'

She forced a smile. 'It's nothing. I'm not interested.' She touched the too soft skin of her grandmother's hand. It used to feel sturdier under her fingers. 'They want me to settle down, don't they?'

'You're nearly twenty-seven, but the war changed things. And since things didn't work out with Daniel... someone soon, I hope?'

'Maybe.' She kissed her velvety cheek, inhaling powder and rose perfume.

'Drive safely. And have fun at the party.'

'Thanks.' Max shut the door behind her and walked towards her car. Granny would have to bring up Daniel now. Max had had no one since the end of their engagement. She climbed into the DB2. The most intimate touch she'd felt in well over a year was the heat of John Knox's hand around her wrist yesterday.

Max edged the car out of the tight parking space, and then sped towards Hampstead. She'd seen Daniel again at Vivian's wedding. She'd stood there in her turquoise bridesmaid's gown while he introduced his new wife, Meredith, whose stomach already bulged against her silk dress. That massive ring weighed down her finger, not Max's. She'd smiled and shaken their hands. Daniel actually looked disappointed that Max didn't shriek in jealousy. One year into her PhD, and the last thing she wanted was to be wife to Daniel Hagan. Dinner on the table, company talk, too much whiskey, too many other women. Too much whiskey she'd gotten in the three years of her PhD, but at least she didn't have to mouth company policy for a husband or laugh at a boss's jokes.

Heat rushed through the open door, and conversation and music swirled dizzyingly. Max shed her old black coat as she entered that house. She couldn't wear the silk coat to this party. Most of the men outside wore open necked shirts. She saw more sweater sets and skirts than the type of dinner dress her mother had suggested. Max tossed her coat in the pile by the door and smoothed her skirt.

'Max!' Emma hugged her, and Max handed her flowers and a bag full of wine.

'It's so wonderful to have you home, Emma.'

'Look at you!' Emma embraced her again, the flowers bashing into her side.

'Colour,' Max said.

'Victor said you had a fantastic red dress yesterday too.'

'Which your American friend greatly appreciated,' Victor said, dropping an arm around Max's shoulders.

She tensed under his touch. 'He isn't a friend.' Her dress's faint red stripe had nothing to do with Mr Knox.

'Well, he said couldn't make it tonight, whatever you want to call him.'

'How long have you known this man?' Emma asked. 'And you asked him to my party?'

Victor shrugged. 'She introduced us.'

'I met him Thursday.' Was the paper in Mr Knox's pocket just Victor's address? There was no double L in their street name.

'You need a drink,' Victor said. He took the bag away from Emma. 'I presume there is decent booze in here, or there's plonk open.'

'I don't care.' Victor had been a constant in her life for four years. She would not let a stupid American make her suspect him. It was probably the place Victor bought his slacks.

'The good stuff,' Emma said. She looped her arm around Max's waist and led her to the kitchen. 'How'd you pick Scotland?'

'I could give you a made up serious answer, but honestly I looked at a map.'

Victor opened a bottle of her wine and poured her a glass. He emptied his and Emma's glasses and refilled them.

'I'm always happy to go to Scotland,' Emma said.

'How was Paris?'

'Lovely. And lonely.' Before she could say more, someone called Emma into the living room.

'I'll head up Monday,' Max said.

'Emma wants to stop and see her parents in Glasgow. I think we could make it there by Thursday. Last time I was on Mull...'

'Victor!' The call came from the hallway.

'Sorry, right back.' He stashed the open bottle in a cupboard. 'Shhh,' he said.

Max laughed. She drifted into conversations, listening to complaints about supervisors and the lack of jobs and plans for the summer. Those with academic posts complained about marking and student performance. It was like every other party she had attended at Victor's house, full of chatter and sporadic dancing. And if she concentrated, she could forget the fear in her mother's voice.

'Max.' She turned and saw Lucy beckoning her. She was another of Edward's PhD students, about a year behind Max. Max squeezed past three people to reach her.

'How's the PhD?'

Lucy made a face. 'Horrid. Don't ask. How are you?'

'The second year is the hardest.' The last four months of writing up, with the pall of death sitting on the house, had been harder. She forced a smile. 'Actually, the whole damn thing is terrible. Until they call you doctor.'

'I'm hanging on for that. It's good to see you out.'

Max nodded. 'What gossip have I missed?'

'I'm sure Victor has told you most of it. Ruth had three months for her corrections—fairly major, as I understand —and they've been approved. What else? I went out with a new chap, but that ended and you missed nothing by not meeting him.' Lucy kept chatting. How tenuous her social grip on the archaeology world had been, Max realised, and how little she'd missed most of them.

'I hear you're striking out solo. Scotland?'

'With Victor.' She rotated her bracelet. 'Edward asked me to Denmark, but honestly I can't face the thought of all those people. The last six months...' She stopped.

'Understandable.' Lucy patted her arm, and Max refused to flinch away. She didn't want pity.

'Plus it's an interesting area. There was a dive in 1950, but only on one site. And I'll do air survey. Are you going to Denmark?'

'Yep. I'll be a trench supervisor, so some income too.' Someone grabbed Lucy's arm, and she turned. Max skirted around three dancing couples to reach the food table. How did Emma have the energy to cook all this? How late had she gotten back last night? Max picked at a few things, listening to the music and general hubbub. Everywhere seemed to play 'Unforgettable.' It only made Max think of George. She drained her glass and refilled it, but the wine was so dreadful she left it on the side.

'Max bloody Falkland.'

She knew without turning that Ruth spoke. Max remained still.

'Her own plane, miss la-de-da! Taking Victor away from any reasonable, real digging.'

'She's had a rough year.'

It was Lucy who spoke. Lucy, who she had thought of as a friend. Why had she confided in her?

'She's not the only one to have somebody die. I bet she won't write it up either.'

'Admit it—you're just cross 'cause she didn't have any corrections, which means she actually finished her PhD before you.' This voice she didn't recognise.

'People wouldn't think she's so fabulous if she wasn't rich.'

'Archaeology has always had rich...'

'Dabblers. That's all she is, PhD or not. Thinks she too bloody good for us, for any sort of teamwork, coming here with her expensive clothes, and...'

Max scanned the room for Victor, for Emma, for anyone she knew well. They couldn't be more than a foot from her. If they turned at all, they'd see her. And if she turned—the look on Ruth's face... 'Dance with me,' Max said instead, grabbing the hands of the man standing next to her. He was thin and tall, and though his mouth opened, he didn't speak. He let her draw him towards the three other couples in the middle of the floor. God help her, he was an MA student at best, maybe even an undergrad, with a neck too small for the collar of his shirt. Now they'd add cradle snatcher to her other sins. Moisture seeped through her dress from his hand, and his feet crashed into hers. Max held her arms rigidly so he could get no closer. He gasped apologies as they collided into a bystander, and then he stepped on her toes again. She'd nearly worn strappy sandals tonight.

Max eased away as soon as the music slowed and retreated to the garden. A few people hung around talking, but Max sat in a free lawn chair. She slid off her shoes and drew her feet up under her. The cool air soothed her heated cheeks. She knew what they thought of her; she just hasn't heard it expressed so baldly before. How stupid she had been to even try opening up to Lucy.

The chair shifted as the boy perched on the arm. 'You ran away fast.' He leaned down, until Max could see his spots. He was so thin that even looming over her, Max couldn't feel threatened.

'It was quite warm.' Rubbing her sore feet would only hurt his feelings. She didn't even know his name, and he was younger than George… would have been.

His sweaty finger dipped into the narrow v of her neckline. Max knocked it away. 'Don't be ridiculous.'

'Clearly they were right,' he said.

'I'm sorry?' Max asked, despite her best intentions.

'You're a tease. Not even a kiss.'

'I don't kiss children,' Max said.

'Bitch,' the boy said. His hand reached towards her again, but she stood quickly. The chair fell and the boy tumbled under it.

'Excuse me,' Max said as the boy spluttered. The people in the garden laughed, and only one offered to help him up. Max picked up her heels and headed to the steps.

'Max?' Emma stood in the doorway.

Max stepped into her shoes before she climbed the rough wooden steps into the house.

'You all right?'

Max nodded.

'Why are archaeologists so randy, all the time?' Emma asked.

'You married one,' Max said. She didn't think she'd be able to laugh, but she did. Emma was good at that. The wet finger still made her shudder.

'You became one.' She took Max's arm. 'You look a bit pale.'

'I haven't been to a party in six months.' She waved a hand. 'Smoke, noise. I'm fine.'

The boy pushed past them, shoving Max harder than necessary. 'Know him?'

Emma shook her head.

'Maybe I should go,' Max said.

'Absolutely not,' Victor said, coming up beside Emma. They never strayed far at parties like this. Max missed closeness, although she couldn't quite remember if she'd actually had it with Daniel. 'What a silly idea. I just got you back in circulation. You don't have a glass.'

'Did you invite any undergrads?'

'Not to my knowledge, unless they came as dates.' He waved her towards the kitchen, wrapping his arm around Emma's waist. 'The chap you danced with graduated last year. Doing an MA, I think. Hardly your type. Now that American...'

'Over the last four years, you've said every single man between twenty and forty-five we've met is Max's type,' said Emma. 'I think all we've established is you don't know her type.'

'By elimination, darling.' He retrieved the good bottle of wine and poured glasses for both of them. 'It isn't tall blond Englishmen.' He shook his curls. 'Despite my example.'

'You're taken,' Max said. She leaned against the counter.

'And it isn't vapid little aristos, or your mother would already have you married off.' He lit a cigarette as Emma clinked her wine glass against Max's. 'Let's see, who else? Clearly not children, or old professors, fortunately, or darkly intense men with academic pretensions. That leads us by elimination to Americans.'

'You forget my esteemed ex-fiancé.' Max swallowed more wine. 'He was American.'

'Too short for you,' Victor said.

'And clearly just wrong,' Emma added.

'And obnoxious and moving towards pudge,' Max said.

'Max's Mr Knox is tall, broad shouldered, dark haired—ridiculously American. Perfect.'

'Victor,' Emma said. 'You're incorrigible.'

'When will you see him again?'

'I doubt I will.' Max swirled her wine.

'Victor,' Ruth's voice came shrilly from the door. 'I don't...'

'Sorry to interrupt, Ruth.' Max pushed past Victor and grasped Ruth's arm. 'I haven't had a chance to say congratulations on your corrections being approved. That must be such a relief.'

Ruth opened her mouth and closed it again. 'Yes,' she said finally.

Max didn't relinquish Ruth's arm. 'I'm sorry, you were saying something to Victor?'

'We need more wine,' she said, jerking away from Max. 'And you really aren't going to Denmark with Edward?'

'Nope.' Victor peered in Max's bag. 'Here,' he said, doling Ruth one bottle of the four she'd brought.

Ruth pulled away from Max and flounced out of the room. Her light petticoat showed under her dark skirt, and Max recalled a sentence from one of her mother's magazines about the importance of coordinating undergarments. Ruth wouldn't have the money.

'Ouch,' Victor said. 'That was a bit harsh. For you anyway.'

Max wanted to reach for her wine glass, but she didn't. 'I actually meant it.'

'I'm not saying you shouldn't have. Ruth isn't in your fan club.'

'I've noticed.' She forced herself to relax the hard set of her face. 'So that last time you were in Mull?'

'Right, the Spanish galleon dive in 1950. If conditions are much the same, we'll need to take as much as we can. And I'm going to have to leave my car on the mainland.' His mouth thinned. Victor loved his car. 'I can hire something once we get over.'

'So I should fly up as much stuff as I can.'

Emma produced a pad of paper from a drawer, and they made a more detailed list than the one in the coffee shop.

'We're going to Glasgow first, so here's my parents' number. I'll see if I can find us a cottage or something.' She handed Max a sheet of paper, which Max tucked in her pocket.

'I really appreciate this.'

'We're happy to go,' Emma said.

'By the way, my mother says I have to come home for my birthday, which makes me sound twelve, I know. But flying again, it's prompted some... issues.'

'Okay. We can keep doing some work.' Victor doodled on the pad. 'Do you want to wait to go up till next week? There's no rush.'

'I want to go. I'm tired of being in London.'

'Sorry we throw such awful parties.' Victor grinned.

39

'You know what I mean.' She spun her bracelet again. 'I need to get out of my parents' house.'

'You could stay here,' Emma said.

'No, she can't. You've been gone for more than two months.'

'I'm happy to fly up…' Max said.

'So why are we having a party if you want time with me?'

'I thought you wanted a party!'

'Where I stay up all night cooking and I'll clean all day tomorrow?'

Max slipped out of the kitchen, and neither Emma nor Victor noticed. Their arguments followed a well-worn pattern, and while the flares never lasted long, she always tried to absent herself. The living room seemed dim after the bright kitchen, and Max eased her way into a conversation about Kathleen Kenyon's excavations in Jericho. The boy she had danced with pointedly left the group, but Max didn't react. She glanced at the door. John Knox stood at the threshold. Damn this dress—everyone around her wore dark colours. She'd shine like a bloody beacon.

The music stopped abruptly and the overhead lights came on. 'Everybody out,' Victor said. His face was as flushed as hers. 'Party's over.'

'It's barely ten o'clock,' said someone.

'Sorry, the neighbours complained. Too much noise.'

Their arguments usually blew over quickly. Victor looked too agitated for her to ask what happened.

'When?' asked Ruth.

'They rang. Go home.' He shoved a hand through his hair. 'We'll have another party soon.'

Max tried to resist, but she looked at the doorway anyway. Mr Knox was gone. Had she dreamt him?

'Come on,' Max said to the people around her. With grumbling, people gathered bags and coats. Her champagne coat would have been easy to pick out, but she had to wait for the pile of black coats to dwindle down. She said goodbye to Lucy, who hugged her as if the conversation with Ruth hadn't happened. When her coat emerged, the heat felt too heavy to consider putting it on. She managed to pat Victor's arm, and he gave her a tight smile. Max stepped out into the cool evening, and the door closed behind them.

She said goodbye to a few more people and walked to her car. The crowd thinned as almost everyone headed for the Tube. What made this argument different from their others? They almost always had some disagreement at a party, but they'd never ended one before.

Why had she parked between streetlights? Silly. Still it was Hampstead and... a tall figure leaned against her car, and her step stuttered. She could hardly go back to Victor and Emma's. Max pushed her arms in her coat sleeves and gripped her handbag. His lighter flared.

'Good evening, Dr Falkland. I didn't mean to startle you.'

'I thought perhaps you were an apparition, and maybe I shouldn't drive home.'

'Do you often find yourself dreaming of me?' Mr Knox asked.

She could hear the smile in his voice. Arrogant as all the American men she knew. Max reached the car. 'A wine-fuelled nightmare, perhaps.' She closed her eyes. Nothing tonight had been his fault. She shouldn't be so harsh.

'Victor assured me it wouldn't be too late to turn up, but it seems I am.'

Max had no need to tell him about their argument, so why did it rise to her lips? 'Too much noise,' she said instead.

Mr Knox caressed the roof of her car. She could think of the movement of his hand in no other way. 'It's

41

beautiful. The 1950 Aston Martin DB2.' He circled to the front. 'And you have the three-part grill.'

'It's one of the first forty-nine made. The rest have... but I suspect you know that.'

He shrugged. 'I like cars. I'd love to see the engine.'

'It's a bit dark.'

Mr Knox pulled something from his pocket. 'Flashlight.'

Max's fingers clenched, remembering the smooth wool of his pocket. 'Do you always travel with torches?'

'If I'm walking at night.' He didn't turn it on. 'My apartment is quite close.' He touched the bonnet. 'I imagined you'd have the convertible, in red.'

'Ge...no.' George tried for weeks to wheedle her into one. His disappointment hadn't kept him from joining her for the first ride when it arrived, just two weeks after her birthday. The wind had blown through the open windows and the May sunshine had gleamed off the chrome as George swore he'd get a convertible for his twenty-fifth birthday present. But he hadn't made it that far.

Mr Knox said something. She couldn't hear it through the roaring in her ears. 'Good night, Mr Knox.' She unlocked the door, and he walked around as she climbed in.

'Good night, Dr Falkland.' With the interior light on, she could see his smile. 'It's a pretty dress.' He closed her door before she could respond.

She started the car and pulled away.

Chapter 4

Max had never considered that her parents would want to accompany her to the airport. That they would pace the hangar as she loaded the baggage compartment with supplies, including Victor's Aqualungs, which she wrestled into place. He'd sent two, full of conviction that she would want to dive. She couldn't imagine anything worse. Her mother clearly could, as she met any attempt at normal conversation from Dad with monosyllables.

Max secured smaller items in the backseat, making sure they wouldn't break free in the event of any difficulty. She circled the plane. Her father came beside her, repeating each check she made.

'Sure you'll be okay? It's been a while,' Dad said.

'I'm fine.' She smiled. 'You go longer than this between flying.'

He nodded, then squeezed her shoulder tightly. Mother clenched her in a hug, and Max breathed in the cloud of perfume, felt the frailty of her mother's body against her own.

'I'll be careful. I promise.' George had probably said the same things.

'Darling. I know you will.' Tears shimmered in her mother's blue eyes, but she found a smile. 'And we look forward to you coming back for your birthday. Just something small with the family, I think.'

Max nodded, then climbed into the plane. She settled herself in the seat and exhaled. This she'd missed. After doing her cockpit checks, she switched on the master and alternator switches, and then cranked the hand wobble pump. With a press of the starter button, the propeller began to whir. Her parents had a hard grip on each other waists, but she waved cheerfully all the same. She eased the plane out of the hangar, the propeller progressing to a full throated roar. The plane moved down the runway, and then its nose rose into the air. The plane's controls smoothly responding to her touch tickled a pleasant buzz in the base of her skull. Max retracted the landing gear and eased her shoulders down. Now to Scotland.

The red barn, the pub's pig weathervane, and the field with the tractor. None of those details were quite as distinctive as the pub landlord seemed to believe. No doubt someone would tell her to move along if she'd got it wrong. At least the field had been cut recently. The plane bounced lightly, then ran into a stop not far from the tractor.

Fortunately, no one came to greet her as she opened the door. She'd had quite enough of dealing with the shocked disapproval of men when flying for the ATA. No cows either. Max tugged out her overnight bag and threw a tattered blanket over the kit wedged on the backseat. The mud squelched high against her boots as she jumped down from the door. This she did not miss about flying.

Walking across the field became an exercise in tugging her boots out after each step. When she rang to make the booking, she hesitated before giving 'doctor' as her title. She ended up giving Maxine Gould, plucking Vivian's name randomly from the air. She couldn't say why she had. Now as she trudged she recited 'Gould, Gould, Gould' under her breath. She would not scrawl her own name on the register.

She went through the kissing gate. The pub's yard was neater, punctuated by a few bedraggled flowers, and a car and one motorbike parked on the loose gravel and dirt. Max scraped as much mud as she could off the soles of her boots before pushing open the door. She stepped into steamy warmth, and silence. Four men, ranging from twenty to possibly eighty, turned from the bar to stare at her, and a middle-aged woman stopped drying glassware. She had focused so much on cleaning her boots she came through the wrong door into the public bar. And judging from the floor, a little mud wouldn't have mattered much.

'Hello,' Max said cheerfully. She let as much American drip into her voice as possible. 'I booked a room for tonight?'

'Aye,' the woman said. 'Come around to the other side.'

Three of the four men turned back around, but the twenty-year-old stared at her legs in trousers. In the ATA, they had to change back to skirts as soon as they landed, but were trousers really that uncommon here? In 1952? Maybe it was the mud. Max walked through the swing doors into the empty saloon bar. Cleaner.

The woman plopped a ledger on the counter, and licked her thumb before flicking to the right page. Although Max wrote 'Maxine Gould' on the top line, along with her parents' address in the country, rather than London, the white lined page already bore grubby marks. Hopefully from a former visitor, not the landlady's thumb.

'Like me to show you to your room?'

'Yes, please.'

'Or a cuppa tea first?'

Would they serve her whiskey in a pub like this? 'I'll just change first, if that's okay.'

The woman nodded and came out from around the bar. 'Where's your husband?' She wiped her hands on an apron.

'I'm not married.' The woman opened a door that led to a narrow flight of stairs lined with faded red carpet. The canvas weave showed in patches where the plushness had completely worn away.

'Well, head on up.'

Max started climbing, counting eight steps before a tight turn to the left.

'Died in the war.' The woman didn't ask so much as state.

'Hm? Oh. Yes,' she lied. The red-haired pilot she'd flirted with—Peter—had survived. Married and living in Leeds, last she'd heard. She could never have lived in Leeds.

'Sad, sad.' Max lifted her bag up three more steps, and she reached a landing with two doors. 'No, up another level. These're ours.'

Max kept climbing, prickles shooting down her legs as the muscles warmed.

'Another American staying here.'

Foolish, foolish, foolish to feel that slight lift in her chest. She could enjoy sparring with someone and feel nothing more, surely?

'Been here a week. Don't worry, his wife's with him. Not sure where she's from, doesn't talk much.'

'Oh.'

'Room next to yours.' The woman puffed. 'Last little bit.'

Max reached the top of the stairs and dropped her bag. The woman fumbled in her pocket for a large iron key.

'This one's yours.' She unlocked the middle door and pushed it open. 'Bathroom there.' She flung open the door to the left. Max took in the bath and a low ceiling before carrying the bag into her room. Another low ceiling, punctuated by exposed ceiling beams. A single bed, lumpy even under the counterpane. A solitary chair and a small bright rug next to the bed.

'This is excellent. Thank you.'

'How long you staying?'

'A few nights only.' When Victor and Emma arrived, they'd move into that little cottage, far from the lumps and tatty stairs of this place.

The woman solemnly handed her the key. 'I'll have your tea downstairs.'

Max smiled and hoisted her bag onto the bed. 'Thanks.'

The woman, whose name she realised she still did not know, closed the door. Max collapsed next to her bag. How many people lived in America? How many thousands? John

Knox did not have to be everywhere, despite his ubiquitousness in London. If the thought of teasing him had raised a frisson of excitement, well, that was too bad. Besides, if he'd followed her to Scotland it would prove that Victor had told him of their destination, and that John Knox was following her. Neither were options she wanted to believe.

Max unlaced her boots and rubbed warmth back into her feet through the thick socks. The temperatures in April couldn't compare to wartime flying, but her feet held a memory of cold each time she took to the air.

She washed her face in water that could charitably be called tepid and changed into a blouse, cardigan and wool skirt. Thank God she'd packed the brown one, with its thick fabric cut into an unflattering shape. Her mother wanted her to throw it out, but it was useful here. She went back to the pale pink lipstick.

Going downstairs seemed easier without the puffing of the landlady and the heaviness of her bag. Halfway down, she turned back around, dashed upstairs and took out her notebook and fountain pen. She needed something to keep her occupied over tea. She pushed open the door. The voices of the men carried through. 'American woman. Trousers.' The young voice cracked slightly, and then there was the sound of a cuff, possibly around the head.

'Over there.' Behind the bar stood a man, who jerked his thumb towards a table near the unlit fireplace. A tray was laid out with a teapot, a pitcher containing a drizzle of milk and a solitary oatcake. Max placed her notebook to the side and poured the tea. The muddy colour did not raise her spirits, and they sank even more as she sipped it. The landlady must have made it as soon as she got downstairs, and from leaves several uses on.

She opened her notebook, and John Knox's card fell into her lap. She stuck it in the back again and flicked past the airplanes she'd drawn in Bar Italia, the ticked off shopping list, and another page of doodles before she reached a clean sheet.

The woman came all the way to her table before Max realised she'd been calling out 'Miss Gould'.

'Pardon me.'

'I need your ration book.'

And it had her real name on it. 'It's upstairs, I'm so sorry.'

'You can fetch it now, please.'

Max dashed up the stairs. She rehearsed it all in her mind as she took the book that clearly said 'Falkland' and gave a London address.

The woman still stood next to her table. Staring at her notebook? No, the fireplace. All the same, Max fingered the dip in the cap of her fountain pen as she reached the table.

'Mrs...'

'Fentiman.'

Max drew the book out of her skirt pocket. 'I have to confess—I'm trying—there's a young man. He won't take no for an answer. So I've come up here, so I gave you my friend's name. Can you understand, please?' Max kept her eyes down. The notebook was open to the picture of the planes, not the next blank page.

'Thought it was funny you didn't answer when I called out. I don't mind. What's his name, in case he comes round?'

'Knox,' Max said quickly.

Mrs Fentiman took the booklet. 'Falkland. And you run away from a young man by plane?' The emphasis on the word 'young' carried as much weight as necessary. Max was judged too old to have suitors.

'It's rather difficult, I'm afraid.'

'I don't mind none. Have your tea.'

Max sat back down and nibbled at the oatcake. Stale. Dinner did not bode well. She reopened the notebook to the next page and left it alone. The public bar door slammed open, and the page did not even shiver in the resulting breeze. Why would Mrs Fentiman leaf back a page —two pages—in her notebook? Max glanced through. Her notes, a shopping list, Victor's suggestions about possible areas to survey. Maybe opening the door to the upstairs caused the pages to shift. Maybe Mrs Fentiman just fulfilled the requisite role of a nosy landlady, particularly waiting on a dim guest who didn't remember her own name, let alone her ration book. Max sipped the now cold tea and unfolded the map she'd gotten upstairs along with her ration book. She could plot out the flight plan for tomorrow. And did it even matter if they knew where she was going? They'd notice soon enough when she flew her plane over fields ploughed by oxen.

She traced her finger over a ridgeline, following the contours carved by glaciers millennia ago. Noted the subtle patterns of the roads and trackways, routes that had stood through hundreds of short summers and long winters. She visualised the detail of the archaeology underneath—the prehistoric stone circles; the medieval castles; even the hints of more modern military activity... She'd flown planes to Scotland in the war, but never this far north.

The door to the public bar had let in clearly another local, if the cries of 'James' were anything to go by. The saloon door flapped open a few minutes later, and the waft of fresh air cut through the cigarette smoke leaking in from the bar. Max glanced up and smiled at the couple. Their boots were as muddy as hers. The woman wore a green coat, and the man a thick scarf. Max looked back at her notebook again as the man went to the bar. The woman made a great show of taking off her coat, fluffing it, arranging it neatly on a chair, and then rearranging the flap.

'Mrs Fentiman,' the man called. 'Can we have the fire lit please?'

'I'm Jane,' the woman said. Abandoning her coat, she sat down at Max's table without being asked.

Max slid her oatcake plate onto her notebook, just over the lists. She'd rather it had been Mr Knox.

Jane stuck out her hand while Max did her rearranging, and Max shook it belatedly. 'That's Adam. We're from the U.S.' Her voice sounded shrill, and she said 'U.S.' with great emphasis on each letter.

'Maxine,' Max said quietly. No doubt Jane would want the entire story of a shortened name, and she simply couldn't take it.

'Where are you from? We're from Maine. But we might move to England. After this trip.'

'London.' One word answers, and maybe Jane wouldn't notice her accent.

'Mrs Fentiman says you're American too.' The man brought a pint and a sherry glass to the table. 'May we join you? Can I get you a drink?' He dragged a spare chair over.

'British. I spent some of my childhood there.'

'We're from Bar Harbor. What about you?'

Max knew Bar Harbor. Her grandmother visited a childhood friend there every spring, and most years Max had accompanied her. These people's accents had never, ever seen the environs of that island, much less that area. Too sharp, too harsh.

'New York,' Max said. They nodded.

'We're on honeymoon. Taking long—' Jane glared at Adam. '—wet, walks.' She touched Max's map, and Max pulled it away. 'Where are you walking?'

'Just around.'

'Say, is that your airplane?' Adam peered at a tiny bit of the wing protruding from the saucer. 'Do you draw? Can I have a look?' He reached towards the plate, his hand close to her body.

'Not well. It's just doodles.' Max kept her hand on her notebook. What had Mr Knox been hiding?

Mr Fentiman came in and started messing about with a few meagre scraps of wood. 'Cost you extra, this will.'

'That's all right.' Adam turned his head, and Max pulled her notebook free. She folded it closed and slid it into her pocket. The map she rested on her lap.

'I believe I might retire. I'm a bit tired. Mr Fentiman, could you tell Mrs Fentiman I shan't need any supper?'

Mr Fentiman swore at the wood, then apologised when Jane squeaked. Max escaped up the stairs. A single oatcake wasn't a great meal, but she couldn't stay with those people. She was half a flight up when she realised her fountain pen still lay on the table. It had been her grandfather's, so she forced herself back down the stairs. Adam, Jane and Mr Fentiman stood by the fire. Not warming themselves, but speaking quietly, and quickly. Max pushed the door back silently, and then flung it open noisily. When she emerged, Mr Fentiman moved quickly towards the bar, while Jane and Adam warmed their hands.

'Pardon me.' Max lifted her pen and waved it, and then went back through the door. She climbed six steps and stopped to listen. Nothing. Probably they had been talking about the crazy American woman who jumped when anybody nearly touched her stuff. Why did she feel so defensive of the page with her plans? Flying air survey over Iona hardly qualified as ground breaking.

Max took the notebook out of her pocket and wrapped the map around it. She started climbing the stairs for the third time in fifteen minutes. On a single oatcake. And with no supper.

She tossed her notebook and map on the bed, and dragged the weight of the overnight bag to the floor.

Two lumps and one particularly deep dip met her back when she stretched out on the bed, and the pillow smelt faintly of dog. Could she last the few days before Emma and Victor arrived? Hell. She hadn't rung her parents. She used to just scrawl a letter to them when she arrived to do fieldwork. She used to go on fieldwork with other people. And she used to do all of that before George died.

Back down those awful grey stairs and out into the pub? Her leg bumped the notebook, and it teetered on the edge of the bed. She grabbed it by the spine. Nothing fell out. A fierce shake, and nothing. Max flicked through the pages. She clearly remembered lodging John Knox's card against the back cover.

She had lost a card and people mumbled together. That did not add up to suspicious behaviour. Max paced from whitewashed wall to whitewashed wall, and crawled on the floor to peer under the bed. Nothing except dust. Go downstairs, ask about a phone box and look on the stairwell. Since when did she see danger everywhere?

She took a thick cardigan and her handbag before she left the room. A slow progression down each step revealed nothing but tatty carpet and a few loose drugget rungs. The tea tray had disappeared and only Jane sat in the saloon, next to the fireplace. The carpet here was a brighter cousin to that in the stairwell, but no white card broke its surface.

'Do you know if there is a phone box nearby?'

Jane folded her coat again. 'About half a mile away, I think. Mrs Fentiman might let you use hers.' She glanced up. The redness of her eyes might be dismissed by the fire, but a puffiness clung to them that had not been there before. 'I thought you had a headache.'

'I'm just tired. Thanks though.' Max brushed the surface of her table, and looked at the chair's seat. No card.

She walked to the bar. Loud conversation carried through from the public bar, but no one came to help her. Jane languidly came beside her, her uncertain movements suggesting she'd downed at least one more sherry. Under the bar lights, the redness clearly came from tears.

'How long have you lived here?' Jane drew on her cigarette.

'A long time.' She didn't want to go into the family's frequent trips between countries, and her degree at Vassar. 'When did you arrive?'

'Here, three days ago. The country, two weeks.'

Her voice managed to be both shrill and whiny. Jane coiled a strand of her dark hair around her finger.

'You *are* pretty.' Her emphasis registered surprise.

'Thanks.' Max leaned forward, stretched out on tiptoe, but she couldn't see anyone on the other side of the bar either.

'Do you think Adam is handsome?'

'I'm sorry?' Max turned to properly look at Jane. 'I didn't notice.'

'He said you were pretty.'

'Excuse me.' Max half swung open the door to the public bar.

'Whatcha want, love?' The elderly man who had been there when she arrived looked up.

'I was looking for Mrs Fentiman?' The smoke made her false headache kindle into life.

'Dunno, love.'

'Could you point me towards a telephone box?'

His muddled directions made a bit more sense than Jane's, and she gathered she should head northwards, towards the church, across a field, and eventually she'd find one near the post office. Why had she chosen a pub out of the way of an already small town?

The door to the public bar closed, and she hadn't heard anyone say anything about her legs. She slid the heavy cardigan on over her light one.

Jane had returned to her perch by the fire, her legs curled under her.

'You aren't going out, are you? It's nearly dark. It gets dark so early here. Ridiculous country.'

Max forced a smile and stepped outside. The chilly air seized in her lungs, but it felt cleansing after the heaviness inside. Three cars now, and another motorbike. Why did Victor have to take so long to get here?

Before she'd gone five steps, a rattle sounded, followed by a crash. She heaved a deep breath and turned to see Mr Fentiman climbing out of the cellar doors.

'Where are you off to?'

'I need to make a telephone call. A gentleman kindly pointed me towards the nearest phone box.'

'Take you half an hour, easy. Be dark by then.' He looked down at her feet. 'Not the right shoes neither. Use our'n.' He slammed the cellar door shut with his boot. 'You can pay?'

'I can pay.' She followed him back into the saloon. Jane's head rested on her carefully folded coat, and her deep open-mouthed breathing indicated sleep.

'Feet off the cushions,' Mr Fentiman said as they passed her, but Jane didn't move. He led Max to a door to the right of the one that hid the stairs to the rooms.

'Office,' he said, as he opened it. Mrs Fentiman jumped and shoved something white, something rectangular, and something with one crushed corner into her apron pocket.

'Scared me, you did.'

'Miss—miss whatever here needs to use the phone.' Male voices from the public bar bellowed 'Fentiman' and Mr Fentiman left.

Mrs Fentiman stood up from the desk, placing her body between Max and the black phone. 'Shall I place it for you?'

'Please. It's my parents. In London.' She recited the exchange and number, and watched as Mrs Fentiman placed the call. The receiver passed from Mrs Fentiman's hand to hers, and her father had already bellowed 'hello'.

'Dad, it's me.'

'You're safe? No problems flying up?'

'None.'

'Your mother's been pacing.' His half laugh sounded forced. He'd been just as worried. 'All okay? Flying again?'

'Absolutely fine. I'm in a lovely pub. The Hare and Hound.' Mrs Fentiman didn't move, so Max looked straight at her face as she spoke. She could try to reach into the apron pocket, but she heard Mr Knox saying she was a terrible thief, felt again his grip on her wrist. And what would it prove? She had no plans to ring him anyway.

'Good, good. Your mother said she spoke to that chap.'

'Victor?'

'No, some American.'

'Oh.' She wanted to ask if they'd told him where she'd gone, why she'd gone, anything, but Mrs Fentiman maintained her stare. 'Look, Dad, I should go. I'll ring you later?'

She listened to his usual fluster of goodbyes, in which he avoided saying he loved her but conveyed it all the same. Mrs Fentiman held her hand out for the receiver and dropped her wrist. No way to ring Victor now.

'Two minutes.'

Max drew out her purse, but Mrs Fentiman waved it away. 'I'll add it to your bill. Is that all?'

'I think I lost a bit of paper, earlier. Nothing really, but I do just hate losing things, don't you?' She left it hanging, but Mrs Fentiman didn't flush, look at her pocket or say a word. 'You haven't seen anything?'

'No supper, right? My husband said you felt poorly.' The hand progressed towards her forehead, and Max shrank away.

'Just a bit of a headache. But I didn't want my parents to worry.' She could ask for a sandwich, but Mrs Fentiman just kept staring at her. 'Thank you.'

She couldn't remember the last time she climbed so many stairs so quickly. Mrs Fentiman had Mr Knox's card.

She woke much later to raised voices from the room next door. Jane's voice shrilled high, but the words didn't make sense. Max sat up. The smack that resonated through the wall made her flesh shudder. A male voice hissed 'English', and only sobs responded.

Max's stomach growled. She had basic provisions in the plane, a flight kit. Stupid to have turned down a meal just to avoid Jane and Adam. Her watch showed one thirty in the morning. How had she fallen asleep for so long? She could creep out of the pub, sneak back in, and no one would be the wiser. Squeaks emerged from next to her. The beds must line up against the wall. Muffled noises matched the squeaks. Far, far too much to learn about Adam and Jane's relationship. Max pushed herself away from her own bed. She had to get out of the room.

She grabbed her jacket and carried her boots to the door, although any clatter wouldn't disturb them. The sounds chased her down the stairs.

By the Fentimans' rooms she tiptoed, but she heard faint snores. She crept down to the pub and slid on her boots.

The pub door was locked. Her key didn't fit.

She parted the thick curtains to peer out into the darkness. A flickering light danced around the yard, but she couldn't see the body that must hold the light. Maybe Mr Fentiman patrolled his land.

Max climbed the stairs again, pushing at the deep creases in her skirt. If nothing else, she could clean her teeth and go to bed properly.

Soft weeping came through the thin wall, not nearly as high pitched as Jane's speaking voice. Adam must be murmuring, for Max could hear an occasional word. And one sounded like 'darling', which her maternal grandmother used to croon to her, but not in English.

Chapter 5

Max woke early and dressed in trousers and muddy boots. The downstairs of the pub remained empty, but the door opened under her hand. She found Mrs Fentiman weeding a garden around the back. Chickens scratched within a cage.

'Could I please trouble you for some breakfast, Mrs Fentiman?'

'Got to finish this row first.'

Max wanted to tell her no, she was starving, but didn't. 'Of course. I need to fetch something anyway.' She walked across the field to her plane. The tractor had moved, but the plane seemed untouched. Inside, she found a chocolate bar and nibbled off a corner. The blue sky through the cockpit window calmed her. She arrived by plane, fussed about, and no wonder the landlord and landlady treated her suspiciously. She'd used a false name, for God's sake.

But nothing hid the fact that Mrs Fentiman had taken that card. And lied about it. She exhaled. Today, she'd fly out, but first she'd talk to Victor.

The bowl of porridge contained mostly lumps, but at least it filled her stomach beyond the tidbit of chocolate. She wouldn't come back before heading out, so she went upstairs to double check she had everything. As she reached the landing, Jane emerged from the bathroom. She tugged her dressing gown higher, but not before Max saw the red patch on her upper arm. It matched the stain on her right cheek that the fall of brown hair couldn't fully hide.

'Feel better today?' Jane asked. Her one visible bleary eye looked anything but fine.

'Much. It's a lovely bright day.' Only darkness emerged from the open door of the room. 'Are you okay?'

'Of course.'

Max watched Jane close the door and opened her own. Jacket, notebook, map, handbag. It would only be a short flight over to Iona.

The directions to the phone box were anything but precise, but after forty-five minutes she found it. The Scottish crown had been newly added to its metal surface.

Max rang Victor and beat her fingers against the cool glass. Manure, dirt and smoke. Not the usual scents of her parents' townhouse.

The phone rang four times. Maybe they'd left early for Glasgow. Just as she started to hang up, Victor answered.

'How can I be waking you up at a quarter to nine?'

Victor mumbled something incoherent.

'Where are we staying?'

'What?'

'What accommodation have you booked? The pub is a nightmare; I can't stay there until you get here.'

'Wait a minute. I have it written down.' She heard paper being shuffled.

'I think...' It sounded stupid to say. 'I think there's something bizarre going on up here.' By the time she'd poured out the story of the people talking by the fire, the argument in another language and the smack, the paper had stopped rattling.

'Okay, here are the details. Maybe they'd give you the key early.' Max wrote it down.

'It doesn't really sound like much, does it?'

'No. Particularly not at this time in the morning. But if you're worried, ring your friend.'

'What friend?' Vivian couldn't do anything.

'That American chap. Knox. Americans like suspicious people. Maybe it was Russian. They'd like that even more.'

'He works for a newspaper. What's he going to do? Call the President?' She stared at the low outline of the post office. 'And it was Russian. I recognised some words.'

'Why?'

'Does it matter? Anyway, I can't ring him. I lost—well, I think the landlady picked up his card. Out of my notebook. I don't have it anymore.'

'Max, you're going mad up there. I'll see if we can come up earlier. Get some food, get some sleep and forget about it.'

'I'll let you know if I move. Bye.' She replaced the receiver. It was mad. And yet she lifted the receiver and asked to be connected to the offices of the *Universal Dispatch*. She barely knew the man. What would she say? She heard a man hit his wife last night? Hardly an international incident. Once upon a time, she acted boldly, without consulting anybody else. Before she'd gone through the scrutiny of the PhD process, before George died. Maybe before she came back to England.

The woman who answered had a full nasal New York accent that should have shamed the chorus boys in *South Pacific*.

'May I speak to Mr John Knox, please?'

'Department, please?'

'I—I don't know.' The card had borne a job title. One so generic that it didn't mean anything.

'Hold the line, please.' Max heard paper rustle, and then the voice returned. 'I would need to take a number and a name. No one is currently available to answer.'

She hadn't asked for no one. 'Max... No, never mind.' She depressed the receiver.

Max took off from the field and turned the plane west. The blue sky of yesterday morning had congealed into lumps of solid grey clouds. Survey would be easier with Victor beside her to examine the ground as she flew, but Max saw the evidence under the cover of grass for prehistoric circles, and a few military installations from the war, now succumbing to creeping growth.

Fog started to seep in from the sea. She should manoeuvre towards to the field and head back to the pub. She stretched her cold fingers.

Suddenly, the controls juddered beneath her hands, the engine moaned, then fell silent. The plane jerked, and she did her best to level it. The fog grew thicker, and Max breathed deep to ignore the metallic fear in her mouth.

The plane plummeted. Max switched the fuel tanks and hit the boost pump, struggling to keep the plane from stalling. The fog—she remembered Peter drawing how to land a plane blind on a napkin in that club. But theory didn't add up when the engine failed to respond. Please God let her be above one of those nice wide fields, and not —she dropped below the fog and saw two trees and a building in the near distance. She wrenched the controls and the plane bounced twice, hard, before skidding into a spin, a wave of mud cascading over the cockpit.

Stillness. Max took six deep breaths and finally looked out the side window. Clear of the building, pretty damn close to one of the trees. Thunder rolled again, but this time lightening split the sky. Max mumbled a prayer and pried her fingers loose from the controls. She flicked the switches on the silent engine. A jagged hole pierced the roof of the barn, so she doubted she'd find any help there.

Fog, normal. Thunderstorms, normal. Neither ideal, but she'd flown in them before. Her engine had never failed like that. Never. Max unhooked her seatbelt and pressed the heels of her hands to her eyes. Had George's plane plummeted like that? Had he found a clear field?

She allowed herself six more deep breaths. She had to focus on the present. Her repair skills stayed pretty basic, but she could at least assess the damage. Thunder crashed, and rain pelted against the plane. The treetop pitched from side to side in the wind and heavy rain. She would have had to set down anyway. And the cockpit kept her dry. She could sit out the storm before inspecting the engine.

In her PhD, she would have outlined an argument, found supporting evidence and defended it. She could do this now. She opened the notebook and uncapped her pen.

Mrs Fentiman misused her ration book. She wrote 'landlady cheating' next to it, and dismissed it.

Mrs Fentiman had taken Mr Knox's card. 'Landlady nosy?' was written next to it. Again, it was possible she had lost it. But the notebook had been moved when she came back downstairs. And landladies were traditionally nosy.

Adam, Jane—who lacked a surname—talking with Mr Fentiman. Speaking quietly did not amount to anything.

The pub door was locked for security, and to be fair, she had not asked for a key to allow her outside the building at night.

Adam and Jane speaking... she wrote 'Russian' darkly and underlined it. Max and George both knew a smattering of Russian from their maternal great-grandmother. Not much, granted, but some. Adam and Jane were not from Bar Harbor. And the argument, the violence, and Jane's tears. She wouldn't write down the sex that followed their argument. Jane said they were newlyweds. Maybe they were embarrassed about their origins, maybe they found another language more comfortable. None of these things were crimes, except perhaps Adam hitting Jane. And no one would care about that.

Her plane. The engine had been checked in London, and she'd checked it before she flew off today. Engines malfunctioned, occasionally, but she'd never experienced her lovely plane failing so spectacularly. The rain drummed overhead. Would it have been better to stay in London? She could be at Vivian's now, listening to music while Bobby begged her to dance him around.

She hadn't asked Vivian's husband Brian about Mr Knox. Brian worked at the Embassy—why had she not thought of it before? He would probably have heard of an American working at a newspaper. Vivian might even know him. She stared up into the rain sheeting against the curved glass and turned the page in her notebook. Mr John Knox. He teased her, in a fashion. He told her to wear more red. She would not write that down. But for all that he occasionally acted out the standard gestures of courting, his tone, his demeanour lacked... heat. Daniel had pursued her at university, before he turned out to be a bastard. Peter, whose quick sketch had just saved her life, had tried repeatedly to seduce her. There had been other suitors, but they all displayed varying degrees of ardour. Mr Knox examined her. Calculated her responses.

Max ripped the page out of her notebook and tore it into six pieces. She had not examined her own responses to him. In tiny letters on the back of one sixth of the page, she wrote Dr Max Falkland. Frightened was the first word to follow. Disoriented, for the entirety of 1952. Accomplished, she wrote next. And dedicated to archaeology, when not imagining espionage around her. She tore that scrap into three and stuck them all in her jacket pocket. As her adrenaline evaporated the temperature fell. She drew her coat's collar tighter. Archaeology. In the backseat, she had eight books that related to this part of Scotland and two books on air survey. She would read until the rain stopped, and then find a way back to another dreary night at the pub.

Max crawled back into the front seat with a book. The rain plummeted against the metal of the plane. Two hours later, it had not abated. Three hours later, the rain continued. Max flexed her feet. Could she spend the night in here? She had the full equivalent of a meal in her bag, plus some of the American tins and chocolate. Her ration book lay in her bag, so it couldn't be stolen again. Eventually, the rain should stop. Getting wet wouldn't be a disaster, but nothing about the Fentimans, Adam and Jane's squeaking bed or the lumps and dips in her own appealed. The plane held both a hip flask of whiskey and a canteen of water. Darkness fell, and Max used her torch to keep reading. She opened a tin and nibbled. When the torch died, she'd sleep. It would be fine. The plane would be secure.

Two hours later, lights bobbed in the distance. Max extinguished her torch. A search party hadn't occurred to her. Would the Fentimans worry, or even know where to look for her? What if Mrs Fentiman had rung her parents?

Three lights flickered and shifted, but none came towards her field. They converged behind her—Max twisted in her seat—and went towards the coast. The reflections shot across the water, not randomly this time, but in sequence. They diffused too much in the rain for Max to distinguish the order, but an answering flash clearly came from too far westwards to be anything but at sea.

The lights turned back towards land, and this time they cast wide, sweeping searches. They would hit the plane. They would hit the plane and come over to investigate. What would she say? Max tightened her boots, shoved her notebook inside her jacket and as quietly as she had ever managed it in her life, unlatched the plane's door. They had gone quite a distance westward, maybe she had time. She leaned out. The wind blasted and the rain lashed her face. She could have opened the door normally. Max jumped down into the mud. Something warm brushed her, and she nearly screamed before the smell of manure told her it was a cow. Max pushed it out of the way and scurried away as the lights drew near to her. They caught the silver of the plane high up, and Max shied away from the bright circle. Even through the wind, she heard the shout. She started running, letting the wind push her away faster. Not the building—they'd go there first. She would have, if it hadn't been for the downpours. Not to the sea, where the other light hid in the blackness. Max ran northwest, circling above the plane and kept going. Eight trees away she stopped and hid, as the lights closed on her plane. Through the wind, they had to shout, so only snatches reached her.

'...landed anyway.'

The smack of the cockpit door sounded as loud as the hand had last night. 'Not here.'

More followed that she couldn't hear, but she kept running in the opposite direction. 'Landed anyway' thudded in her head in time with her feet. Did that mean that her plane had been tampered with? That the engine... she twisted to look over her shoulder and fell heavily. Lights swooshed over her head. Three bodies stood near her plane, rotating their torches around.

Max stayed perfectly still as one patch approached her, closer and closer.

'She's gone. Wouldn't have seen anything.'

The bodies followed the lights away, past the building. Max remained in place for five more minutes before cautiously standing. She expected someone to shout and grab her, but nothing happened. She wiped the mud from her face. Dare she go back to the plane? What if they left the door open in the rain? Three of the books were library books. Max closed her eyes. She could not fret about that now. The notebook pressed into her side. Did this qualify as something?

More slowly now, she walked north. For the first time the cold wind registered with her. The rain and mud saturated her clothes and her boots started leaking. The map had indicated a road that way, and Tobermory. The town she had considered stopping in that first night. If only she had.

Forty minutes later, she heard the press of boots against the ground. Lots of boots. More than three men, and torches didn't accompany these feet. Max ducked behind a tree and stayed still. The rain had ceased, although the trees still bent in the wind.

Chapter 6

She heard a voice, regulated and even. The feet kept time. She heard commands issued, recognising them from the ATA. Military.

Max pushed through the trees and came out to the road. Twenty men halted on the tarmac.

'Excuse me,' Max called.

The men didn't break formation, but the commander whipped around. A torch flicked on, and the beam shone directly into Max's eyes. She squinted, imagining her mother's horror at the mud festooning her clothes and smearing her face. The odour convinced Max it contained more than simply dirt.

'Can I help you, miss?' The commander—Max couldn't see his uniform clearly enough to discern rank—sounded as calm as if she'd stopped her car to ask directions.

'My plane—I had to make a crash landing. In the field.' She motioned behind her, but how far had she gone since leaving the plane?

'Just now?' A hint of suspicion crept into his voice.

'Hours ago—I was waiting out the rain, but...' The bizarre night's narrative froze on her lips. 'I got frightened.' Muddy, soaked, cold—and now an idiot, nervous ninny. 'I'm Maxine Falkland. I was doing air survey, or trying to.'

'Lieutenant Angus MacDonald at your service.'

He sounded more relaxed. Playing the scared girl card had been correct. The torch swished away from her eyes, and Max could see the outlines of the men again. The lieutenant spoke, and one figure detached from the mass. They conversed in voices too quiet for her hear, and then the second figure barked a command and the column moved off again. Lieutenant MacDonald came off the tarmac towards her.

'Can you walk?'

'Of course. I've just come, I don't know, two miles or so.' What did he plan to do, sweep her manure-covered body into his arms?

'I thought you... You landed in Red's field? The long, low barn?'

'I think so.'

'That's four miles away. It's too late for any pubs to be open, but I'll take you to our camp. The medical officer can look you over, and you can kip there till morning.'

Max slept fitfully, aware that she had kicked the medical officer out of his tent, and despite shedding all her mud soaked clothes before climbing into his cot, the smell of manure mingled unpleasantly with the odour of strange man. Entirely unlike Daniel's expensive cologne, the blankets exuded industrial antiseptic and sweat. If she hadn't been down to an undershirt and briefs in the April chill, she would have elected to sleep on top of the covers.

Besides, she wanted to be fully dressed before anybody entered the tent. So by 4:30, Max had donned her still damp clothes, although she elected to leave her leaking boots off as long as possible. Lighting the small lantern in the tent, she opened her notebook to the previous night. The two pages of rational, archaeological notes from her reading. Geographical features of Iona, the limited history known. A small doodle of the horrible pub, three stars and a few sketched boxes. The next page had her ramblings. Mrs Fentiman, Adam and Jane, her plane. She refused to delve into her pocket for the scribblings about Mr Knox.

The flashing lights. Did they make her ideas about the pub more fanciful or prove that she had been right? Max counted the rolls of bandages in the medic's open cabinet. Twenty-five visible. He shouldn't leave that door open, so the surfaces could gather dust and dirt.

What could she write about the lights? The voices? Her pen was missing from her notebook. She checked her coat pocket. Maybe she left it in the plane—lying next to the book she hadn't closed either. If they didn't shut the door, the book would be ruined. Maybe the pen fell as she dashed from the field.

Could she have dreamt the whole thing? What if the three lights had, in fact, been a rescue party? Her parents rang the pub to check on her, the Fentimans explained she had not returned, and her father insisted they go out and look for her. She could all but hear his booming voice cowing the Fentimans into doing precisely what he demanded.

But the flash from the sea. It didn't even bear writing down, assuming she could find a pen or pencil in the tent.

'Miss Falkland?' The soft burr came from outside the tent. She padded over to the flap and opened it. In the dim grey morning, Max could finally discern that Lieutenant MacDonald had dark blond hair and blue eyes. Either sunburn or shaving reddened his cheeks.

'Good, you're awake.' Lieutenant MacDonald smiled at her. 'Breakfast?'

Angus, as he insisted she call him, kept apologising for the state of the breakfast. Yet the porridge had no lumps, and the tea came strong and hot—vastly superior to the Fentimans' effort. He drove her in a jeep to the field.

'You walked over four miles before you found us. What made you decide to set off?' He spoke loudly over the rain still drumming on the canvas top of the jeep.

'I—I thought my torch might die.' She hoped he wouldn't notice she hadn't brought the torch with her. 'How long are you here for?' The camp certainly wasn't a permanent base, not with the small number of tents.

'It's beautiful around here. Must be amazing from a plane. Do you think you can get it started again?'

Max shook her head, then said 'no' aloud as Angus didn't take his eyes from the road. 'I need to get some stuff

67

from it. Would you mind terribly driving me back to the Hare and Hound after? I know I've already taken you away from your duties.' The taciturn commanding officer had okayed the trip over breakfast. His nose wrinkled slightly at Max's clothes, but otherwise he remained impassive.

Angus laughed. 'Let's see, a choice between normal duties or driving a pretty American girl around. That's a hard one.'

Max flushed. She'd last brushed her hair and her teeth nearly twenty-four hours ago. Nothing about her, from her ruined clothes to her bare face could be called pretty. 'I appreciate it.' She stared out the window at the driving rain. 'I'm not American though. My mother is. And I've spent a lot of time there.'

'And your father is a solid Scottish gent.' His burr increased.

'English, I'm afraid.' She omitted the title. 'Where are you from?'

The conversation took them to the field. Max had no clear memory of climbing the fence, but she saw the stand of trees she'd hidden in on the far side. She should be able to remember it.

'Nice plane,' Angus said.

She pushed away the nausea that rose at not being able to remember to tell him it was a Beechcraft Bonanza. And how long it had taken for her to fly from London. And a million other boring, concrete facts that grounded her in the daylight and the practicality of stepping carefully through the mud. The rain had dropped to a drizzle that misted Angus's hair.

The plane lay on her belly in a sea of mud. No clear footprints that Max could identify as bigger than hers, no sign that men had been here.

'What did you need?' Angus asked.

'I'm sorry?'

'From the plane.'

'Sorry.' Max walked to the door. Pushed to, but not closed. She had closed it. She hoisted herself inside. The library book remained open, the pages spotted with damp. She lifted it and her ration book, and then she shook out the blanket. No fountain pen rolled out. She'd inherited it at ten from her paternal grandfather, and she'd written almost all her of university work with it. She covered her kit with the blanket, but reached under it for the whiskey bottle.

Outside in the damp, Max touched the dents on the undercarriage. Even if the fountain pen had been lost, she'd still had fantastic luck yesterday.

'You did quite a bit of damage there.'

'The engine failed. I'll ring a garage.'

'I guess you are British.'

If Max had walked south, she might have reached the pub again after not much more time than she had reached the troops. Angus didn't mention the relatively short distance— he chattered away about a film he'd seen when last on leave. Max's head ached.

'Have you seen it? *The African Queen*?'

'I've read the book.' She didn't want to explain she'd been in mourning when the film opened, but he filled the gap by telling her how fantastic it was and how she ought to see it.

The rain had ceased by the time they reached the pub, and the jeep's wheels crunched over the scattered gravel.

'It sounded nicer when I booked it over the phone,' Max said. The grey skies did nothing to offset the peeling paint, and even the two pots of flowers looked grim.

'How long will you be here?' Angus turned off the engine, and cows lowing filled the silence.

'I'm going back to London tomorrow.'

Max closed the door of the jeep, and if Angus replied, it was lost. Could she manage to avoid telling her parents?

Not if she arrived by train. They would expect to collect her at the airport, not King's Cross.

'I'll see you in,' Angus said. He held the pub door for her.

'I really do appreciate this,' Max said, as her name was bellowed from within the pub. A tall blur ran across the dim lounge towards her, but skidded to a stop just shy of a hug.

'What the hell have you done to yourself?' Victor demanded. 'And where have you been?'

'Let her get in the door, Victor,' Emma said. She actually touched Max's arm, pulling her into the pub.

'When did you get here?' Max asked. She glanced back at Angus, and saw his face set as he took in Victor's pale trousers and pink shirt. Angus's blond hair and blue eyes dimmed a little in attractiveness.

'Victor insisted we drive up overnight after you rang.'

'Then we get here, and no Max. Where the hell were you? Is that manure?'

'Victor, Emma, this is Lieutenant Angus MacDonald. My plane went down yesterday, and Angus was kind enough to look after me. Victor is an archaeologist I work with, and Emma, well besides being an all-around amazing person, is Victor's wife.'

'The pub is closed,' Mrs Fentiman said, emerging from the office. 'I said you could stay here long enough to see if Miss...'

'Falkland,' Max interjected.

'...turned back up, but she's here now, and I'll thank ye to leave. And I don't allow manure in the lounge.'

'I'll just go change,' Max said.

'And no guests in the rooms.'

'We've sorted the cottage, Max. Why don't we wait outside while you settle up?' Emma asked.

Max nodded, then turned to Angus. 'I can't tell you how grateful I am.' She thought about touching his arm, but her nails were grubby, although she had washed her hands at the camp repeatedly.

'You're welcome. Maybe I'll look you up when I'm next in London. See if *The African Queen* is still playing anywhere.'

'That would be lovely.' Max felt she should sound enthusiastic, but all she wanted was a shower, clean clothes and sleep in a real bed.

'I'll sort your bill,' Mrs Fentiman said, retreating into the office. She slammed the door behind her. The door that held that apron, and the pocket that held Mr Knox's card.

What would he say about the lights? The ache concentrated behind her eyes. She couldn't think about the lights, John Knox, or her poor plane. Once she was in the hopefully clean and dry cottage Emma had chosen, she could analyse her situation.

'Thank you again, Angus.'

'Anytime. I mean, not that I hope...'

Max managed a small chuckle, although it intensified the headache. 'Understood.'

'Well, let's go outside,' Victor said finally, and Max waved goodbye to Angus. Her thigh muscles ground up the stairs, but eventually she reached her room. Everything seemed to be the same. She stripped out of the filthy clothes and turned them wrong side out before rolling them tightly. More mud caked her fingers, but she wiped it off on the trousers. God knew how she'd clean her jacket. Max weighed up hurrying against Victor's reaction to a hint of mud and manure in his car—even a rental car—and decided to go for a bath.

The towel provided was thin, but that at least meant it had dried since yesterday morning. Max wrapped up in it and dashed next door. No sign of Jane or Adam. The sink tap produced icy water to wash her hands. Maybe the bath would trigger the boiler. She let the water run for a few minutes, then closed the drain. A cold bath it would be.

*

Max shivered as she carried her bag downstairs. Her hair drizzled trickles of moisture over her shoulders and soaked the collar of her shirt.

Mrs Fentiman's office door stood ajar.

'That'll be extra for the bath. The hot water.'

'There was no hot water.' Max's teeth set. Mrs Fentiman handed her the bill. 'And I didn't ask for the fire, Adam and Jane did.'

'You used it too.'

'I had gone upstairs by then. And you didn't have to feed me either night, although you've noted both.'

'I planned to feed you. Had to buy the food, didn't I?' Mrs Fentiman waved her right hand above the desk.

Max stared at the black pen in her hand. Lots of people owned black fountain pens. But the cap, lying on the desk, had a small dent at the point. Her fountain pen had a dip at that exact same point. She'd dropped it at Vassar onto a sidewalk, and put the dent in that her grandfather had avoided making over the previous twenty years.

'Are you going to pay up, Miss Gould?'

'Yes.' She dug in her bag and fished out the correct money. 'Did I have any calls yesterday, Mrs Fentiman?'

'No. Did you collect everything from upstairs?'

Except for Mr Knox's card and the fountain pen in her hand. 'Yes. Thank you.' Max crumpled the bill and headed for the door. So the lights weren't a rescue party. And her pen—which she had had in the plane, which she had written with in the plane—had made its way back to the pub and into Mrs Fentiman's graspy hands.

Victor lounged against the hood of the car. 'It took you long enough. That chap eventually took off—I think he was holding out for one more word from your lovely lips.'

'Max, you daft girl, you don't go out with wet hair in Scotland in April.'

72

Max looked at the bit of paper in her fist. Surely she had been overreacting since she got to Scotland. Pens got lost. And lots of people had black pens with dents in the cap.

'Max? Are you okay? Take her bag, Victor.'

The bag's weight eased out of her hand. 'I'm fine.' Emma propelled her to the car and put her in the front seat.

'You're shivering.' The car doors slammed around her, and Victor drove them away from the pub.

'Bloody useless heater,' Victor said. 'This is a ridiculous car.'

Emma used her handkerchief to mop at the water dripping from Max's hair. 'It's not far.'

'I'm okay,' Max said.

'You're grey. Did you sleep at all?' Emma asked. 'Victor, pass me your handkerchief.'

Max closed her eyes. How long had it been since someone fussed over her like this? Her collar still stuck damply to her skin, but Emma lifted her hair into Victor's handkerchief.

'If your plane crashed, how did you get covered in manure?' Victor asked.

'I got out.' Please God, he wouldn't ask why. 'My plane's in a field. Where is the cottage?'

'About 200 yards from the coast. Perfect for diving, which is all we're going to be able to do now.'

'Victor, shush. Archaeology can wait.'

Max roused herself as Victor parked the car at the base of a dirt track. Trees surrounded them, the path kinking around the trunks. She climbed out of the car. The mist had stopped, and the sea roared nearby.

'I'll grab my—what is this car?' The dull crimson of the roof had no relation to the black bonnet. No attempt had been made to ease the seams or remove the rust.

'It's a bastardised Mull car,' Victor said. 'They all look like this.'

'Come on, Max.' Emma pushed her up the path.

After a few turns, Max saw the small stone cottage. The door had fresh coat of pale blue paint, and Max prayed it would be warm.

Emma unlocked the door. 'I'll run a bath. Victor, put the kettle on.'

'I don't want tea,' Max said. The large open room had a kitchen to the left and a living room area to the right. A saggy chair and sofa huddled around a fireplace, the stack of logs beside it as high as the chair's seat. Victor obediently filled the kettle at the tap in the kitchen and placed it on the range.

Emma returned to the living room. 'It's for a hot water bottle. You're going to bed.' She pulled Max from the chair. 'And I'll come scrub your back if you don't comply. So get moving.'

Max laughed. She had no questions now as to why their party had ended. Emma had decided. 'Okay, fine.' She hugged Emma. 'Thank you.'

She woke in the box room, barely big enough to hold a bed and her bag. She dressed and found Victor and Emma eating baked potatoes in the kitchen.

'Yours is in the oven.'

Max pressed a hand to Emma's shoulder to keep her in place.

'I'll get it.'

'Do you want to talk about what happened?' Victor asked.

Max found a plate warming in the side oven, and fished the potato out of the main oven. She stood next to the warmth, letting it soak in to her legs. 'The engine failed. I managed to land it, and wait there for a while. In the rain. Anyway, we should go...' The overhead lights were on and the curtains drawn. 'I slept all day? Get the stuff from the plane. I have tinned food, all the kit.'

'Well, we aren't going to be doing air survey now. Not unless it gets mended quickly. Did you get the stuff to make a dive suit?'

'I'll buy it in London.' The chairs had cushions embroidered with chickens. She chose the one with a blue chicken with a red beak holding a bucket.

'Eat, Max. Stop talking about work. That lieutenant was handsome,' Emma said.

Chapter 7

As the clock swept towards six, Max looked in the teapot. If she had much more, she'd jitter herself out of her skin. She could scrub under her nails again. She could make another list. She could worry about the marks on Jane's face. She could think about John Knox. Instead, she dressed in warm clothes and pulled her hair into a ponytail. Her boots were stuffed with newspaper, but her shoes would suffice. More shoes, she added to her London list.

The bracing wind brought tears to her eyes, but seared the thoughts from her mind. Pink barely glowed through finger gaps in the clouds. Nothing like the heavy fog that shrouded her plane. Today would be beautiful, the perfect day for a flight. Instead, she picked her way down the path and past the dew-drenched angles of the rental car.

She walked down to the shore and let the pounding of the surf calm her. Her shoes sank into the sand and clattered over the stones as she headed north, away from the cottage. The growing light showed a house a mile away or so, and she set her path that way, at the single light shining in a window.

The lights off shore. Had it been code? It could have been kids. It could have been a friend joining them, and the light may have come from another torch, not the sea.

Ahead, an upright structure emerged from the water's edge. It could be a fragment from a shipwreck. Max sped her pace. Maybe the day wouldn't be completely wasted.

It was too thin to be a ship's rib or spar, even broken. She sighed. Just a walking stick, which had been dug into the sand. A lump of folded clothing rested next to it. What kind of lunatic went swimming at dawn in April in Scotland? It wasn't a decorative stick, but medical grade metal, cold and solid under her fingers.

She jerked her hand away when the shout came from the sea. Farther out than she had anticipated, a head bobbed above the surface and a hand waved. The figure moved across the swells swiftly.

No one knew where she was. She'd left no note, and she'd walked to the same coast. How stupid could she be? She moved back from the walking stick, and turned back towards the cottage.

'Stop.'

The man used a walking stick. How threatening could he be? But his pace across the water exceeded hers in shoes over damp stones. Did he need the stick? The sky had lightened so she could see the pale brown hair slicked wetly across his head. Then he was close to the shore, and heavily muscled shoulders emerged from the water. He reached for the base of the stick, and pulled himself upright. Max stepped back. She saw a flash of pale skin, interrupted by a scarlet scar down his left leg. He swam nude. She spun towards the pile of clothes, and fumbled for the towel draped on top. What would motivate a person to swim naked in April? She threw the towel behind her.

'Tell me you were a nurse in the war. Or you're married.' He was English, not Scottish.

'Air Transport Auxiliary.' At nearly twenty-seven, she shouldn't feel the flush in her cheeks.

'My apologies.' The stick emerged from the stones with a clatter, and Max paced away a few steps to allow him to reach his clothes. 'You must be the woman who flew up the other day.'

Max flinched.

'It's a small island. Richard Ash.' He coughed. 'You can turn around now.' His fingers fumbled at his buttons.

'Max Falkland.' She gestured to the left. 'I'm staying in the cottage that way.'

'I'm your landlord then. But I didn't think it was let to Americans.'

'My friend, Emma, booked it.' He skidded his feet into slip on shoes, resting his weight heavily on the stick. 'Isn't it dangerous to go swimming alone?'

Richard thumped his leg, scarring hidden beneath woollen trousers. 'This hurts. All the time. If I were to succumb, well, I've lived a life. Not a great one, but a life.'

'What happened?' She wouldn't normally ask, but if he would be so blunt about the chance of death.

'POW. Pacific theatre.' The thin planes of his face didn't match the muscle on his shoulders. 'I used to fly.' He dragged the towel over his hair. 'Would you like to come have breakfast with me? Do say yes, I don't ever have visitors and it will shock my dog delightfully.'

'I have friends waiting. And a train to catch.' Victor had to drive her to the ferry for the connection.

'Leaving so quickly?'

'Just a quick trip to London.'

'I look forward to your return then. And again, I don't say that lightly.'

Max walked back slowly, carefully placing her feet on the rocks. POW. The RAF seemed so sure that George had died. She'd imagined it over and over, the bullets ricocheting off the fuselage, the punctured fuel tank, the spin, the flames. A dogfight, or the munitions coming from the ground below. No details had ever been provided. She tried to keep to those images, horrific as they were, as opposed to considering that George survived the crash and died in the plane's broken fuselage. Or now, with the scar freshly blazed in her mind, in a POW camp. Would it be better to think George could still be alive? The sun, fully risen, warmed her face, despite the strong breeze. Maybe she should ask John Knox how hot it would be now in Korea. If she saw him again. She inhaled the sea air. Smoke puffed from the cottage's chimney. They must be awake.

Max opened the front door.

'Will you please stop bloody disappearing?' Victor said as she came into the kitchen. The neutrality of his working clothes always surprised her—no pastels, no colours, just heavy weight trousers and normal collared shirts.

'It was just a walk.' Max slid out of her cardigan. 'I met our landlord.'

'Really?' Emma flipped an egg. 'Have you eaten? The agent said he never goes anywhere.'

'He swims at dawn apparently.' And nude. 'He was a POW. Uses a stick.'

'Are you ready?' Victor asked. Emma slid an egg on the plate, and he carried it to the table.

'Of course. I'm going to travel for ten hours and turn up at my parents like this.' Max flicked her ponytail.

'I want to do some work too today.' He flapped his hands at her. 'Get dressed. We don't know what the traffic will be like.'

'She needs to eat first,' Emma said.

Traffic turned out to be one tractor. The longest delay came from cows crossing the road, plus a dog and a herdsman.

'Twenty. Twenty-one,' Max counted.

'We'll make it.' Victor lit a cigarette. 'Did you ask that Knox chap about the Russian?' he asked. His thumb patted the steering wheel casually.

Max shook her head. 'Twenty-three. He works at a newspaper. What could he do?'

'Oh, I don't know. He was somebody in the war. You can tell. He'd know people. For that matter, tell your father.'

'Right. Tell my father. And exactly how does that fit into me coming back to do archaeology? They've already lost one child to communism. They'd lock me in my room. It's going to be hard enough to keep my mother from impounding my plane, once it's fixed. Look, I'm sorry about this. Leaving and all.'

79

'Your mother is insistent. We'll make up for it when you're back. Are you going to drive or take the train again?'

'Train, I guess. We don't need another car.' She looked out the window. 'I'll sort a garage for the plane when I'm back. Would you mind getting the things from it we need?'

The herdsman waved as he ambled across the manure-strewn road.

'Since it has half my kit, plus all the wine, of course not. Write down directions to that field.' He flicked his cigarette out the window, and the car moved forward. 'Listen, go see Honor while you're in London.'

'Why?' Honor Frost mostly did underwater archaeology, and Max didn't know her well. 'Isn't she in France?'

'Home for a bit. I rang round, and she's the only one I could find with some spare rubber you can use to make a suit. I sort of hoped she'd have a spare suit, but no dice. I would have gone, but...'

'You didn't want to?'

'Remember how I drove through the night to rescue you from Russian speaking mad landladies?'

'She didn't speak Russian,' Max muttered.

'Whatever. Otherwise, you can call rubber producers all weekend—wait, that's right, they'll be closed. If you'd sorted this before you left the first time...'

'All right, all right.' The twisting road still meant Victor had to drive slowly. 'Why does Honor want to help me? I barely know her.'

'She likes getting archaeologists diving. Especially women.'

Victor walked with her to the dock. A few people milled around, and Max looked at the sign posted on a railing. One timetable for Wednesday, and another for the other weekdays. 7:30 this morning, which got to Oban at 10:30. That couldn't be right.

'Three hours?'

'It's like a bus. What'd you expect?' Victor asked.

'I hoped to get the 9:12 train. I'll be on the afternoon one at this rate, and it doesn't get in till tomorrow morning.' Her mother would kill her if she arrived on her birthday itself.

A woman standing near them tapped Max's shoulder. 'You could go in my husband's boat. Expensive though, cost you three times the price of the ferry.' She pointed to a man repairing fishing nets further down the dock. 'Not like he's doing any bloody fishing today anyway.'

Max looked at Victor, who shrugged.

'Your husband going too?' the woman asked.

'I'm staying,' Victor said. He smiled at Max.

'Oh, well, I'll go along too then. Keep it all proper.'

'Thank you,' Max said. The woman wore a plain blue dress, with a rather grimy apron over it. She walked towards her husband.

'Stop messing about with those nets, George. Lady here wants to go to Oban. She's the one who flew up in that fancy plane.'

Max flushed. 'If you don't mind, that would be much appreciated. I can pay.'

George hauled himself to his feet. 'All right.'

Fifty, portly, and he smelled of fish. He couldn't be any more different than her own George.

Victor patted her shoulder. 'Don't forget to see Honor.'

Max watched the waves from the boat. Mercifully, George and his wife didn't try to talk to her. But on the train to London, she made a new list. Bar Harbor she knew. She would call Marjorie. She would get her plane repaired, and she would stop letting things happen to her. And when Richard Ash asked again, she'd say yes to a meal.

She'd rung her parents from Oban and explained briefly about the plane. Despite the fact that she'd told them she'd get a taxi from the station, her parents stood together at the end of her platform, their arms around each other's waists. Last summer, they wouldn't have even considered coming to a train station at ten o'clock to collect her. Max endured the fussing of her mother, the hugs, the fretfulness, and the fierce tight embrace from her father. She claimed tiredness from the train, and as soon as they arrived at home, she retreated to her room for the night.

In the morning, she paced into her study and touched the typewriter she'd written her PhD on. The bookcase held a mass of photos, from the war, from Vassar, from her grandparents in New York. Of George, of her parents. The books reminded her of a sane, rational world. She went back into her bedroom and pulled apart the sheer curtains to look out into the garden. Sun shone on each vegetable, each flower. Far from a world with Jane and Adam, and her poor plane.

The phone shrilled in the hallway, and kept ringing. At least six people in the house, and she had to answer the phone? She let her door bang shut behind her.

'Hello, may I help you?' Her father's government job embedded automatic politeness into her voice.

'Dr Falkland. This is a surprise. You're a difficult woman to locate.'

'I've just returned yesterday, Mr Knox.' With a voice like that, she didn't need to ask.

'You called me, a couple days ago, I think. A partial message.'

'Only because you rang me. Here, my parents said.'

'I did?'

It had been Vivian's husband her mother spoke to, the American, and now she looked crazy.

'Of course. Sorry, I did.' His lighter clicked. 'You didn't call direct. When you didn't reach me.'

'I, I didn't have your card with me.' It sat in the pocket of Mrs Fentiman's apron.

'Where have you been?'

'Out of London. For a bit.' With odd people, frightening people. She wouldn't complain. He would laugh. Anyone would.

'Could I interest you in meeting for coffee?'

'Not today, no. My parents—I have plans.' Her mother must have made plans for her birthday. Something made her add, 'I'll be here for a few days.'

'Before you disappear again?'

Max felt again the sickening lurch of her stomach as the plane faltered, heard the smack from the room next door. 'Do you think it's automatically suspicious if people speak another language?'

'Depends on the language.' He exhaled. 'Are you confessing to speaking French? Or have you heard something... wherever you were?'

The violence in Adam's voice saying 'English', even without the slapping sound. The bruise on Jane's arm. The redness across her cheek.

'Dr Falkland, is something wrong?'

The card was taken, a man hit his wife, and her plane plummeted, when it had been checked. She saw odd lights. Did any of these warrant even a British police officer's notice? And a newspaper man from the South could do nothing, despite Victor's suggestions otherwise.

'Dr...'

'Of course not. I simply wanted to return your call.'

'My secretary is sick.'

'I'm sorry?'

'That's why you missed me before. But I'll give you my number again. Just in case. I would answer this line. Ready?'

Her father insisted on notepads next to the phones. She wrote down the number. 'Thank you. Bye.' She depressed the receiver before he could answer. She picked it up again and asked the operator for a line to Bar Harbor, Maine.

She waited for the phone to ring again, doodling around John Knox's phone number. She'd write this one in her notebook, although she had no intention of calling him.

Marjorie answered, and went through the rapture of talking to Maxine, and then the sympathy of losing George. Max thanked her for the flowers, although she knew her mother had dutifully written cards while Max sat upstairs typing her PhD.

'Aunt Marjorie, I met some people who said they were from Bar Harbor. Newlyweds.'

'In London? I don't know anybody who is visiting London now. I would have sent you a little something. What do you miss? I could put something in the mail for you. Your grandmother showed me the pattern of that red dress she sent. It's good to be out of mourning. It can be too long, dear, and...'

'They said they had a bookstore,' Max interrupted.

'Adam! Oh, it is such a shame he's left. But his fiancée— can't remember her name—she didn't like it here. He said she wanted to be in a big city. Did they decide on London?'

'I'm not sure. He ran a bookstore?'

'For about a year, maybe? A really good little one. And he'd get books in for you. Really quickly. He got loads of deliveries. That fiancée though, she came out a few times, and clearly put her foot down. Within a few weeks he shut up the shop and moved on. A real loss.'

'Oh.' Hard to imagine Jane imposing her will on anyone.

'How is he? Give him my best, and tell him how much I liked the last book I ordered, please. Now, how is your lovely mother? Wait a minute, it's the twenty-fifth. Happy birthday, darling. What are you going to do?'

'Just dinner.' Max kept doodling around John Knox's number as Marjorie talked. Planes broke, and people could speak other languages. She did. George had.

Chapter 8

'First my mother insists I have to spend my birthday with her. Then she sends me to you!' Max dropped her handbag onto the floor of Vivian's sitting room. 'Where's Bobby?'

'With the nanny upstairs.' Vivian hoisted her large body off the sofa. 'Don't get comfortable.'

'Why?'

'We're going out.'

'Vivian, I just want to tell you about Scotland, and be still. I'm tired.' Max hated the whinging tone in her voice. 'Sorry.'

'Humour the pregnant lady and come along.' Max followed Vivian. 'We'll take a taxi.'

Fifteen minutes later, Max and Vivian sat in a beauty salon, with Vivian energetically discussing styles for Max's hair.

'It's just dinner. With my parents. Why does it matter?' The smell of chemicals made Max light-headed.

'Should she go lighter? Maybe all the way to properly pale blonde?' Vivian asked the stylist.

'No. Absolutely not.' Max pressed her hands to her head. 'I've spent the last six months getting my hair done. This is my summer to do something different.'

'It's your birthday.'

The woman led Max to a sink and washed her hair. The massage of her scalp did soothe some of the aches away from her neck, and she nearly fell asleep in the chair. Soon, sections were twined around enormous rollers and Max sat next to Vivian under dryers. The lights and the plane seemed very far away.

Another woman appeared beside her and started shaping her nails. She didn't need this; she needed to go back to work. Her mother would appreciate it though, so she didn't fist her fingers. Maybe they could get out the residue of dirt and dung from the corners. Vivian examined her own.

Vivian and the women had a discussion about nail varnish that ended with a dark scarlet being chosen, without any input from Max at all. The polish was smoothed on as the original woman brushed and pulled, twisted and tucked Max's hair.

'So what did you want to tell me about Scotland? Meet anybody? Your mother said something about a soldier...'

'My plane went down. He—I met him after.'

'Oh my God. Are you okay?' Vivian flung her hand towards Max. 'Of course you are. You're here. But...' The nail girl eased Vivian's hand back onto the chair's armrest.

'I'm fine. The plane isn't.' The crimson spread, tiny brush stroke by tiny brush stroke, across her hands. 'When did you see my mother?'

'The other day.' Vivian's eyes skidded away from Max's in the mirror.

'You're a terrible liar.' And just like that, John Knox invaded her mind again. 'Have you ever heard Brian mention an American named John Knox? He works for the *Universal Dispatch.*'

'Ow,' Vivian said, as a particularly strong tug with the brush pulled her head back. 'Don't think so. I can ask.'

Conversation turned to the pregnancy, to Bobby, and even to golf, Brian's latest pursuit.

The hairdresser held the mirror so Max could see the complicated whirls and curves of the up do—far more elaborate than anything she'd do herself.

'You ever going to cut it?' Vivian raised a hand to her own cropped curls.

'My mother keeps asking me that.' Max liked her hair long, but the new Queen's cut was proving very popular. 'That's lovely; thank you.'

Max followed Vivian to the front of the salon.

'Back to mine? We should do our makeup and...'

'Vivian, this is sounding suspiciously like more than just a dinner.' Max paid and replaced her wallet in her handbag. How could her hands look so different now?

'It's dinner. But how lovely to go out properly.' Vivian turned to a mirror and fluffed her hair, rather than looking at Max.

When they arrived back at Vivian's, Max found that her mother had had two boxes and all her makeup delivered. The crimson bow on the large box matched her nails. The small one held jewellery came from her mother's stash. The diamond necklace fell into the 'will inherit one day', not the 'wear now' category.

'This isn't dinner.' Max dropped the necklace back onto the velvet. 'She's planned a party, hasn't she?'

'Of course it's dinner. But since you're back from the wilds of Scotland, why not have fun?'

Vivian sighed as Max opened the lid of the second one, revealing a white taffeta gown. 'It's beautiful.'

'I didn't ask for a new evening dress.' She hadn't asked for anything, actually. She'd opened the present from her American grandparents at breakfast—a tiny diamond pendant, and even that seemed too much for her twenty-seventh birthday.

'Darling, you have no sense of fun. You've worn dreary clothes for ages. Let's play dress up. I'll do your makeup.' She pushed Max towards the lavatory. 'Go wash your face. I'm glad she sent your own stuff over. Your colouring is so much fairer than mine.'

Max found a washcloth and gingerly wiped her face, avoiding her hairline. Everyone wanted her to get married. What else could explain the expensive dress? The evening certainly held a party, rather than dinner. Why else would they have given her the American present already?

The weave of the cloth pressed into her eyes. They'd gotten through the first Christmas, the first New Year's.

Hers was the first birthday without George. Max could force herself, for Mother's sake. She rinsed the cloth and hung it neatly. 'Just bloody cheer up,' she said to her reflection and headed back to Vivian's bedroom.

Bobby had danced around the room while Vivian outlined, powdered and shaded Max's face. But Vivian whisked him up to the nursery when it came time for Max to dress. Max lifted the dress from the box carefully. Balenciaga. The shirred bodice had a bow under the bust and another at the waist. A strapless corselette rested in the box. Mother had thought of everything. Max took off her clothes and fastened the underwear around her chest. A knock sounded at the door. She prayed it wasn't Brian, although why would he knock at his own door?

'Only me,' Vivian said, as she pushed the door open. 'My God, I'd kill for your figure.'

'Get the baby out first.' Max stepped into the dress and fumbled for the zip.

'Let me.' Vivian tugged up the zipper.

Max turned and examined her reflection. Yards and yards of taffeta domed over a visible black underskirt. It dragged to the floor in the back, but bared her ankles and a bit of her shins in the front.

'Here. You'll want these.' Vivian handed her a pair of strappy sandals.

'We don't wear the same size. How long have you been plotting this?'

'I have no idea what you mean.' Vivian held her gaze for half a second before she laughed.

'She didn't have this delivered, did she? The dress was already here.'

'So I asked her to find you something really nice. Sympathetic dressing up. Look at this.' She pulled a pale blue maternity dress out of the wardrobe. 'I'm wearing this. I had a waist once. Here are the gloves.'

Max pulled the white gloves up to her elbows. 'Forget terrible—you're a horrendous liar. It's clearly a party. How big is it?'

'No party. Dinner.'

Brian drove them, with Vivian sitting in the front seat, but twisting as best she could to talk to Max in the back. With the width of Max's skirt, no one else could have sat beside her. Seventy hours ago, she had been covered in mud and frightened; now she had been sprayed, manicured and poured into a designer dress. Why did she feel just as uneasy?

'Brian, do you know somebody—what was his name, Max?'

'John Knox.'

Brian tapped the steering wheel. 'Sounds familiar. What's he do?'

'Something at the *Universal Dispatch*.' Something with a secretary, and a private line. 'I've never read it.'

'It's mostly aimed at Americans overseas, I think. We get a copy,' Vivian said. 'Does he write for it?'

'I'm not sure. He's Southern.'

'Oh. I do know him, I think,' Brian said. 'I'm pretty sure I've met him at some event or another. All right, for what he is.'

'What does that mean?' Vivian asked.

'Well, Southern.'

'Don't be horrid, Brian.'

'Army, I seem to remember. Had quite a distinguished war, I believe.'

The conversation changed to something Bobby had done that morning, as Max filed away those tidbits. Had Brian simply meant that Mr Knox hailed from below the Mason Dixon line?

*

Brian parked around the corner and they walked towards the house, their shoes clacking in rhythm. Vivian held onto Brian's arm.

'My feet hurt,' she said.

'You did insist on those heels.' Max eyed the stilettos.

'I'll sit down in…' She stopped speaking.

'It's a party, isn't it? Please, please don't make me face people shouting at me.'

'Okay, yes. But your mother really wanted to do it, so do act surprised.'

'You weren't supposed to tell,' Brian said.

'How big?' But she already had mounted the steps to her front door, and it opened as they reached it. It wasn't a servant Max knew, so her mother had brought in extra staff. The number of guests multiplied in her head.

Vivian and Brian propelled her towards the room that had been a ballroom before the First World War and the slide in the family fortune that precipitated her father going abroad to marry a wealthy woman. Mother had insisted on restoring it during the Depression, despite all contrary opinions, or perhaps because of them. Max listed these facts, trying to keep her calm despite the muffled giggles that emerged from the room and the crash of a breaking glass.

'How big?' she whispered, but Vivian opened the door and the shouts of 'surprise' nearly deafened her. She numbly tried to count, but stopped when she reached more than forty.

A body collided into her, and she flinched before she recognised her cousin Charlie hugging her. She forced herself to close her arms around his back.

'Tell me about the plane crash. It sounds spectacular. How did you…'

Her mother glided towards them and kissed Max's cheek. 'Happy birthday, darling. Do you like the dress?

Please, Charlie, talk about the, the incident later. Not now. Max needs to greet her guests.'

Max saw Edward, and picked out over a dozen archaeologists amongst the children of minor peers. Her mother had tried. Even Ruth was there, hiding behind a knot of archaeologists. 'Did you invite every person from the Institute?'

'I didn't know who were your particular friends, dear. Except for Victor, and he said he had to go ahead to Scotland. Although speaking of Scotland, there's a young man here to see you. And luckily Edward hadn't left for Denmark yet.'

Adam? She'd invited Adam and Jane?

'A kilt!' Vivian whispered ecstatically in her ear.

Max saw him then, Angus, in full Scottish dress uniform, standing at the far side of the room, talking to her godfather Uncle Gerald and Dad. The bar had to be three deep in archaeologists. Dear God, if it included Wheeler, he'd hit on her mother.

'Was this a bad idea?' her mother asked. She looked forlorn.

'Of course not. Thank you.'

Max forced one high-heeled foot forward, and then the other and pressed into the mass of people. She counted fifteen 'lovely' comments before she remembered she couldn't compare tallies with George after the party. They'd played the lovely game since the first parties they'd been allowed to attend. She blinked away the pressure behind her eyes, keeping up a flow of chatter. Ruth complimented her on her lovely home. For all her disdain at Max's money, Ruth certainly didn't mind drinking her parents' champagne, if the high colour in her cheeks marked anything. But she noted the pre-war style of Ruth's dress that gaped too large around her waist. Max gripped Ruth's hand. 'It's very nice of you to come along. Thank you.'

Ruth nodded and drew her hand away. Max floated through happy birthdays and meaningless chats with archaeologists and society people she'd avoided throughout her writing-up period until she reached the bar. Edward handed her a glass of champagne. He wore an impeccable dinner jacket, although most of the archaeologists she saw wore suits.

'Nice party.'

'Odd party. The whole Institute?' She watched Charlie talking to Ruth, leading her to the dance floor.

'Rik Wheeler's back in India.' Edward smiled. 'The bar is going fast. You should drink up. What have you found so far?'

'Not a thing. My plane went down. There's something strange up there, Edward.'

'Archaeological?'

'No.' Before she could explain, a light cough sounded behind her.

'Miss Falkland.' She and Edward both turned, and Angus stood behind her. She tried not to stare at his knees.

'Doctor,' Edward said.

Angus looked puzzled.

'Doctor Falkland.' Edward extended his hand. 'I'm Edward Sinclair. I'll leave you two to talk.'

'I hope this isn't intrusive—I didn't—your mother invited me.'

'Of course not.' She smiled. 'Please, call me Max. Thank you for all your help the other day.'

'You look simply splendid, Mi... Max.'

'Better without all the mud? That's a relief.' Her mother had certainly latched onto the mention of his name. His blond hair shone under the lights.

'What will...' he started.

'Max, darling, I just had to say happy birthday. What an amazing dress.'

Max turned and found a smile for Matilda, who clearly wanted to meet Angus. 'Angus, this is my friend Lady Hays. Matilda, Lieutenant Angus McDonald. I met Angus in Scotland this week.' Max drained the rest of her champagne as they swapped greetings. She closed her eyes as the buzz tickled high in her head.

'Another drink?' Angus asked. 'Lady Hays?'

Max decided to not shock him by asking for a whiskey. Glasses of champagne appeared for her and Matilda, although he received a tumbler of whiskey.

'Max and I were at school together in the States. I heard you had a dramatic plane crash,' Matilda said. Her pastel pink nails gripped Max's arm. 'Were you all right?'

'I'm fine. My plane isn't. Angus was very helpful.'

Uncle Gerald appeared, sliding his arm around Matilda's waist. 'Hello, pet.'

'Darling, this is…'

'We've already met, and I've had a chance to thank him for saving my goddaughter.'

Angus hadn't saved her exactly. She'd managed perfectly well until the lights and… But what would she have done in the middle of the night?

Matilda shuddered. 'I can't imagine why you want to go off to the wilds of Scotland.' She flushed slightly, her complexion nearly matching her pink dress. 'My apologies, Lieutenant McDonald.'

He smiled. 'No need.'

Uncle Gerald laughed. 'Come along, pet.' He drew Matilda away from them.

Max sipped her champagne. 'Sorry about that.' Surely Matilda hadn't been quite so silly before her marriage.

'Is his wife American too?' Angus asked.

'Matilda *is* his wife. I actually introduced them.'

'Oh.' His expression was guarded.

'It was as awkward as you can imagine, given it was at a school concert.'

93

Angus laughed. 'I'm glad you said it. How long did you live in the States?'

'I was born here—in case I was a boy—and then lived in New York till I was eight. Then my mother took us...' She took a deep breath. With George. 'We went back at the start of the war, and I returned in '43 to join the ATA. Then back for my degree, and then I came home for my PhD. A bit of a ping pong life, honestly.'

'I've never met anyone with a PhD before.'

'Do you mean a woman?'

'I meant anybody.' He looked down at his shoes.

She shouldn't be so acerbic. 'Well, there's Edward, and my father. You've met a couple tonight already. And I've only had mine for a few months.'

'What will you do now with your plane out of operation?'

'Land survey. Victor, my colleague, is doing some dive work. I may join him.' His mouth puckered as she said Victor. 'He and his wife are still in Scotland.' His expression didn't ease much, and his attractiveness dropped accordingly.

'What type of training were you doing out there at night?' she asked. Angus picked up his tumbler, and they drifted away from the bar and the mass of archaeologists.

'Just training.'

Max skirted the central floor where three or four couples danced to 'Unforgettable'. Why did they keep playing that song? 'I'm very grateful.'

'I'm surprised you stayed out there as long as you did. I know that it was raining and all, but what...'

'I don't mind the rain. The pub I was staying at was pretty dire. The plane seemed more comfortable.'

Angus laughed. Max caught movement at the door, a bright dress heading out perhaps, and she saw John Knox, standing tall and straight in a dinner jacket, just inside the room, watching her. Her crimson tipped fingers sketched a tiny wave, and he nodded. Then a man in a white coat, one of the hired waiters, approached him. He pivoted and left the room.

Angus asked her to dance twice before she processed the question. At least the song had changed as they moved to the middle of the room.

He put his arms around her, and the hem of his kilt bounced against her skirt as they moved. He danced well, and Max knew that wherever her parents and grandmother had positioned themselves, they would be smiling.

'Who were you waving at?'

'Someone I thought I recognised.'

'You know a lot of people.' They whirled past family friends, Institute acquaintances, Vivian tapping her toe as she sat on the sidelines.

'My parents invited a lot of people. Some I hardly know.' A flush rose in her cheeks. He certainly qualified for that status. 'And some it would be lovely to know better.'

'I'd quite like to know you better.' His hand tightened on her back, and Max wanted to sidestep him all together. One point of his upper lip tilted infinitesimally higher than the other. How bad would marriage be to someone like him? She'd have pretty children, a man with handsome knees to go to bed with, and her family would stop throwing suitors at her.

'Yes. I would too.' The song drew to a close, and Angus waited a fraction too long before dropping his arms.

'Would you like some air?'

Max smiled. And she led him, not towards the garden, but towards the front of the house. The door had just closed behind a tall figure, and Max stepped ahead to reopen it. John Knox rushed down the last three steps and let himself into a black car. Angus slid his arm around her waist.

'Are you all right?'

Max nodded. Mr Knox drove away. And he didn't even wave, or stop. Or say hello.

'When do you have to get back to your base?' Max asked.

'I have three days leave.'

Max filled the gap with inane chatter, and Angus didn't seem to notice. He didn't ask why they went to the front instead of the garden, and he didn't ask why she had followed the man in the black suit to the front door. She didn't relax into his arm around her waist; however, nor did he try to pursue the kiss she knew he had intended by suggesting they get air. Max allowed herself to shiver, and Angus immediately suggested they go back inside.

Her mother swept up to them as soon as they slid back into the room.

'Darling. And Lieutenant MacDonald. I was telling him earlier how grateful we were that he was there to rescue you. The thought of your plane...' She stopped, her fingers clenching into a tight clasp. 'I'm glad you won't be flying for a while.'

Max danced with Angus again, as well as with friends, and even Edward, who turned out to be surprisingly graceful. Charlie only stepped on her toes three times, as opposed to his usual eight. At the end of the evening, Angus squeezed her hand when saying goodbye, although he didn't offer a kiss.

'Archaeologists drink rather a lot, don't they?' her mother asked at breakfast.

'I could have told you that. I'm sure I have told you that.' A dull headache wrapped her temples, but she woke cheerfully for the first time since she could remember. 'Thank you for having it.' The phone rang in the distance, but she didn't move.

'You looked so horrified when the door opened, I was quite worried.'

'I think I needed it. Needed to remember.' That's what life in the States had been like, parties and happiness and being free. The PhD, George—she would remember how to enjoy herself again.

'Irene Sterling said Harold has almost finished his PhD. At Cambridge, I believe. Maybe if things don't work out with your lieutenant we can have him over for dinner. At least you wouldn't have more education than he does.'

'Mother, I've met Angus twice. I hardly think we can plan a wedding.' She'd known Harold since childhood. George always called him Horrid Harold and more than once he'd made Harold cry.

Her father walked into the breakfast room. 'There's a chap on the phone for you, Max. American. Knox, he said.'

'I invited him, but he didn't turn up,' Mother said.

'He did. He left. Would you mind telling him I'm out?'

Her father rested his hand on the back of her chair. 'That's not like you.'

'Is it because of a certain lieutenant?' her mother asked.

Max kept her eyes on cup of tea. 'I'm simply not interested in speaking to him.' Being cheerful meant letting go of what bothered her. No more worries about Scotland, no more wondering about the mysterious man who didn't speak plainly and didn't stay to wish her a happy birthday.

'Okay.'

'What about Angus? Do you like him? You seemed to.'

'It was only the second time I've seen him. And the first time it was rather muddier.'

Her father came back in and dropped a piece of paper next to her cup. 'Said to ring him back. Where's Charlie?'

'Still asleep, I think,' Mother said.

Her father, it seemed, had tried to write neatly. The two phone numbers had been carefully inscribed. 'Two?'

'Different ones at work. He'll be at the second one after eleven. Something about being in different offices. Seems rather serious about you getting in touch. Very precise about them. Nancy, do you know what happened to that chap, what's his name, with that odd wife. Southern, the pair of them.'

Her parents started talking about the old days in New York, before she remembered very much of anything, long before they moved back to the UK. Max sipped her tea. She wouldn't ring him. But she slid the paper into her pocket all the same. The phone rang again, and her father stood.

'Since when do you go to answer the phone?'

'You can't pretend to be out and then answer, can you?' He kissed her forehead as he passed. 'Glad you look happier.'

He came back a moment later. 'The Scottish one, now. Are you out?'

'I'll take it.'

'How are we supposed to keep up with your suitors?' He laughed, but Max could tell how pleased they were. How delighted they would be if she just married Angus.

His soft burr was pleasant as he asked her to dinner and the cinema. And she said yes before replacing the phone with her scarlet nails.

Angus kept apologising about taking the Tube as they walked to the cinema.

'I didn't think you'd have a car in London when you're posted in remote Scotland,' she said.

'I don't actually have a car at all. It's mostly jeeps for me. I'm afraid I couldn't find *The African Queen* still on anywhere, but I thought we could see *Angels One Five*. It's about flying.'

War flying. Max fought a wiggle of panic in her stomach. 'Could we see something else?' They drew close to the bright lights of the cinema.

'Sure.' He pointed to a poster. '*Wings of Danger*. Looks exciting.'

A plane plummeted on the poster. Max shifted. 'Maybe not?'

'Of course, yes. Sorry.'

Max looked for any other poster. 'There. *The Tall Headlines.*'

'That film was terrible. I'm sorry,' Max said. She'd never been to the café he'd chosen, but she knew the prices on the menu would horrify her mother. She'd rate the wine as worse than the regular bottles at Victor's party.

'It was rather gloomy, wasn't it?' He lifted his wine glass. 'I didn't think there would be so many films about flying. Will you fly again?'

'Definitely. As soon as it's mended.' She smiled. 'I just wasn't ready to see one with a crash quite this quickly.' Or one that made her think of George.

'How long have you flown?'

'Since I was seventeen. My father flew, in the Great War, and, well, my family likes planes, I guess.'

'That's a sore subject?'

'My brother. He was shot down in Korea. Last year.'

Angus pressed his lips together, and she remembered his face when she introduced Victor.

Victor and Emma, in the little house, doing archaeology. While she saw silly films and fantasised about having children with sturdy knees.

'Do you know anything about the Hare and Hound? Or the Fentimans?'

'Who are they?'

'The couple who run it.'

'It's not a great pub. A better one would be the Bull and Last. But I don't think they do rooms.'

'I'm staying in a little house with Emma and Victor now.' She saw it again, the slight tightening of his cheeks. 'When I'm back up there, I'll have to introduce you properly.'

'Are you going back?'

Max waited for the waitress to deposit plates before them. Her meal seemed to have more gravy than anything else. 'It's my work.'

'I thought maybe, after, well I thought you might stay in London.'

'I really love archaeology.' She wouldn't dip her head; she wouldn't look anywhere but in his eyes. 'I'm very good at it.'

'I'm sure you are.' He smiled. Perhaps she imagined that flicker of emotion. 'Frankly, I'm pleased. I thought I'd have to wait until my next leave to see you again.'

He kissed her on the walk from the Tube, a sweet, gentle kiss, and then escorted her up the steps of her parents' house. She kissed him again, there at the door, before going inside.

A note sat next to the telephone on the table in Charlie's scrawl. The top definitely said Max, the second line had what might be a J and a K, and something approached a phone number on the third line. Max exhaled. She certainly couldn't return a call based on that.

'Max,' her father said. He stood just outside the library door. 'Nice evening?'

'Dreadful film, but Angus was pleasant company.' Was that all he was?

'See your note?'

Max nodded.

He withdrew a piece of paper from his pocket. 'Your Mr Knox rang again. I fear he didn't find Charlie a reliable message taker. Perceptive of him, of course.'

'Of course.' Or bloody-minded. He had no reason to expect she'd be home on a Saturday evening.

'Do you want it, darling?'

Max stepped closer and took the sheet. Every digit was perfectly legible.

Her father gripped her hand. 'Are you all right? We haven't talked properly about the crash or…'

'I'm okay.'

'Come in.' He tugged her into the library. The lamp next to his chair was lit, illuminating a thick sheaf of papers.

'You're working late.' She slid off her heels and curled her legs up under her on the sofa.

'Lots to get through.' He folded his glasses and dropped them on top of the papers. 'So what happened?'

'I don't know, exactly. The engine failed. I managed to get the plane down—do you remember Peter, that pilot I saw briefly in the war? He'd talked to me about landing blind, thank goodness. I couldn't get the landing gear down either, so she skidded.' She opened and closed her hands, remembering the wrench of the controls, the wave of mud. 'It's still in the field. I'll find a mechanic when I get back.'

'So you are going back?'

Why did everyone think she wouldn't? 'I haven't managed to do any work yet.'

Her father smiled. 'I told your mother that. She'd like you to stay.'

'She'd like me to be married with three children.'

He laughed. 'That, too. I'm glad you'll head back up.' He rubbed his forehead. 'I wish I could go with you.'

'Where is Mother, anyway?' Ten o'clock seemed early for her to have retired.

'She thought I'd get more out of you about your date alone. Although I'm not supposed to tell you that.' He lit a cigar and puffed. 'Nor do I believe it.'

'Has it been that long since I went on a date?' Before the six months of mourning.

'One that she didn't arrange?'

'I suppose.' Max rose and scooped up her shoes. 'He was perfectly nice. I'll probably see him again on Mull.'

'We don't have to talk about your love life,' he said. 'Anything else on your mind?'

Max saw again the lights flashing off the coast, but she shook her head. 'I enjoyed flying again, before the crash. And it's nice to be out of London, back doing something real.'

'Tell me about it. Maybe I'll come up and visit later in the summer. I could even help with some survey.'

'Victor wants me to go diving.'

'I won't join you doing that.' He laughed. 'Sleep well, darling.'

Max stepped close to his chair, and he squeezed her hand. She leant down and kissed his forehead. Surely the wrinkles had spread in the last six months. And was the salmon pink of his parting wider? She rested her hand on his head.

'I'm not ancient yet, Max.' He shooed her away.

'Don't stay up too late.' Max climbed the stairs slowly. In her room, she removed the bits of paper from her handbag and looked at the one bearing her father's hand. A Hampstead number. Close to Victor and Emma, Mr Knox had said. She stuck the papers with the other in her notebook and undressed. Old Max fit more comfortably into her party dresses. And Old Max ignored the whisper from post-PhD Max that Angus would expect her to give up archaeology, to raise a family, and eventually he'd ship out to some other war. Max closed her notebook on John Knox's phone numbers and went to bed.

She twisted under the covers. In Scotland, she would focus on archaeology and forget her suspicions. She would be cheerful again.

Chapter 9

After church, Max changed and sat at her desk. She rolled a sheet of paper into the typewriter. She could... but she lifted her notebook instead. It fell open to the scraps bearing John Knox's numbers. She flicked past them, back to the notes she'd written in her plane. The whole train journey, she'd resisted writing about the flashing lights. She rolled the pencil between her fingers. Was Mrs Fentiman writing with her fountain pen even now?

Something banged against her door, but before she could answer Charlie came in.

'Could you wait till I say come in, please?'

'Why? It's not your bedroom. I figured you'd be decent.' Charlie perched on her desk, next to the typewriter.

Max turned her notebook to a clean page. Charlie stayed silent, and she started to sketch a plane. Her plane.

'Hey, will you drive me back today?'

'Why? I mean, sure, I'd be happy to. But why?'

'Cause you have an amazing car, and you're pretty.'

Max smiled. 'Thanks. But the other boys know I'm your cousin, right?'

Charlie nodded. 'Sure. But usually Uncle Max's car disgorges me, and it's just faceless like all...' He stopped. 'Mum brought me at the start of term with *him*, and if I could have somebody else...'

Max patted his knee. Charlie's mother's remarriage was only a month after Charlie took up the mantle of heir. 'Of course.' The new husband had not improved in the intervening time.

Charlie swung his legs, his heels thudding against her drawers. 'Thanks. Can you wear something different?'

Max laughed. 'You're as bad as Mother. What did you have in mind?' She held her oversized shirt away from her body.

'Something sharp. Like a film star. And sunglasses.'

Max glanced out the window at the cloudy sky. 'All right.'

'Why do you wear that stuff? What does Aunt Nancy call it?'

'The Vassar look.' Max tapped a cartoon pinned over her desk. The illustration showed a woman in similar clothes, and the caption said 'a dramatic silhouette for 8.15 to 6'. 'We wore it to classes, and it's comfortable to work in. But I would have changed anyway before taking you. When do you need to be back?'

'I should be back for dinner at six, but if we had a meal on the way...'

'Seven thirty? We could stop by and see Granny, if you like.'

'She already inspected me at your party. I'm taller, apparently. And I look like my father.'

'Charlie, come on,' Max said. He disappeared back towards his room. He'd been here for less than forty-eight hours—how much could he have to pack?

The phone rang, and she lifted the receiver. 'Falkland residence, may I help you?'

'Hello, Dr Falkland. It's John Knox.'

'Hello.' Why hadn't she let someone else answer? How many messages had he left now? Her face flushed.

'I thought perhaps you had already left. Back to wherever you were.'

'Tomorrow. I'm...' The apology stopped on her lips. She didn't have to call him. 'I'm taking a sleeper.'

'Would you have time for a drink before you go?'

'I'm driving my cousin back to school now.'

'And tomorrow?'

'I'm busy, I'm afraid.' She had to see Honor Frost. 'I have to procure a large amount of rubber.'

'Excuse me?'

'Never mind. It's for archaeology.'

'I'll take your word for it.' His lighter clicked. 'I'm sorry I had to miss your party. That was quite a dress.'

'Thanks. My mother chose it.' Did he mean it was a pretty dress or awful? 'If you'll excuse me...'

'Why are you avoiding me, Dr Falkland?'

'I scarcely know you, Mr Knox. I don't know what you anticipated, but...'

He exhaled. 'Very well. Again, I apologise for my absence from your party.'

'No apology necessary. Good afternoon, Mr Knox.' She replaced the receiver. 'Charlie!' she called.

'Darling, must you bellow like a fishwife?' Her mother came into the hallway.

Max never had learned the name of the woman who had offered her the lift on George's boat. She hadn't bellowed.

'What are you going to have?' Charlie asked.

'Chicken,' Max said.

'Okay. So I'll ask...'

'Don't you dare.'

Charlie looked up from the menu. 'Isn't that what I'm supposed to do?'

Max exhaled. 'If we're on a date, it's traditional. Dad does it for me. But I'm perfectly capable of ordering my own food. And I'm the one bloody paying for it.'

'Okay. So would I do it on a date?'

'Most girls expect it.' The waiter approached and they both ordered. 'Mother says I'm odd.'

'You're fun. I think if you were a normal girl—I mean not my cousin—I'd be afraid to ask you out though.'

Max laughed. 'The PhD?' Her mother's voice whispered: *How will you ever get married if you have more education than all your suitors?*

'Nope. You're fierce. Well, maybe the PhD too. You

going to marry that lieutenant?'

'Did Mother say that?' Charlie didn't answer. 'Charlie, going on a date with somebody doesn't mean you're headed to the altar. We went to the cinema.'

Charlie started chattering about films, and Max let it wash over her. Fierce? George called... used to call her ornery. Mean, sometimes. What would John Knox say? Angus didn't seem to find her fierce or mean. But he didn't realise she had a PhD until the party.

The waiter brought their dishes and they ate in silence.

'You going to finish that?' Charlie asked. He pointed to her plate. 'You've been picking at it for ages.'

'Probably not.'

'Can we swap?'

Her mother would be horrified, but Max swapped her nearly full plate for Charlie's empty. 'Do they feed you at school?'

'Never enough.'

'Are you going to go home at all this summer?'

'I'm going to Norfolk with you lot. I've already arranged it with Aunt Nancy.'

'Don't you need to see your mother eventually?'

'I had Christmas with them. I'll do a weekend, maybe, and they came for my birthday. That's plenty.'

'What does she say about it?'

'I don't think she's noticed.'

'Charlie...'

'Look, you know what it's like at boarding school. You're barely home normally. She's tied up with what's-his-name.'

Charles. He was hardly likely to forget it.

'Leave it alone. Please.'

Max smiled. 'You're getting very grown up.' He'd have shouted even a year ago. But George was alive a year ago, and Charlie's prospects consisted of finding his way to university and progressing into a job at some Falkland enterprise.

Max walked Charlie up to the entry hall of the school. It smelled just the same as it did when George was there, dinners and sweat and leather.

'Do you have any of George's teachers?'

'Yep. They compare us a lot. Or they did.'

'I'm sure you're doing better than he did. He hated it here.'

Charlie nodded. 'I know.' A few boys passed through the hall and eyed her curiously. 'Hey, have a safe trip back to Scotland. Call me if you crash anymore aeroplanes, okay?'

'I've only got the one.' She hugged him. 'Take care.'

Charlie laughed and pushed her arms away. 'That's enough mushiness.'

'Bye.'

Stones crunched under her feet as she walked back to her car. Fierce. Maybe children with sturdy knees wouldn't be too bad after all.

Max parked her car in Wimbledon. She closed her eyes briefly. She hadn't spent much time with Honor. Would she expect money for the rubber? Should she offer? Max pressed her hand against her stomach. Why had her lovely plane failed? She wouldn't need a rubber suit if it still worked.

She forced herself up to the front door, and Honor's ash blonde hair approached the glass pane in the door.

'Hello, Max. Come on in.'

Max followed her through the house to the garden, where a cocktail shaker rested on the metal table.

'Have a seat. Martini?'

'Thanks ever so much for doing this.' Max fidgeted with the glass Honor passed her.

'You don't look enthused.'

Maybe because she didn't usually have gin before noon? 'I've never been sure I wanted to dive.'

'But you study Vikings, don't you? You'll love it. It'll be an addiction soon, mark my words.' She sipped her martini. 'My first dive was in a friend's garden at a party. In snow. Victor was there—such a lovely man.'

Max nearly laughed, but restrained herself.

'I climbed into the suit through a rubber apron in the belly, and then Victor and some others helped press the air out of the suit with planks. The canvas—it was a suit from the war—closed around me—and I descended into the blackness. It's like flying. Euphoric.'

'If you say so.'

'Anytime out of water is a waste.' She lit a cigarette. 'But you seem ill at ease. Is that just my reputation?' She grinned.

What to tell her? The lights? The plane? George? 'It's nothing. I had some plane trouble and...' She exhaled. 'You know what it's like. Being a woman in archaeology.'

'At least you have the degrees.' Her lips thinned. 'Does it change how they treat you? Or do you have to be somebody like Kathleen? Old and respected?'

Victor had said once she was touchy about not having degrees. 'The PhD hasn't made a blind bit of difference in how I'm treated.' What would Honor have done to that boy at Victor's party? But she probably would have told off Ruth and never danced with him in the first place. 'They— it doesn't help to sound like this.' Honor had the clipped vowels of Max's father and all her aristocratic friends. Max could ape it, if she concentrated. But Ruth wouldn't dare mock Honor in person.

'Or this.' She laughed. 'I suspect the size of your purse has an impact too?' She took the cocktail shaker into the house.

Max sipped her own drink. Honor's glass had less than a quarter of an inch remaining.

Honor returned with an armful of black foam rubber and dumped it in Max's lap. The weight surprised her.

'It isn't made up into a suit. I hate this stuff. Woollen ballet tights and combinations are the way to go.'

'Victor said I should try the suit.'

'He would. They fit men properly. All the talc and salt water brought me out in a rash.' She swung a small bag onto the table that clunked. 'Here's some spare lead weights too. Take a belt and you can…' She laughed. 'Or Victor can sew them on for you.'

'I can probably manage that level of sewing.'

'I'm impressed you managed to avoid that at your schools.'

'Dad had me going out for private tuition in Latin and Greek.'

'I'll be right back.'

Max picked at the foam rubber. She was supposed to encase her body in that?

Honor came back with the cocktail shaker. 'Another? Drink up, Max.' She tipped the shaker over her own glass. 'You could come back to France with me.'

Max stretched out her legs. 'I'm quite happy in Mull for now. Maybe another time.' Was she happy there? She'd resolved to be cheerful after her birthday.

'Or go find Kathleen Kenyon. She's doing some excellent work on radiocarbon dating.'

'I've heard.'

'What do you think you'll find up there?'

'I have no idea. It's just the two of us, so it's not a true season.'

Honor started talking about the Tobermory dive, and Max relaxed. Forget dates with lieutenants. Archaeology was all she needed.

Chapter 10

Max walked through the grand hall of Euston station. The ludicrous quantity of dive equipment and yards of rubber far outweighed the few extra clothes and shoes she'd packed. She had planned on coming back with just an overnight bag. Her mother would get a porter, but Max prided herself on carrying her own kit for a dig. Although she didn't normally travel by train in a formal suit and heels. By the time she reached her sleeper compartment, her arms ached. She shoved the bags under her bunk, took off her heels and sat down. She read the *Antiquaries Journal* for a while and then tossed it down. Cheerful. She'd resolved to be cheerful, so she reached past a book about Mull in her bag. Instead, she drew out *Mrs McGinty's Dead*, the new Agatha Christie novel. Her father had sworn she'd enjoy it.

Max put down her novel and stretched. The excitement of Poirot nearly being pushed under a train subsided quickly as a man tested an electric meter in the next chapter. She should try to get some sleep. She made her way down the swaying corridor. She'd obviously stayed up later than the others in the compartments around her—the train's chugging was the only noise. She went to the WC, and then headed back. Still another nine hours to Oban.

Her door—she had latched it behind her. Why was it slightly ajar? A cool breeze whipped through the passageway and she shivered. Maybe it hadn't quite caught. She slid it open, and something barrelled into her with a hard blow to her stomach. She struggled for breath, tears obscuring her vision. Hands seized her upper arms, propelling her backwards. Towards that chilly breeze. The roar of an approaching train sounded. Everything slowed until her back slammed into the heat of a body, not a wall. The first man released her and ran. The second man pushed her upright, gently touched her shoulder. Did he speak? Max saw a flash of brown eyes, a faint smile, a black hat and the man released her and ran down the train corridor, after the brown suit. The retreating back wore blue.

Max took six deep breaths, her stomach burning. The attendant emerged at the far end of the corridor.

'Are you all right, miss?'

'Just a collision with someone,' Max murmured. 'Good night.'

The attendant jerked up the window on the external door. It hadn't been open. She couldn't have been pushed out, even if the man hadn't been there to stop her. She swallowed. Surely her imagination had been carried away by reading about Poirot.

'Are you certain you're all right?'

Max nodded and walked back to her compartment. She closed the door firmly and turned to chaos. Her cases had been dragged from under the bunk and tipped out, and the foam rubber thrown on the bed. She lifted the glue bottle, thankfully still intact. Her handbag's contents lay strewn across the floor, and although she couldn't find her change purse, her wallet remained in the bottom of the bag. Max rubbed her aching stomach and began repacking methodically. The little drawstring bag of lead weights Honor had given her had disappeared. Maybe they thought a bag of round heavy things had to be valuable?

Because clearly this had to be a case of theft. An empty first class sleeper. Small amounts of money and possibly what they thought were coins. They'd be disappointed to find worthless lead.

Theft. Random chance. Max checked her makeup case but refused to look in the mirror. The powder cake in her compact had cracked. She smoothed the dust back into the middle with the puff slowly.

She lifted the foam rubber. Her novel still lay underneath, undamaged. Her father would have been cross if it had been. A slash bisected the middle of the rubber, but maybe they could cut around it to make a suit. Her hands trembled slightly. She shoved the rubber back in her bag and tossed her hip flask on the bunk. The book's scarlet cover looked more lurid than it had just twenty minutes ago.

Who had chased the man in the brown? Max slid out of her own suit jacket and rubbed her arms. Red marred her skin, in the shape of a man's hands. She brushed her thumb over the worn silver of her hip flask. Why should it make her think of Mr Knox's silver cigarette case? Lots of men had silver cigarette cases.

A face swam before her eyes. The buzz of Bar Italia. Mr Knox's colleague. Mr... Fuller. Like the brush. He'd had brown eyes, a blue suit.

But that was craziness. London newspaper men didn't venture up to Glasgow very often, surely.

The sip of whiskey warmed her. If it was theft, why didn't she call the attendant?

She stood up and wedged her bags against the base of the door. It'd slow down anybody who... not that anyone would. Random.

But instead of her pyjamas, she lifted trousers and a dig shirt out of her bag and changed out of her formal suit. She slipped under the covers fully dressed and lifted her book.

She'd read and sleep. No more wild conjecture. The lead weights were useless, and her change purse had contained a negligible amount of money. She exhaled. And yet she didn't sleep for hours, watching the door in the darkness.

*

Max shifted the two large suitcases as she waited to disembark from the ferry. Her arms and stomach ached.

Emma waved and ground her cigarette under her shoe as Max stepped out into the sunshine. Max progressed down the gangway and lifted the bags into the backseat.

'How was the party?' Emma asked.

'Don't tell me you knew too?' Why didn't she tell Emma about the train?

'Of course. Your mother was quite cross when we insisted on staying up here.' Emma slid behind the wheel. 'Victor's working. Did you get the stuff to make a dive suit?'

Max unbuttoned her suit jacket. 'Yep. I'm not great at sewing though.'

'Neither am I. Victor's pretty good though.'

Max stared out the window and saw a blue suited man talking to a tall man with a familiar build. But the tall man wore a hat and very normal clothes—it couldn't possibly be Victor. Why would Victor come to meet the ferry too, but not travel back with them?

After dinner, Victor prattled on about diving. Emma read a novel next to him on the sofa as he sewed. Max examined her straggling stitches in the trousers. She'd managed about three inches. Victor held up the top. He'd finished the left arm entirely. He'd cut the suit out efficiently, and he hadn't asked at all about the slash.

'This is going to take forever,' Max said. The saggy chair didn't offer any more comfort, no matter how much she wriggled.

'It'll get quicker. Now, my mate Dave had a real crisis, when he was at about thirty feet. His diving partner had to...'

Emma touched his leg. 'Darling, go check the car.'

Max gripped the needle too tightly. What did Emma suspect?

'That thing? Who cares if it gets damaged?' He kept sewing. 'Besides, it's fine.'

'Then just go away.' She smiled. 'For a little while.'

Victor took a deep breath, and then laughed. He stood, dropping the dive suit top in Emma's lap. 'My, I fancy a walk on the beach. Bye.' He slid on his shoes and went out the door.

'Was it that obvious?' Max asked. Of course Emma didn't fear anything unusual outside. Who would? The lights didn't signify.

'He adores diving. If you don't stop him, he'll go on for hours.' She held up a seam in the dark rubber to the light. 'Besides, we haven't seen each other properly in months.'

'No.' There'd been a tight hug at George's memorial service, and she'd seen them in pubs a few times since.

'Victor said he saw you a bit while I was in Paris.'

Max smiled. 'He forced me over for dinner a few times.'

'Mourning doesn't have to mean burying yourself.'

'I didn't feel like doing much, to be honest.' She kept stitching. 'I really don't see how this is going to fit.'

'You want it tight.'

'Did you have fun in Paris?'

'It was work. But I saw some plays and went to museums. I'm really glad you asked us up here, Max. I couldn't bear the thought of Victor going off to Denmark for months, just as I got home.'

'Even if it is ridiculously ill thought out and on the fly?'

'It makes it more fun.'

Max looked at her nail varnish from the party. A chip had already formed. Had she packed remover? 'Are you and Victor okay?'

'Of course. Why?'

'The party.'

'Ah.'

'I assumed—maybe wrongly—that a neighbour didn't complain.'

Emma shook her head. 'We didn't communicate well about the party.' She put down her sewing. 'Partly I spent most of my first night and day back cooking. But mostly I'm ready to have a baby. I don't want late parties.'

Max couldn't imagine glamorous Victor and Emma with a baby, but then she thought of Victor dandling a baby, and the way he took care of everyone around him. 'What does Victor say?'

'Sure, if it happens. But I'm getting older. And I lost— well, it went wrong a few times.'

'Oh Emma. I'm sorry.'

'The last was a couple years ago, so we stopped trying for a while.' She started sewing again. 'So I was happy to come up here. Not so many people, fewer parties...Ow.' She sucked her finger. 'You seemed upset too. More than just that stupid boy.'

Max shook her head. The plane crash had forced thoughts of Ruth's comments away, but they returned fiercely now. A flush rose in her cheeks. 'I overheard something I shouldn't have.'

'Ruth?'

Max picked at a log in the pile of wood next to her chair, the grain rough against her skin.

'She's simply jealous, you know. You can make life seem, well, effortless at times, Max. The PhD, your freedom.'

'Never underestimate the veneer you acquire after years at a finishing school.'

'I said seems. I'm well aware it isn't the case, but I don't think many other people see that.'

'Ruth would hardly be my first choice for confidant.'

Emma smiled. 'Agreed. Just remember Victor and I are both happy to listen.' She dropped the sewing. 'This is taking ages. Let's try my dive suit on you. I'm not going to go diving on this trip, whatever Victor says. Maybe we can tailor it. Get your bathing costume on and I'll get the suit.'

*

115

Max came back in her swimsuit. Must she think of Mr Knox every time she put on anything red?

'That's pretty,' Emma said.

'Last year's.' Last year George had been alive, if flying somewhere over Korea.

'Okay so it's two parts. You cinch these ring things around your neck and waist, although it isn't really watertight. It's not bad.' She handed Max the trousers first. Powder floated to the floor. 'Talc, I'm afraid. What's that?'

'What?'

Emma touched her upper arm where bruises marked her skin. She circled around Max and brushed her other arm. 'You have one here too.'

'Someone bumped into me on the train.' At least she couldn't see her stomach.

'That must have been frightening.'

Max shrugged and stepped into the trousers. They clung to her ankles and then she pulled them higher. 'Ick.'

'It's worse when they're wet.'

'I can imagine.' Even dry, the coolness unnerved her. She'd never worn anything like it. It gaped a bit at the waist, and once fully pulled up, a couple inches of her ankles showed.

'I'll take the waist in, but it isn't cold enough for the length to matter.' Emma sprinkled talc into the top and then helped Max lift it over her head. 'You tend to peel it back off.'

'Oh, good.'

'Victor will help. You pretty much have to do it in pairs.' She tugged the top down. 'Well, it's a bit tight in the bust. Can you breathe?' She smiled. 'There isn't much to do in terms of letting it out.'

Max took deep breaths experimentally. 'Yeah I think so. What about underwater?'

'You just breathe normally.' Emma pinched the waist. 'Maybe this much? Tighter? You can't pin rubber.'

'Are you sure you don't mind?' Max held out her arms. Again an inch or so of her wrist extended beyond the sleeve.

'Not in the slightest.'

The door opened slowly. 'All okay?' Victor put his hands on his hips. 'That was fast.'

'It's mine,' Emma said.

'But…'

'I'm not diving this trip. In case.'

Victor wrapped her in a tight hug, and Emma laughed as he kissed her neck. Victor released her and studied Max. 'It's too tight.'

'She can breathe.'

'Well, that's something. Can you move your arms? Like you're swimming.'

Max reached and stretched with her arms, laughing. Thank God Victor had never ogled her, or she'd just want to hide away.

'I guess it'll do. At least we can go out tomorrow.'

Emma pulled the waist tight again. 'At our rate of sewing, I think it'd be at least a week before you could do anything otherwise. Plus, there's the gluing.'

'I bought that pot you recommended. Where does it go?' Max asked.

'All the seams. It's vile. The worst smelling glue you can imagine,' Emma said.

Max could see Richard's house in the distance as they walked down to the shore. No lights burned. It was past dawn, but maybe he still swam.

'Ready?' Victor asked.

Max nodded. She dropped the towels, unease curling in her stomach. New didn't mean bad, she reminded herself. And if she saw lights, well, she'd have a witness. They undressed down to their swimsuits, and Victor helped Max tug on her suit. His was much more straightforward—just one piece to step into and a straight zip up.

'Why is yours so easy?'

'Military issue. I can't even tell you most of the places I've worn this.'

'Right.'

Victor hoisted an Aqualung and hitched it over Max's arms. 'Let's hope we don't run into anybody. I'm fairly certain your mother would call that indecent. Are you sure you can move your arms in that?'

'Yes.' She buckled the front straps. 'And I'm positive she would.'

Victor lifted a black hose with a rubber hollow at the end. 'This is your mouthpiece. The most important thing to remember is to breathe normally, but only through your mouth.' He grinned. 'Proper Aqualungs are bloody hard to get in Britain. I had to do a lot of deals to get these, but they're the best.'

'So be careful?'

'They're not easy to damage. You'll be fine. Okay, last thing—the weight belt.' Victor handed her Emma's weight belt. He'd planned to sew her belt while she and Emma glued the altered seams outside, but she simply said she'd forgotten them. Thank God the glue pot hadn't broken in the compartment. If she'd known how hideous it smelled, she would have wrapped it every protective fabric she could find.

'I'm not heavy enough in all this stuff?' She buckled it around her waist.

'Nope. Let's go in.'

'How?'

'Just walk, of course.' He laughed. 'Tomorrow we'll hire a boat, and I'll teach you how to flip yourself off the side. But today, we'll just play around. I doubt we'll see much.' He leaned down to put on his flippers, so Max did the same.

'This is the most ridiculous get up ever.'

'You should see some of the old dive kit. This is positively streamlined.' He walked into the water, and Max followed slowly.

'Bloody hell,' Max yelped as the water closed around her knees.

'It's Scotland in April. What did you expect?'

'Emma said it wouldn't be too cold.'

'She's Scottish. Her ideas of temperature don't match our thin English blood.'

Max exhaled. 'She's the one who keeps telling me to dry my hair.' No way would she be able to add woollen ballet tights under this suit.

'Precisely. Okay, dip your mask in the water before you put it on.'

'Why?'

'You get condensation otherwise. Now spit in it.'

'You're joking.'

'A good gob. Like this.' He hawked into the mask. 'Then you spread it around.'

'You're doing this to torture me.' Victor grinned. Max spat.

'Oh Max, you're in remote Scotland. Nobody can see you except me, and I won't judge.'

Max coughed and spat again. The spittle felt warm and thin against her fingers as she smoothed it to the edges of her glass mask. 'I hate you.'

Victor laughed. 'Now dip it in the water again.'

'So what the hell was the point of that?'

'It works. Otherwise, all you'll see underwater is fog.' He pulled his mask easily over his short curls.

Max tugged hers over Emma's hood. She couldn't imagine the mess it would make of her own hair without the hood. She closed her eyes, trying to forget about the spit so close to her lashes.

'Basically, it's like getting in a pool. Just go underwater, but remember you can breathe, but only through your mouth. Follow me, and if you have any worries, we'll be shallow enough that you can just stand up, or at the very least tread water.' He smiled. 'You'll be fine. Did Honor tell you about her first dive? Down a well in Wimbledon?'

Max could have reminded him that Honor was an orphan, without the pressure of parents who thought she was doing safe land archaeology right now, or she could have told him she'd seen lights off this very coast only a few days ago. But instead she just followed him into the water, biting back swear words as the cold water enveloped her head, her vision blurring.

Victor's flippers kicked in front of him, and she emulated him, gradually warming as she moved through the water. She breathed carefully and slowly. The mask's pinch over her nose helped her to remember to use only her mouth. Tiny brown and white fishes flashed along the seabed, riffling the sand as they passed. She'd imagined total darkness under the water, not unlike what Honor had said about that London well. But Max could see fishes and rocks and waving ferns and kelp. She simply didn't find much of it very interesting. Maybe once they got to a proper depth and archaeology it would make a difference.

She saw no bright lights. No ships, no submarines. Maybe the answering flashes came from the shore, not at sea.

Victor swam around her, giving her a thumbs up. Then he pushed his way down to the bottom, parting the kelp with his hands. He mimed drawing, so Max followed him. Excitement traced up her back. Finally, she'd see something worth wearing all this. He showed her only sand. Max frowned. He lifted his Bakelite tablet from his belt and used the crayon. 'How to record,' he wrote.

Max nodded. Icy water leaked in around her neck seal and she shuddered. How could he love this so much?

Max took the crayon. 'Find something?' she wrote, her letters awkward.

Victor shrugged and pointed away from the shore. He reattached the tablet and swam into deeper water. She followed until he motioned to her to stop. He drew an imaginary line, so she assumed he meant this was their boundary. She wouldn't be able to reach the bottom if she stood, but only by a little. Victor swam deep again and shifted the vegetation, moving precisely in a grid formation she recognised from land archaeology. She copied him, the disciplined search soothing her, despite the loud noises of their breathing and her constant search for lights or sources.

They found nothing.

After half an hour, Victor pointed to the watch on his wrist and they kicked their way back to the shore. When the water was no more than waist deep, they rose to the surface. Max spat out the regulator and breathed deeply.

'Great, isn't it?'

'Dull.'

'It's better when you find stuff.' He took off his flippers and walked out to the sandy beach. 'Remember, this is just learning. And Scotland isn't the best place to see sea life. You want warm water for that.'

'So I should have picked someplace tropical over Mull when I went looking for a site?'

'I doubt I'd have gotten Emma there.'

Max sat down on the shore, struggling to unclip the Aqualung.

'Was it that awful?'

'No, no. I'm sorry.' He pulled the Aqualung from her shoulders. 'It was much better once we actually starting doing something. And it was easier to see than I thought.'

'We'll make a proper diver of you yet, Dr Falkland. Just wait till you have your first find.' He looked at his watch again. 'We'll go again after lunch. And maybe a third after tea. Then we can go do real diving tomorrow.'

Max came out of the bathroom. Thank God the cottage had enough hot water for both Victor and her to have baths. Diving made her far colder than flying ever had, not to mention the crusting of salt and talc all over her body. She followed the smell of meat to the kitchen. Emma sat at the table writing, while a pot bubbled on the stove.

'Have I said how amazing you are lately?' she asked Emma.

Emma laughed and put down her pen. 'It's only stew.' She stood and stretched. 'Is Victor in the bath?'

Max nodded, squeezing water out of her hair. Emma started to shift her papers.

'Should we eat outside? It's a nice evening.'

'Only if you dry your hair properly, young lady.'

'Young lady?' Max laughed. 'Does marriage make you older? You're only three years ahead of me.'

'And you keep forgetting it's April.'

'Fine. I'll take another chair outside first.' The small table pressed up against the house only had two chairs, although the kitchen table had four.

'Victor can do that. I need to slice some bread anyway.' She flapped her hands at Max. 'Go dry your hair. You aren't in centrally heated London now.'

Max retreated to her room, and extracted the hand-held dryer she'd packed in London from her bag. At home, she would have carefully rolled her hair first then covered it in her bonnet dryer, but she'd only submerge it in salt water tomorrow. She leaned over and waved the dryer at the roots of her hair. Her mother would have a heart attack, but she wouldn't see the result. She tried to shake water out of her left ear, remembering the blur of the world as she descended. Victor clearly loved it, and despite her boredom under water, the elation of doing something new, something physical, still buzzed through her body. She hadn't felt this awake in a long time.

Max straightened up and looked in the mirror. Her normally wavy hair hung around her face in a wild frizz. Even for dinner with Victor and Emma, she'd have to do something. She persuaded her brush through the tangle and wove a braid. God knows what her hair would look like after a summer of diving in salt water. It'd give her mother even more reasons for her to cut it. For dinner with Emma and Victor, she would eschew make up.

The braid was damp enough to leave a faint coolness against her neck, but she went out to the living room. Victor lifted the record player from the coffee table.

'You look like a teenager,' Victor said. 'Sure you're okay?'

Max nodded. 'I'm never going to love it.' She picked up the records. 'But I see why you do.' They stepped outside. 'It's invigorating, isn't it?'

She stopped as Emma and a man turned towards them. Richard Ash. A flush climbed her cheeks.

'This is our landlord, Richard Ash. Max I think you've met, and this is my husband Victor.'

Victor dropped the record player on the table and shook Richard's hand. 'Nice to meet you.'

Richard had no visible reaction to Victor's pink shirt or her own trousers. He reached for her hand, and she shifted the records to her hip. She tried to forget about her bare face and braid.

'Lovely to see you again, Dr Falkland.'

'Please, call me Max.'

'Then it's Richard.'

'I was just saying Richard should join us for dinner.'

'I couldn't intrude,' Richard said. 'I just wanted to see if the cottage was up to scratch.'

'Oh stay,' Victor said. 'We're grateful to find such a nice cottage. The least we can do is feed you.'

'Well, thank you.' He sat at the small table, leaning his walking stick against the back of the chair. He'd taken the kitchen chair, the one with a cushion, not one of the rickety wooden slat ones.

'Excuse me for a moment,' Emma said.

Max dropped the records beside him. 'I'll help.' Richard offered Victor a cigarette as Max followed Emma inside. She took another plate out of the cabinet.

'Don't,' Emma said.

Max added another glass to the tray. 'Don't what?'

'Put on makeup. Even if you're interested.'

'It'd feel like a retreat,' Max said. 'And I'm not.'

'Besides, you're beautiful.'

'Bah.' They laughed as they carried the dishes and stew pot outside. Victor dropped the needle on a record. 'Unforgettable' started playing. Max stared at a wedge of paper Victor had put under the left table leg to stabilise it.

'Max?' Richard asked.

Max smiled. Even Emma didn't notice the falseness. She should throw the record away.

'Darling, can you get another chair please?' Emma asked. 'Grab an ashtray too, please.'

'Sure.' Victor kissed her cheek as he passed.

Emma had said she was old for babies. What did that make Max? She handed Emma plates and Emma began ladling out the stew.

Richard placed a card on the table. 'Max, here are the details of a chap named David McPherson. He's a fisherman now, but he was an RAF mechanic in the war, so I'm sure he could mend your plane.'

Max slid the card in her trouser pocket. 'Thanks. That's very kind of you.' Emma must have noticed the yellow tinge of Richard's fingertips. She and Victor barely smoked, not enough to have an ashtray on the table.

Victor emerged with a chair, and then disappeared again. He returned with a bottle and an ashtray. 'It's a celebration.'

'Why?' Richard asked.

'First, none of the wine broke when Max crash-landed her plane. Second, she had her first dive today.'

'On holiday?'

'Archaeology,' Max said. 'We were going to do air survey, but my plane failed.'

'So I've convinced Max to let me teach her to dive. That's what I did in the war—Navy frogman.' He eyed Richard. 'I could teach you, if you like. Max said you swim.'

'Where are you diving?' His fingers gripped his cane's handle.

'Today, just off the shoreline there.'

'Open the wine, darling. The stew's getting cold fast.'

'Did you find anything?' Richard asked.

'Today was mostly just practice.' Victor eased out the cork. 'Tomorrow we'll do some proper work.' He tipped the wine bottle over the water glasses.

'Aren't there any wine glasses?' Richard asked.

'No.'

'That is embarrassing. I'll sort that out.'

'For a rental cottage, this is pretty well equipped,' Emma said. 'The cooker works, for one.'

'The floor is dry,' Max said. 'Plus a distinct lack of cobwebs, roaches and mice.'

Richard's face twisted. What had the POW camp been like? She wished she could take back her words.

'For archaeologists, this is luxury,' Victor said. 'We can do without stemware.'

'Come on, the food's going to be freezing. Sit down.'

'I should have moved the table out before we loaded it up,' Victor said. Max sat at the end of the table in one of the outdoor chairs, while Victor insisted that Emma take a comfortable chair. They crowded together opposite Richard. No one suggested she could sit next to Richard.

'So Richard, what brought you to Scotland?' Max asked.

'Escape,' Richard said. His smile held no warmth. 'And I had no family left in England. Are you based in Scotland, Emma?'

'London,' Emma said. 'I went south for art school, and then I met Victor. So I stayed.'

'Did the cottage come with your house?' Victor asked. 'Do you get a lot of renters?'

'Not really.'

The silence stretched. 'I met Victor on my first English dig,' Max said cheerfully. 'He was my trench supervisor.'

'What does that mean?'

'Rik Wheeler says the top man on a dig is a colonel, and he equates a trench supervisor as a lieutenant. Or is it a captain?' Victor topped up their glasses. 'With rather lax discipline, comparatively.'

'The top person isn't always a man, Victor. There's Kathleen Kenyon, and before that Tessa Wheeler...'

'Point taken.'

'But whatever the rank, Victor and Emma took care of me.' The first day of the dig matched what was meant to be her wedding day to Daniel. She'd felt fragile, but it bore no comparison to the last six months.

'Who is Rik Wheeler?'

'He's legendary,' Emma said. 'You've probably heard of him as a war hero. Both wars. His actual name is Sir Mortimer Wheeler.'

'He's a professor at the Institute of Archaeology. And a very good archaeologist.' Max smiled. 'But his exploits are renowned.'

'Particularly with women,' Victor added. 'Supposedly he saw a beautiful woman getting out of a taxi outside the Ritz and just walked up to her and said they were meant to be having lunch.'

'So she slapped him, said "you're late" and took him to lunch. Mavis de Vere Cole was in the middle of an affair with Augustus John, but she left him and became Wheeler's second wife.'

Richard didn't respond, so Victor and Max continued to tell their most outrageous stories about Wheeler. Max was fairly certain that Victor invented some of them, and she didn't bother to share the times Wheeler had hit on her. At least he was always a perfect gentleman when she refused, unlike the boy at their party.

Eventually they ran out of stories, and the meal dragged. Cigarette stubs filled the ashtray, as Victor smoked as much as Richard. Richard seemed incapable of starting a conversation. When the second side of the LP ended, Emma didn't move to put on a new record.

Max began counting the stones making up the wall of the cottage and reached thirty-three before she couldn't stand the silence anymore. 'I thought there'd be rabbits here.'

'Myxomatosis,' Richard said.

How long had it been since he'd spoken? 'I'm sorry?'

'The rabbit population was infected.' Richard stood. 'Thank you for a lovely meal, and the company.' He glanced at Max, but she didn't rise from the seat. He was their landlord, not a date. He went down the path alone, leaning on his cane.

'See you soon,' Max called.

Victor stretched out his legs. 'It's a beautiful evening.'

'And wonderful food. Thanks, Emma.'

'My pleasure.' Emma sorted through the records and pulled out a single. 'I haven't heard this one. A new Rosemary Clooney?'

'My grandmother sent it.' It had come with the red dress and tins of food.

The opening notes sounded as Victor touched Emma's hand. Max jumped up and collected their plates. 'Stay,' she said, when Emma started to rise. She carried the plates indoors and peeked through the window. They were kissing.

Max filled the sink with soap and the blessed hot water and started washing the plates and cutlery. She was drying them by the time Emma brought the stew pot in, with Victor following with glasses.

'Richard is a deeply unhappy man,' Emma said.

'I think he's in a lot of pain,' Max said.

'So many men came home broken,' Emma said.

'It's made me think that maybe George was lucky after all.' Max dunked the pot in the soapy water.

Emma touched Max's shoulder. 'I can take over.'

'Not a chance.' She found a smile. 'Go relax or... be together or whatever.'

Victor laughed. 'Subtle, Max.'

'Thanks,' Emma said. Their bedroom door closed a few minutes later.

After finishing the washing up, Max retrieved her flight jacket and hip flask from her room and went outside. She walked along the path until she could see the sea. Only the moon reflected on the water. No lights. She trudged back up the path, rubbing her arms.

She changed 'Tenderly' out for Nat King Cole. She could listen to 'Unforgettable'. The stunted trees waved in the breeze. George's buttons on his dress uniform had pressed into her in their last hug, and his whispered command—but she pushed away the spurt of anger that had marred their goodbye. She thought instead of his white blond curls as a child. He'd say 'come on Max, be a pal,' as he talked her into some ridiculous scrape. Five years older, she inevitably reaped the blame. At school, his judgment hadn't improved much. It never had, despite the platitudes that filled his memorial service.

Her fingers found scraps of paper in her pocket. She pulled one free. The notes she'd written about John Knox. She took a sip of whiskey and twisted the paper into a tiny snarl.

How on earth had George been friends with Mr Knox? He had to be at least a couple years older than she— George would have dubbed him ancient. Maybe the RAF and war had steadied George more than years of parental entreaties had. He'd won medals, been commended, but his letters had still sounded like George, careening from one adventure to another. Tears pressed behind her eyes, but she wouldn't let them fall. Cheerful.

The needle thumped and scratched. She lifted the arm but didn't flip the record. The ocean blurred with the wind. George hadn't survived. The RAF wouldn't lie to her father, of all people. He'd have access to their reports.

The door creaked. 'Bloody hell, Max. I nearly locked you out,' Victor said. She didn't turn. 'Have you been out here all this time?'

'Not long.'

'It's past one. Get some sleep.'

Chapter 11

The blade nestled on the seabed beneath the crushed kelp. Had anyone else seen it in the thousand years since a storm washed it overboard from its Viking ship? Or had it slid out of a man's dying grip as the vessel tipped into the water? Max tilted her neck, fighting the constriction of her suit, and a finger of icy water cascaded down her spine. She yelped against her mouthpiece, but the sound simply absorbed into her bubbling expiration. Her crayon floated away on its string. She reached out to recapture it, the slow movement of her arm, encased in black rubber, still baffling her. She had rendered the sword fragment as accurately as she could in thick gloves. On land, her drawing would have been precise.

She let the current drift her away from the area of bruised kelp. Half an hour in this murkiness. Time to surface, wrap herself in a blanket and consume as much coffee as the thermos contained. The damage to the kelp looked recent. Whatever caused it had to be bigger than her plane, and unlike the Viking ship, it had not remained on the seabed long. Her fin brushed over the waving fronds, and another dull glint emerged. Max forced herself lower and parted the long leaves. A blade, yes, but one not forged by Viking hands.

It matched the one strapped to her right thigh, but instead of being shiny and new this knife's handle bore dents and scrapes of long use. The water gave a startling crispness to the shape imprinted on its side. Worn, partial, but a letter. And not a Roman letter.

A tiny space remained on her tablet, and she made a rougher, faster sketch of the knife. The half letter she drew enlarged, positioning it beside the knife, and then she hooked the tablet on her weight belt. Thirty-five minutes underwater, but still she hesitated. The Viking sword needed to stay in situ. But this? This couldn't be more than ten years old.

The knife slid easily into the sheath on her leg, and she kicked her way towards the surface. The shadow of her boat broke, shuddered and then reformed. Max floated, staring at the silhouette above. Maybe it always shifted like that. The down line she held stayed constant. She blinked. One mass. She continued to ascend, tracing her hand along the rope.

On the surface, Max spat out her mouthpiece and gulped air. Air that didn't taste like rubber, that she could inhale and exhale without the cacophony of noise underwater. How could Victor prefer diving to land archaeology? The grey clouds overhead matched the dark water breaking around her as she treaded water.

'Shame we missed each other in London, Dr Falkland.'

Max shuddered. His conversational voice couldn't reach the half-mile from shore. She could dive back down, escape —hide—but for how long? Maybe fifteen minutes of air remained. Pale sunlight glinted against her mask, and then she saw him. John Knox leaned against the wheelhouse of her boat.

'How did you find me?' she asked. If her voice wavered, well, the wind blowing against her wet hood made her teeth chatter. Would make anyone's teeth chatter. Her tablet knocked against her leg, tapping the blade. He would see the sketches. More to the point, he'd see the knife's Cyrillic letter.

'Guess how many pretty American women rent boats on the Isle of Mull in April.'

'I'm not American.' She peeled off her mask, the chill assaulting her eyes. Smoke curled from his cigarette. The narrow shape disrupting the left side of his blue jumper had to be a gun. She detached her tablet and kept it under the shadowy water.

'You sound it.'

His own accent had blurred into neutrality, a generic American that couldn't be pinpointed to a single state or even region. Was anything about this man honest?

'I'd appreciate it if you kindly got the hell off my boat.' Her cold fingers worked to tie the tablet by its crayon's string to the line, but she had to bite off one glove to manage it.

'What are you doing?' He stepped towards the ladder and flicked his cigarette overboard, towards the small sailboat moored to her boat.

Her tablet plummeted, but at least he wouldn't reach it. She unfastened her weight belt quickly and heaved it over the side of the boat. He jerked his boot out of the way just in time.

'Not nice, Dr Falkland.'

'Bad aim.'

Max tossed her flippers into the boat, flicking water up onto Mr Knox's trouser legs.

'You're doing this on purpose now.' He held his hand out. With a deep breath, Max put her ungloved hand into the heat of his and set her foot on the wooden ladder. As soon as she stood flat in the boat, she jerked her hand out of his. She unbuckled her Aqualung, and before she could stop him, he drew it off for her. Max inhaled freely.

'You shouldn't dive alone.'

Maybe if he shot her, Victor would feel a reverberation and come up to find her.

'What are you doing here?'

'Fishing.' He gestured towards the sailboat, where a reel rested across the seats.

Max suddenly remembered how tightly her suit clung. Indecent, Victor had said. The towels and blankets lay behind Mr Knox. She tried to reach around, but he shifted at the same time. She crashed into his chest, and with a shock of warmth, his arms closed around her.

Max pushed at his shoulders, her face burning. His arms dropped.

'My apologies,' Mr Knox said.

'I need a towel.' He handed her two, and a blanket, and turned to face the coastline as she wrapped the blanket around her body. Max retreated to the short bench on the far side of the boat. She would not remember the pressure of his chest against hers. Much more importantly, nothing solid interrupted the line of his jumper.

'Okay?' Mr Knox asked.

'Yes.' If he were going to shoot her, he wouldn't turn his back on her, surely. Water printed the front of his jumper when he faced her. Water from her body. Her flush didn't diminish. 'Why are you really here?' Max peeled off her hood. Her hair spreading across her shoulders made her even colder. The towel only seemed to spread the chill, not dry her hair. This could convince her to cut it.

'You didn't return my calls.'

'You didn't stay at my party.'

He pulled the thermos out of her bag and passed it to her.

'You've been up here a while.'

He reached towards the edge of the wheelhouse, where he'd stood before, and Max half rose. Where could she go?

'Here. Happy birthday.' He extended a long, thin shape to her. The neck of a bottle. A bottle, not a gun.

She took it with trembling fingers, and saw the familiar label of Oban.

'You're shaking.' He took the other blanket and threw it around her shoulders.

'Thank you.' Max slowly sat back down. Forget the coffee. She opened the Oban and poured a slug into the thermos cap.

'Who did you hear speaking another language? And what language?'

Max decided against offering him any whiskey. 'I heard a man hitting his wife. I know that's barely a crime, but it upset me. That's all.'

Mr Knox sat next to her. 'That's all?'

'Yes.'

'Max. Can I call you Max? Are you telling me the truth?'

'Why would you care?'

A splash, and Victor surfaced. His mask cleared his hair easily. 'You nearly brained me with this thing. Why'd you drop it?'

'Drop what?' Mr Knox asked.

Victor spluttered and swam over the boat. Max leaned out to help him. 'He's stronger,' Victor said. He threw his Bakelite tablet in, then hers.

Max sat back down as Mr Knox helped Victor in.

'Why are you here?' Victor asked. He unbuckled his Aqualung. Mr Knox did not help him to remove it.

'Waiting on you. What'd you find?'

'Her, not me. A dive knife. Modern. She drew it.'

'There were subs here during the war,' Mr Knox said. He rubbed his chest above a drying damp patch.

'I'm sure that's it,' Max said before Victor could volunteer anything else. 'Nothing to worry about, nothing to pay attention to.'

'You should show him that sketch you did.' Victor grabbed her tablet before she could stop him. 'Here.' He handed it to John Knox. 'I assume you can do something with that?'

Mr Knox studied it. 'Nothing to report, Max?'

'Why are you here, anyway?' she asked.

'Fishing.'

Victor shivered, and Max shrugged off the blankets. She draped them around Victor's shoulders, and turned to Mr Knox. She extended her hand.

'Can I have my tablet back, please? And would you kindly leave?'

'I'll get it back to you.' He smiled, and Max wished she could throttle him. 'See you later.' He gracefully stepped into his own boat and sailed to the shore.

'Right then,' Victor said. 'Shall we record our finds here or on land?'

'How the hell do I record my finds when you gave him my tablet?' She drained the whiskey from the thermos cup.

'Fair point. I'll do mine.' He lifted the bottle. 'Nice.'

Max closed her eyes as Victor transferred his notes from his tablet to paper. She stayed silent for the short trip back to land. She didn't speak even as she tied the boat up and Victor refilled the Aqualungs.

'What is going on, Max?' Victor finally asked.

'You know him!' She paced the shoreline.

'You introduced us. Of course I know him. I don't know what the hell he was doing here, but...'

'What did you give him?' Max demanded. Victor spread his hands. 'Not here, at Bar Italia. You wrote something down for him. Did you tell him we were coming up here?'

'He asked me for some essentials in London. For a gentleman.'

Max blinked. 'You gave him a name of a bordello?'

'You think I know where there are bordellos? Emma would kill me. Tailor, barber, that sort of thing. It seemed harmless. After all, you introduced us!' Victor sat down on the bank. 'Stop pacing.'

'What the hell is going on here, Victor?'

'I think you fancy John Knox. Or you wouldn't automatically jump to thinking about sex.'

'I'm talking about that knife. And why he cares about what we're finding.' She was not interested in John Knox. Not sexually, not romantically, not even as a friend.

'Are they even called bordellos? Outside of Westerns?'

'Oh, shut up.' She sat down heavily and bent forward over her knees. 'And if you ever see him again, don't you dare tell him I said that.'

'Then admit you fancy him.'

'I don't.'

'He does.'

'I'm an intellectual problem to him. A bother.' Max dug her fingers into the sand of the shore.

'Yes. And all men look at intellectual problems the way he looked at you in that dive suit.'

'He made a distinct point of not looking.'

'You really are ridiculously bad at telling when men like you, aren't you?'

'I'm sorry?'

'Ash, Knox—tell me at least you noticed with your lieutenant.'

'Shut up,' Max said.

Victor retreated into the boat's wheelhouse with their Aqualungs. Max stared at the surface of the water. Cheerful. Mr Knox said there were subs here in the war. The knife didn't mean anything.

'What are you going to do with it?' Victor extended his hand and pulled her to her feet.

'I don't know what you mean.' She took a deep breath.

'The knife.' He pointed at the sheath on her leg. 'I can only assume Knox was so blinded by your charms he missed it, or I suspect he would have taken it too.'

'Nothing. I should have left it down on the seabed. Just forget it.'

Chapter 12

Just because she drank the man's whiskey didn't mean she liked him. The cottage didn't stretch to tumblers or ice, so she put three juice glasses on the tray beside the bottle of Oban and a deck of cards. She had assumed he hid a gun. Did newspaper men usually carry guns? What made her leap to that conclusion? She'd stuffed the knife under her mattress after her bath.

Emma's laugh floated in through the open living room window, and Max paused. Through the net curtains, she watched as Emma dropped the needle on a new record. Rosemary Clooney's voice poured into the little front garden, caressing the refrain of 'Tenderly'. Victor kissed Emma's neck and then spun her away from the table, drawing her into a dance. Even while engaged to Daniel, Max had felt nothing like the joy so clearly on their faces.

Max opened the door and put the tray on the table.

'Marvellous,' Victor said, still twirling his wife around the grass. 'I like this song. Good job your grandmother posted it to you.'

Max tipped the bottle over her glass, pouring more than she should. Why not? She sipped. Had George really told Mr Knox she liked Oban? The evening breeze caressed the trees, but the midges and the persistent thought of John Knox standing in their boat made it feel less than tender. Max closed her eyes, the low sun warming her face.

'Will you bloody cheer up? We found some valid archaeology today,' Victor said. 'A good meal and now whiskey, free whiskey too. I'll dance with you next, if you like.'

'You gave that man my sketch.' Max drew her feet up on her chair.

'She's cross because she fancies him, Emma.' Victor dipped his wife low, and she laughed again.

'Why does he bother you?' Emma asked.

Max's gulp of whiskey burned beautifully. 'He's smug; he has a poorly defined job; he left my party; he told me I was a terrible thief...'

'Do you aspire to be a good thief?'

Max's glass skidded in her hand, and liquid sloshed on her knee as Mr Knox strode into view. Damn. Heat flooded her cheeks, and Victor didn't help by laughing.

'Emma, darling, this is Max's Mr Knox.'

Pride kept Max from running or burying her face in her hands, but she gulped another mouthful of whiskey.

'John, please. And don't stop on my account,' he said, as Emma slowed.

'Ask Max,' Victor said.

Max would cheerfully throttle him as soon as Mr Knox left. She watched Mr Knox's boots as he crossed the garden towards her. She would look no higher. He placed her Bakelite tablet next to the tray. Max stared at the weave of his blue jumper, the nubbled texture she'd felt under her palms when they collided on the boat. Her flush intensified.

'Do you...' His hand came into her view, and she batted it away.

'No.' Her mother and both her grandmothers' voices whispered chastisements in her head, so she added, 'thank you.' He laughed. She could chalk a pleasant laugh up with everything else that irritated her about the man.

'May I sit then?'

Max nodded. He sat to her right, and at this angle, she couldn't avoid seeing his smile. Had he heard Victor say she fancied him? 'Whiskey?' she asked.

'A small one.'

Max had to put down her generous glass to pour his.

'How do you like diving?' he asked. 'And the spitting?' He grinned, and Max considered not passing him the drink at all.

Victor laughed. 'I told you I didn't make it up, Max.'

She managed to hand Mr Knox the whiskey without touching his fingers at all.

'Were you a frogman too?' Emma asked. Victor's laughter subsided.

'Army.'

'But you've dived?' Max asked.

Rosemary Clooney sang the last 'tenderly' and the song ended with a small scrape. Mr Knox reached over her to lift the arm of the record player. 'I've said before, a well-rounded gentleman should have many interests.'

'A whiskey for me too, Max,' Victor said.

'I'll just get a glass for Emma,' Max said, half rising.

Emma snagged Victor's. 'I'll share his. Inside.' She steered Victor towards the door, and closed it pointedly behind them. She shut the window next, although Victor's voice could be heard protesting before the frame settled into place.

Mr Knox hadn't disturbed her drawings—the Viking sword or the dive knife. What had he done with it for three hours? 'How long were you lurking out there?' Max drew her feet up to the chair again, wrapping her arms around her knees. He didn't seem horrified by her trousers.

'Not long. Come to the pub with me?'

'I have a drink.'

Mr Knox pulled the stack of records across the table. 'I'll buy you another one.'

'Which pub?'

His fingers flicked through the sleeves. 'I don't like men who hit their wives,' he said, his voice as mild as if debating the merits of Nat King Cole and Dean Martin.

'What do you propose to do about it? Beat him up in the car park? It's out front, people would notice.'

He drew out an album and stood to swap out 'Tenderly'. 'Just come to the pub.' The needle bumped, then Ella Fitzgerald started singing 'Someone to Watch over Me'.

Max stared at an ant meandering across the surface of the table, heading for a tiny crumb of bread from their dinner. Emma would pester her if she didn't. Victor would talk about it all day tomorrow. And she would never have pegged Mr Knox as an Ella Fitzgerald fan. 'I won't change.'

'Can I suggest shoes?'

Max wiggled her bare toes, still scarlet long after the nail polish had gone from her fingers. 'Perhaps.'

They listened to the first side of the album in silence while she finished her drink. When Max went inside, Emma and Victor didn't emerge, so Max took a few minutes to take down her ponytail and refresh her lipstick. Victor had stayed remarkably silent about her wearing makeup to dinner. The knee of her trousers remained damp. She pondered the way the men in the pub had looked at her legs. She slid out of the trousers and tucked her oversized shirt into a black high-waisted skirt.

Mr Knox swept the cards up from a half-finished game of solitaire as she emerged.

'It's a pretty old fashioned pub,' she said, gesturing to her skirt. Why did she need to explain herself?

Mr Knox nodded and then drained the end of his whiskey. They walked down to his car. He'd managed to get a rental car that was all the same colour. He opened her door.

'How did you know they were speaking Russian?' he asked.

'How do...' Standing in their boat. 'You read my notebook.'

'You didn't call me back.'

'So you followed me here, boarded my boat and read my notebook.' Max pivoted on her heel and started walking back to the cottage. 'Took my tablet.'

'Max, honey...'

'I never said you could call me Max, much less honey, Mr Knox.'

'I apologise, Dr Falkland.' He slammed the car door. 'I, however, did give you permission to call me John.'

Max closed her eyes. At least she had ripped up the page she wrote about him. Those slips still lay in the pocket of her flight jacket, and it had hung safely in her bedroom all day.

'And I returned your tablet.'

'Thank you.' She turned towards him. John leaned against the car, his arms folded. He didn't look nearly as angry as the slamming door led her to expect. 'If I come with you, will you accept that it's so that Victor and Emma actually let me do some work tomorrow?'

'I don't care why you agree.' He moved away from the car and opened her door again.

Max walked the few steps to the car. 'I speak four languages fluently, and George and I both know—knew— some Russian. Our great-grandmother was Ukrainian, so my maternal grandmother speaks it.' A bright smile plastered over the tug in her chest at George's name. What possessed her to mention him? 'And call me Max.'

Mr Knox went straight to the bar. Following his instructions, Max chose one of the two large tables, despite the completely empty lounge. He was served by Mr Fentiman far more quickly than she had ever been, and returned with a tumbler of whiskey for her and a pint for him. He placed the drinks evenly on the table, and then sat down next to her, rather than opposite.

'What are you doing?' The bench she sat on easily could hold three people, and his body felt entirely too close to hers. She didn't even have a handbag to put between them.

'We can talk.'

'What if they've gone?'

'Then we have a drink and I drive you home.'

141

Mrs Fentiman came out of the office. 'Miss Gould. I thought you'd gone back to London.' She walked towards the table, smoothing her apron over her hips. The apron that held Mr Knox's card. 'Still trying to avoid that suitor? Knox, wasn't it?'

Max refused to look at him. Gould plus Knox, what would he think? 'Just showing my cousin around a bit. He's visiting.' She drummed her fingers on the table.

'James Carter,' Mr Knox said. 'Distant cousin. Mother's side.' He covered Max's hand with his own. 'You didn't tell me about this Knox fellow.'

Max resisted the urge to pull her hand away. His hand dwarfed hers. 'He, um, follows me.' The heat of his skin distracted her.

'Want me to have a chat?'

'Please.'

Mr Knox smiled at Mrs Fentiman. 'It's important to take care of family.'

'Is Jane still here, Mrs Fentiman?' Max asked.

'Aye. You going to stay again?'

'I have a place with some friends now.' Something kept her from specifying where.

Someone shouted from the public bar, and, spouting apologies, Mrs Fentiman walked away.

'Who's Mr Carter?'

'I couldn't very well be Knox, could I?'

Max tried to pull away, but Mr Knox lifted her hand and cradled it between his. Her notebook. She should concentrate on that, not on deciphering the texture of his palms. 'Cousins don't hold hands,' she hissed.

'You clearly aren't from the South. And most of the crown heads of Europe do.' He released her fingers. 'Besides, I said distant.'

Max folded her arms firmly over her abdomen. Why couldn't he act like a normal man? She had no question that Angus admired her—he made it perfectly clear. Mr Knox veered from one extreme to another. And yet that very complexity made him far more interesting than Angus. She watched him drink from his pint and relaxed one arm to pick up her whiskey. 'When did you arrive in London?'

'Not quite six months ago.'

With hair like that, he'd have a barber by now. Victor had lied.

'Why are you in Scotland?'

'Fishing. Holiday.' He barely touched her shoulder. 'And I heard...'

The outside door slammed, and a female voice said, 'Maxine!' at high volume. Jane rushed over to their table, with Adam trailing behind. 'Mrs Fentiman told us you'd gone back to London.'

'Just to see family.' Adam kept his eyes firmly on the floor. 'Jane, this is my cousin, James Carter. And Adam, her husband.' Mr Knox rose and shook hands.

'Join us. Let me get you drinks.'

With some simpering, Jane settled on sherry, and Adam asked for a pint. Jane went through the ridiculous fluffing of her coat again. Adam walked over to the bar with Mr Knox.

'He's very handsome, your cousin,' Jane said. Her makeup had been applied much more thickly than before. No redness showed through the mask.

Max forced a smile. 'Are you okay, Jane?' Jane shook her head. 'The last time I saw you, you seemed to have hurt— well, you just looked tired.'

'Me? You're the one whose plane went down. You must have been so frightened.'

Mr Knox placed Jane's sherry in front of her. His face didn't reflect the shock she expected.

'Mr Fentiman said you came back the next morning all muddy.' Adam returned with his pint as John sat down next to Max. 'Of course, Adam will insist on these long walks, so I get muddy nearly every day.'

'It wasn't that bad,' Max said, willing herself not to experience the stomach-churning drop again, the run through the mud.

Mr Knox settled his arm over her shoulders. 'Your mother said you were quite shaken up.'

'What did you do?' Adam asked.

'I just walked to the next town,' Max said. 'I got lost for a while.' Could she shrug the warmth of his arm away? When did her mother start talking to Mr—John?

'You have to be more careful,' he said, crushing her into his side in what he obviously considered a cousinly hug. Max pried herself free. 'Where are you folks from?'

They told John the same story they'd told her. But John managed to wheedle out that Adam had a brother, and Jane an older sister.

'What about you, Max?' Jane asked.

'I'm the youngest. Two big brothers,' John volunteered. 'One takes care of my mother, and the other lives all of ten miles away. I definitely win on going the furthest from the farm.'

He'd kept her from having to answer. From saying George's name aloud. She took a deep breath. They chatted more about a farm in North Carolina that Max doubted existed, and Adam and John went to the bar for another round of drinks. Adam looked dubious about ordering a woman whiskey.

'Is that Mr Carter's?' Jane asked.

'Beg pardon?'

Jane pointed at Max's chest. 'Your shirt, it's a man's shirt. Is it Mr Carter's?'

'I bought it. For myself.' Max had gotten it at Brooks while at Vassar, like all the other students. In what possible world did Jane think a shirt this size—admittedly big on her —would fit over John Knox's shoulders?

144

Adam placed a double shot before her and another sherry for Jane. How many shots was this now? Max sipped slowly.

'It is *her* shirt,' Jane said.

'It's...' How to explain Vassar fashion in rural Scotland?

John touched the collar point, and only the collar point. 'It suits you.'

Max kept her hand flat on the table, hoping he wouldn't see a tremor. 'What made you decide to honeymoon in rural Scotland?' she asked.

'The coastline,' Jane said, draining her first sherry.

'The walks,' Adam said, rubbing her arm. 'With the pretty views of the coastline.'

Had Adam held one of the torches she'd seen? Lots of people came on holidays for coastlines, although April in Scotland seemed extreme.

'Marjorie said to give you her best,' Max said, lifting her glass.

Adam's fingers tightened on Jane's arm, and Max tried to not react to her hissed exhalation. 'I beg your pardon?'

'Marjorie Spencer. From Bar Harbor? She and my grandmother are friends. I happened to speak to her when I was London.'

'How is she doing?' Jane smiled.

'Apparently missing you and your shop. She said it was a such a brief joy to have it there.'

'Yes, well, it wasn't quite the right market.'

Mr Knox held the car door for her again, and then retreated to his side.

'Are you okay to drive?' When she closed her eyes, the world felt lightly dizzy. She used to hold her alcohol better.

Mr Knox started the car. 'I'm fine.' He reversed from the car park, and they drove past the field that had once held her beautiful plane.

'I want my plane back,' she said to the window.

'Did you find out what happened?'

'The engine failed. A mechanic was recommended to me, but he still hasn't figured out why. Or he hadn't yesterday. I couldn't get the landing gear down, so the chassis is a bit banged up too.'

'You were lucky.'

Max thought of those lights bobbing towards the sea. 'What did you think about Adam and Jane?'

'Their accents are pretty variable.'

'They aren't from Bar Harbor. And it's not suspicious that I know that.' She traced a seam on the seat's upholstery.

'I take it you called Mrs Spencer?' Max stayed silent. 'Good investigating. Anything else she shared?'

Max glanced at Mr Knox, his face faintly illuminated by the dash lights. His upright posture, and the shape of his hands on the wheel. The tiny bit of his neck visible through the open collar of his pale shirt. He stayed silent as he changed gears and turned corners smoothly. No question about directions, he simply drove.

'Is there anything else you haven't told me, Max?' He turned towards her, and she flicked her eyes away. 'What did you do with the knife?'

He had noticed it. 'I haven't told you about my PhD.' Max tried to sound as flippant as possible, willing herself to forget those lights. And the answering flash from the sea. And the blade under her mattress.

The car bumped along the track to the cottage. 'Why won't you trust me?'

Max closed her eyes. Why didn't she? The lights, the voices, the knife underwater...

He stopped the car and turned the key in the ignition. 'Okay, what is your thesis about?'

She opened her eyes, and he faced her, one hand balanced on top of the steering wheel. The engine ticked in the silence.

'I'd settle for anything at...'

Max couldn't explain it, didn't want to consider it, but somehow she'd scooted along the bench seat and pressed her lips to his. He stayed perfectly still.

'Too much...' Before she could say 'whiskey' his mouth covered hers, and his arms wrapped around her. Faint stubble scratched her palm, and then her fingers slid into his hair. The taste of his beer and smoke blurred into the sweetness of her whiskey, and the world felt more than dizzy.

When the kiss—kisses—stopped, John held her, and she didn't pull away. His cheek rested against her hair, and their breathing blended with the soft clicks of the engine. At least his was as uneven as hers.

'Can I call you honey now?'

Max laughed against his throat. 'Not if it's to mollify me. Or if it's the way you talk to your secretary.'

'Am I still an unwelcome suitor?'

At least he couldn't see her blush in the darkness. 'Can you pay suit to someone you find so highly suspect?' She wanted to press her lips to his neck, the way she hadn't with Angus, a voice whispered, but Mr Knox eased the pressure of his arms.

'Exceptions have been made.'

He didn't deny it. He just wanted information from her. And clearly he'd done the same with other women. 'I think I've had too much whiskey.' She pulled away, but a few strands of her hair caught against his stubble. She tugged them free and smoothed them back. Why did her hand movements feel so awkward?

'I'm heading back to London tomorrow.'

Max nodded, inching back to her side of the car. Her cardigan. No handbag. Mr Knox wrote on a card.

'I'm giving you home and work. If I don't answer, call that one. It's Joyce, my secretary, who would never, ever let me call her honey. She can usually find me. The fourth one

147

is her home number, but don't call that one lightly. She has her niece and three great nieces staying with her right now. Don't lose this one.'

'I didn't...'

'So why didn't you tell me that in the first place?' Mr Knox lifted her hand.

'I think I like James Carter better. I know more about James Carter.'

'Almost everything I said as James Carter was true. I have two brothers. And Luke does take care of our mother.' He pressed his lips to her palm, and then placed his card in her outstretched fingers. She willed them not to tremble. 'Next time tell me about your thesis.'

Max closed her hand. She would not be silly about this man.

Before she could open the door, he had gotten smoothly out of the car and come around to her side. Max fumbled the card into her pocket and stepped out. She swore she would not kiss him again, but she still found herself turning towards him. 'Good night.'

'Thanks for coming to the pub.'

He leaned against the car as she walked up the path. She turned to check halfway up. Just enough moonlight shone to illuminate his shape, the disrupted line of his hair. Her fingers twitched, remembering its softness.

'I think I'm pretty safe here.'

'Just making sure.'

Just watching her. 'Why did you really come up here?'

'You sounded upset on the telephone. And I heard about the crash.' He pushed a hand through his hair. 'I had some leave owing. I like fishing.'

'So you followed me to Scotland. That trumps the theatre.'

'Or chasing me out your front door?'

Damn it. But if she couldn't see his face, he couldn't see her blush.

'I had an urgent phone call. I would have stayed, otherwise. At least long enough to say happy birthday.'

'Good night, Mr Knox. Thank you for my drink.'

'I prefer to call people I've kissed like that by their first names, but that's up to you.'

'Would that be James or John?' She forced her feet to carry her towards the cottage. Max didn't hear him move, didn't hear any shifting pebbles, but suddenly he grabbed her arm.

'Max. Be careful. And call me. Whether you crash any more planes or not.' This close, he honestly looked concerned. Maybe because he knew George. Maybe because he too thought Adam and Jane left too many unanswered questions. Maybe she should tell him about the lights.

'My birthday resolution was to be cheerful,' Max whispered. She reached upwards, towards his stubble, but he released her.

'You can cheerfully report suspicious behaviour.'

Max shifted so it looked as though she had aimed towards her hair all along. 'I would call the Scottish police, not some journalist.'

'Or your regimental friend?'

He'd noticed. He noticed everything.

'If nothing else, call me when you get back to London. I'll graduate to buying you food next.' She watched as he walked back to the car.

'Adam and Jane,' she called out. He turned, his profile sharp in the dim moonlight. 'Marjorie said Jane wanted to live somewhere else, although having heard his version of an argument, I'd guess he wanted to live somewhere else.'

'Good to know. Anything else?'

'My thesis is in the British Library.'

He laughed as he climbed into the car.

Chapter 13

Max stared into the darkness. What had possessed her? Nothing about the man should be attractive, and yet she'd kissed him. She'd initiated it. And he kissed well, better than Daniel, certainly, better than An... That line of thought had to stop. She threw back the covers and pulled on her dressing gown. Two hours of lying awake did her no good.

In the kitchen, she filled the kettle and placed it on the hob. She tucked her hands under her arms. A cottage in Scotland didn't compare to the central heating in her parents' house. He had been warm... but she knew practically nothing about him, and he thought she was untrustworthy. Two brothers. And a farm. If she believed him.

The record player, the cards and her tablet sat on the kitchen table. On her very first dig, a girl named Daisy Bryson asked if Max had brought servants to clean up after her. Max prided herself on doing more than her fair share, something the Daisys and Ruths of the archaeological world never protested. And now she'd left Victor and Emma to tidy up after her while she traipsed off to the pub with that man. She rescued the kettle before it whistled, and poured the water over the tea leaves.

'I'm not even going to ask if you're hung-over,' Victor said. 'How much tea have you had?'

'Your dressing gown still hurts.' She shielded her eyes from the intense red and purple stripes. 'Where did you find that?'

'Don't you mean why?' Emma asked. She peered in the tea caddy. 'You didn't bring any more tea from London, did you?'

'I'll get some posted. Sorry.'

Victor drew out the loaf of bread and a knife. 'So last night.' He sliced efficiently, thick doorstops.

Max eyed him warily.

'You were back late.'

'Victor,' Emma said. She pressed a hand to his lower back.

'Right. You need breakfast before diving.'

'Why do you like it? It's cold, you can't draw properly, it's...'

'Fun.'

Victor disappeared to the bathroom, and Emma tipped more hot water into the teapot.

'Sorry if he pushes you about John today. I've asked him not to.'

'It's what Victor does.' Max drummed her fingers on the table. Should she tell Emma about kissing John?

'For what it's worth, he seemed like a nice man. Even if he irritates you.' Emma smiled.

'I don't—I don't know what I want any more, Emma. Maybe I didn't ever, I mean.'

'You've had a hard time since the war.'

Edward had said that to her, it felt like months ago. 'Lots of people have.'

'Your problems feel as big to you as theirs do to them. It's difficult to come out of mourning.'

The black dresses her mother had had removed from her closet, the black day gloves that disappeared from her drawer. 'It doesn't stop.'

Emma poured tea into Max's cup. 'But you don't either. And look, you're here. Back doing archaeology, rather than just writing about it. And doing what you want, rather than doing a quarter of a trench for Edward. So that's good.'

'And you have two different men—maybe three?— focusing their attentions on you,' Victor said from the doorway.

151

'Which may not be what she wants, Victor.'

'It's what my parents want.'

'Yeah, well, screw 'em.' Victor laughed. 'I don't mean literally, of course. Do whatever the hell you want, but go get ready to dive.'

As they moored their boat after the afternoon dive, a voice called to them. Max heard a vague thump, and looked up from tying a knot to see Richard Ash standing on the shore.

'Hallo there. I wondered if I might run into you.'

Max felt acutely aware of her dive suit, but smiled and forced herself to stand upright.

'Come over for dinner tonight?' he asked.

'Um, sure.' Her mother's voice chastised her again. 'That would be lovely, thanks.'

'Max,' Victor said, emerging from the tiny wheelhouse. 'Aqualungs are sorted for tomorrow. Oh. Hello, Richard.'

'Richard's just asked us...'

'I'll pick you up at seven-thirty then, Max. Nice to see you again, Victor.'

'Wait, Richard. I'll just walk over.' It couldn't be a date.

He nodded and limped back to his car.

'We'd best get home, Max. I think Emma's sorted tea, and I'm ready to get into real clothes.'

Max watched as Richard closed the car door. 'So not dinner for all of us.'

'Nope.' Victor reached for the ring at the neck of her dive suit. 'Good to find more sword fragments,' he said.

'You're being restrained.' She shivered as the cool air hit her skin as Victor helped peel the rubber over her head.

'And no more knives.'

'Eat up,' said Victor. 'You have to eat more when you go diving. Never mind if you have a dinner engagement.' He pushed the plate of scones towards her.

They sat outside again, although Doris Day sang this time. Max broke her scone into small pieces.

'I could get used to having imported American stuff,' Emma said. 'It's lovely having dried fruit in them again.'

'I've got to remember to ring my parents to send more tea. Sorry about that.'

'You had—' Emma kicked Victor under the table and he stopped. 'You were clearly thirsty.'

Max laughed.

'Back in the war, we'd have huge meals after diving. Our rations would be bigger than the other sailors.'

'Hello?' It was a Scottish burr that called, but still Max stiffened. Angus stepped into view. 'Ah, I do have the right address. Hello again.'

'Hello.' Max held out the plate of scones. 'Fancy some tea with us?' He wore trousers, hiding his sturdy knees.

'I came to see if you wanted to go to dinner, actually.'

'Too late, mate, she's got another date.'

'It's not a date. It's...' Max didn't know quite what it was. 'I'm having dinner with our landlord.'

'All of you?'

Max shook her head. She didn't want to consider it a date. And the kisses with Mr—John last night far eclipsed the ones she'd shared with Angus. What had happened to her social life?

'Another time, maybe. When I have leave again.'

'Stay for tea,' Emma said. 'I'll get you a cup.'

'Didn't you just have leave?' Max asked, as he sat down beside her. The song ended and Victor started sorting through the records.

'I swapped.' A flush burned in his cheeks. 'I should have asked before, I—I just hoped.'

'Sorry.'

Victor dropped the needle, and 'Someone to Watch Over Me' started. He smiled blandly at Max. Surely he had heard it playing last night. 'I'll grab another chair,' Victor said.

'It was a silly idea,' Angus said. His hand found hers, a brief touch.

'It's lovely to see you.'

'Have you found anything interesting? I've seen the boat out.' He grinned. 'The whole island is talking about you.'

'Just some sword fragments,' Max said quickly as Victor returned with a chair. 'But they are possibly indicative of...' She stopped. 'Sorry, I've been told archaeology talk is very boring to non-archaeologists.'

'It can be,' Emma said. She placed a cup in front of Angus.

'I'd love to hear it.' Angus couldn't sound more eager.

Victor coughed, clearly smothering a laugh.

'Come for a walk on the beach?' Angus asked, after the scones were finished.

'I just need to help tidy up,' Max said.

'Go on,' Emma said. 'What time is Richard coming?'

'Seven-thirty. But I'm walking over.' She had an hour. Would Richard be able to see her walking with Angus from his house? They walked down the path, but Max kept her hands firmly in her skirt pockets. She turned to the left, away from Richard's house, once they reached the shore. Maybe he'd think she was walking with Victor, who was a similar size and blondness. She didn't consider tonight a date, yet walking out with another man seemed inappropriate. Betty, her Southern roommate at Vassar, would have called it tacky. She'd been from Virginia. Mr Knox—John didn't sound much like her.

'You're very quiet,' Angus said.

'Sorry.' She hooked a hand on his arm. 'How's your training going?'

'Your work is much more interesting. I can't imagine diving.' They picked their way along the stones.

'Neither can I, really.' She laughed. 'It's very odd—and completely different to any other archaeology I've ever done. I'm hoping my plane is repaired quickly. I much prefer flying.'

'Mull must be pretty from the air.'

'When it's mended, I'll take you up for your next leave. How long will it be?'

'Not for weeks.'

'We're here all summer.' Angus smiled at her, but her pulse stayed perfectly flat. Did kissing John make that much of a difference?

Chapter 14

Max expected a servant to answer Richard's door, as surely as they would have at her parents'. Instead, he opened the door himself and ushered her into a living room lit with—she counted—fifteen Tiffany lamps. It didn't seem possible that the room had enough flat surfaces, but it held more tables than chairs.

'I collect them,' he said, gesturing around. 'This one, for example, has Favrile glass.' He indicated the one closest to the window.

'What a lovely turquoise,' Max said.

'Do you know what makes it Favrile?'

'The colour is embedded in the glass.' She smiled. 'My grandmother—my American grandmother—likes Tiffany lamps too.' Although she'd never place fifteen in one room. Rather than putting off his explanations, Richard launched into a discourse on the seven major categories of the lamps.

'My brother once broke one of my grandmother's flowered globe lamps with a baseball.'

'I can't imagine how horrible that would have been.' He kept talking about the colours in his flowered globes, but Max remembered the tears staining both George's and her grandmother's faces. George always said that if she had caught the ball instead of letting it soar into the open window, he would have never gotten in trouble.

'I'd love to meet your dog,' Max said. Richard could hardly be construed as a threat, but she knew what Nancy Falkland would say about her being in a man's house alone. If he kept talking about lamps, her only worry would be extreme boredom.

'Mmm?' He turned around with a glass of wine.

'Your dog.'

'I don't have a dog.' He passed her the glass.

Max took a sip. He had definitely mentioned a dog on the beach. A date with Angus sounded more and more appealing.

'I did, years ago. But he had died when I came home from the war. I'd have had a hard time walking him anyway.'

'I'm surprised you don't have any servants. Not because of...' She stopped. 'I just assumed you would, with a house this size.'

'There's a woman who comes in to clean. But I manage.' He smiled. 'I'm even a decent cook, you'll see.'

Despite his protestations, Max had low expectations of the meal. Richard refused all offers of help as he carried the soup bowls from the kitchen one at a time. The meal would take forever.

The soup was surprisingly good, if a bit heavy with cream. Richard proved a pleasant conversationalist, once away from his lamps. He took the soup bowls away, and Max stared into the surface of her wine. She wanted to ask him about being shot down, but she'd already suggested he needed help because of his leg. As the door from the dining room slapped shut, she heard another male voice. She rose and went to the door. Two voices rumbled down the hall. She had just returned to her chair when he limped in with a dinner plate.

'Lamb,' he said, placing it before her. Max thanked him and watched his painfully slow progress back out the door. This time she opened the door and heard two voices distinctly. One was Richard's, and the other seemed to reply.

'I thought you said you didn't have help. I heard another voice just now,' Max said, when he had seated himself with his own plate.

Richard swallowed a bite of his lamb. 'The radio. I have a horror of silence.'

It had not been the RP tones of the radio she'd heard, but a conversation. He must have brought someone else in to cook. She wouldn't press.

Why had she had tea with Victor and Emma? Four courses were more than she expected from Richard, and by the time the cheese arrived, Max couldn't even pretend to eat any more. She gripped her napkin under the table. She had to ask now. 'This may seem tasteless, but I… I mean, my brother—he was shot down. Over Korea. He died.'

'I'm sorry to hear that.' He snorted. 'Terrible cliché, isn't it? But I am sorry.'

'I hadn't, I never allowed myself to think he hadn't died. They told us he did. Until I met you.' She took a deep breath. 'Now I have all these visions of what might be happening to him.'

'It's not pleasant. But the military are usually quite— well, I found out that they knew I was captured, they just didn't do anything about it.' He tipped more wine into her glass, but only a trickle emerged. 'If they said he was shot down, they probably know what happened. Pardon me. I'll be right back.'

Max smoothed her napkin carefully over her skirt. Her father showed no doubt. The thump of Richard's cane sounded as he returned with an open bottle.

'So archaeology. What are you looking for?' Richard poured her a full glass and Max curled her fingers around the stem.

'Signs of Viking occupation.' The sword fragment gave a good indication, and they might find more tomorrow. The knife still rested under her mattress, and she wouldn't think about it.

'Do you want a tour of the place? I won't talk about lamps any more, I promise.' His laugh was pleasant when it came without bitterness. 'I've just put in a cinema.'

'In your house?' Max stood and followed Richard down the hallway and to a flight of stairs. He opened the door for her to precede him, and she faltered slightly before the darkness.

'Oh, pardon me.' He flicked a switch and the stairwell, normal, carpeted, was illuminated. Max's feet sank into the new carpeting. His tread followed unevenly.

Why would he build something he had to go downstairs to get to?

'Who do you work for, Max?'

'No one.' She turned at the base of the stairs, and he flushed as she saw him lurch down the final two steps. She turned back to the abstract print on the wall quickly.

'No one?'

'I'm financing this myself. It's only survey, so it's not like it's a huge project. Not like people undertake in say Denmark.'

One open door showed exposed floorboards and bits of piping. 'The downstairs WC isn't finished yet.' He stepped ahead of her to open a door. 'When did you get interested in archaeology?'

'My father always has been, so I went to digs as a child. And I did my degrees, of course.' She saw why the cinema was downstairs—it extended most of the length of the house. Three velvet sofas faced a full screen, each with a footstool before them.

'What do you fancy?'

'I beg your pardon?'

'What film? I have a range.' He gestured towards a deep bin holding film canisters.

'I don't know if...' She stopped. She couldn't remember when she'd last seen a film before her date with Angus. Before the mourning period, she'd been finishing her PhD with frantic speed. Maybe a year ago. 'My friends expect me back soon.'

'So a short. A cartoon.'

Richard opened another bottle of wine before he loaded *The Philadelphia Story* into the projector. She'd forgotten James Stewart played a newspaper man, but she laughed at the pratfalls and—mostly—forgot about John Knox. Halfway though, Richard paused the projector when she asked. Her leg muscles felt slippery when she climbed the stairs to find the toilet. As she emerged upstairs, she heard two male voices, and then a door slammed. Why did Richard want to lie about having help?

She didn't ask when she returned downstairs, although the question swirled as she watched James Stewart carry Katherine Hepburn into the house. When the film ended, Richard insisted on driving her home rather than letting her clamber across the beach by moonlight.

'I had a nice time tonight,' Richard said in the car.

'You sound surprised.' The weave of her skirt beneath her fingertips felt nubbly, far more than it would have if she were sober.

'I am a bit.' He laughed. 'Not your company, of course, but I don't... It's why I built the cinema. I look for escape. Wherever I can.'

'Since?'

He nodded. 'Most nights I wish I'd died in the crash.' He stopped the car at the bottom of the path to the cottage. His laugh was harsh. 'Most days too. Your brother was lucky.' He sighed. 'I mean, I'm sorry for you. But that's a better way. In a war.'

'Police action.' The bitterness in her voice shocked even Max. 'He didn't die for a proper, declared war.'

'You aren't committed to halting the Red Menace?'

'I think if the government was, they'd call it a bloody war.'

'Good point.' He covered her hand with his smooth, narrow fingers. 'It was a lovely evening.'

Max nodded, seeing George's eager face over his RAF blues. The press of Richard's lips to her palm shocked her, and she jerked. 'I'm sorry. I was, I was thinking about my brother.'

'Understandable. I apologise.'

He released her hand carefully. The lights from the dash illuminated his faint smile. The rush in her chest sprang from pity, not desire, but she leaned forward to kiss him. A chaste peck. He didn't press for another.

'Thank you.' Max opened her car door quickly, imagining his awkward walk around to open it.

She climbed the path and stopped behind the pine trees as he drove away. Lust had motivated her to kiss John Knox, and she couldn't blame it on the whiskey and loneliness. The wine hadn't made Richard similarly attractive. A wave of heat rushed over her, thinking about John. Very well, she could label it a physical attraction and deal with it.

She opened the cottage door.

'What the hell do you think you're doing? We were worried sick,' Victor shouted.

'Victor's practicing for our unborn child,' Emma said. 'I hope you had fun.'

'He has a cinema. We watched *The Philadelphia Story*. I didn't mean to worry you.'

'In his house?'

Max nodded. Before Victor could ask how she would compare Richard, Angus and John, she told them good night and retreated to her room. Nothing since she ended her engagement with Daniel, and now she'd kissed three men in the last week.

A rap sounded on her door.

'Yes?' Max didn't want to open it.

'Drink water,' Victor said. 'Hung-over diving isn't safe. Good night.'

Chapter 15

'How are you feeling?' Victor asked as they walked down to the waterfront. A heavy rainstorm in the morning had pushed them to work on site reports all morning. Under the watchful eye of Emma, Victor hadn't ribbed her at all, at least not about Richard. Her handwriting was up for grabs.

'Four glasses of wine with four courses. For the last time, I wasn't drunk. Besides, it's two in the afternoon. I don't think I've ever had a hangover last this long.'

'No whiskey? You shock me, Dr Falkland.' He batted her with the pile of towels and blankets he carried. 'Presumably he had some servants doing it all?'

'Oddly, no.' She shook her head. 'He said not anyway. I heard voices.'

'Maybe he thought it made him look self-sufficient. That leg. How does the fair Mr Ash compare?'

'It was not a date. How many times are we going to dive today?'

'Now, and then maybe once more after tea. Depends on what the weather's like, I suppose.'

'Oh goody. Climbing into a wet dive suit.'

'Well, if someone still had a plane...'

'The parts are on order, the mechanic says. Maybe a couple of weeks?' She gazed across the water and shivered. 'It's still choppy.'

'Be all right under the surface.' He took the dive suits from the bag Max had carried down. 'But we should get kitted up here.'

Max threw her capris and jumper into the bag and dragged the rubber over her legs and up to her swimsuit. Her skin recoiled at the chill.

'I still prefer land archaeology.'

'There's two of us. You should have gone with Edward if you wanted that.'

'I'd rather be here. You know that, right? I'm terribly grateful. I don't mean to moan.'

'A turbulent love life can lead to that, I've heard.' He laughed and helped her finish cinching her suit's neckline. They clambered on board the boat.

She untied the boat as Victor started the engine, and soon the boat cut cleanly across the waves.

They'd agreed this morning to move to a new location, fifty feet along from where they'd been yesterday. Soon they anchored and put on their masks and fins. The backward flip off the boat felt less terrifying this time, and the rush of adrenaline didn't throb quite as loudly in Max's ears. They'd slightly miscalculated the position of the boat, so they swam down to the seabed then above the broken kelp. The clear water they'd enjoyed yesterday had turned grey, but each frond could still be distinguished. The seabed fell away sharply beneath them, but Max followed Victor's flippers.

Victor slowed, then gestured around the area they'd pinpointed this morning. The depression didn't extend this far, so they used their hands to part the strands to examine the sandy bottom. Max prayed she wouldn't find any more dive knives or anything bearing Cyrillic letters. She rolled and looked upwards. Only water. They'd come farther from the boat than she thought. As she flipped back, her breath caught. Breathe normally, Victor had drilled into her. Breathe normally. She tried, but only a thin trickle of air came. Victor floated a few feet away from her, but he didn't respond to her hand gestures. She pushed herself forward and grabbed his arm. Now no air flowed at all. She held the last precious breath she had, trying to explain with gestures. Victor pulled the mouthpiece from her mouth and shoved his into its place. She gulped one mouthful of air, and then it slowed as well. She shook her head and handed it back to

Victor. He pushed it back to her as they started to ascend together. Victor nodded reassuringly to her. How could she make him understand? She held out the mouthpiece and tried again. It felt like hours before he took the mouthpiece, and when almost no air arrived, his face finally registered concern. He forced it back into her mouth, and she gasped in reflexively. Victor swam faster, linking their arms.

Max could see the shadow of the boat, but not the down line. She took a shallow inhalation, and the airflow stopped, just as Victor's swimming slowed. She ripped her focus from the boat just as his grip on her loosened and then dropped.

Max grabbed Victor before he floated away. His head lolled to the side. Surface. She had to reach the surface. She fumbled at her weight belt but unclipping it one handed was taking too many precious seconds as her lungs started to ache from not exhaling. She grasped Victor's, holding him steady, and the belt fell from his waist. Her ears popped as now they ascended too quickly. Finally, the down line blurred into focus in front of her and she grabbed it.

If only someone was on the boat, but Emma had stayed home to finish tea. She kicked desperately, dragging Victor's body. Her lungs burned. Finally, she broke water and spat out the useless regulator. She ripped off Victor's mask and puffed air into his mouth as he floated. His eyes remained closed. She tried again, then unclipped the Aqualungs and crawled with him the few feet to the boat. His weight seemed unbearable as she climbed into the boat, then pulled him after her. She heard a rip, felt cold air touch her bare skin. He had to breathe. She pushed on his chest, on the stupid rubber, and after a few agonising seconds, he choked out water. Max rolled him, and heard his first breath, but he didn't open his eyes, and his breathing didn't deepen. Max flung open the door of the wheelhouse and stumbled to the shortwave.

Max switched it on, praying it would work as she checked the frequency. She depressed the handset's button.

'Mayday, mayday,' she called. 'Mayday,' Max repeated, and as she started a fourth time, the crackle of a response came. She gave their location and explained the lack of air, diving, and the voice reassured her a helicopter was on the way.

Max fell back onto the deck. Victor's chest rose and fell beneath her hand, although the rhythm stayed erratic and light. What could she say to Emma? She imagined the helicopter roaring overhead and the delay until she heard the actual rotors felt interminable.

A line dropped over their boat, and a man descended to check Victor. Soon, Victor was hoisted upwards and the man followed.

He'd told her to seek medical attention once on land, but she had to talk to Emma. Max turned on the engine and steered back to the shore.

Regulators failed. But both?

Max forced her attention back to the choppy water as rain started to pelt at her. As she approached the shore, she saw a jeep parked by the mooring and Emma pacing frantically.

Max stepped out of the wheelhouse and Emma's body slumped. Angus took the rope Max threw and tied the boat up. She wrapped her arms around herself, her fingers fumbling at the edge of the rubber at the torn seam.

'Max?' Emma asked.

'He's breathing. They're taking him to County Hospital. In Oban.'

Tears started flowing down Emma's face.

'I'll drive you,' Angus said. 'What happened?'

'Both our regulators—and Victor's lasted longer but he shared and...' Max pulled Emma into a hug. 'Go. Take her.'

'I'm radioing for the medic to come look at you,' Angus said as they pushed Emma into the jeep's front seat.

'I'm fine. Don't bother. Go.'

The jeep bounced away. He'd driven her to her plane in that jeep, or one like it. Max trudged back up to the cottage. Her plane. The regulators. Both regulators. They'd checked them carefully.

In the cottage, she struggled out of the dive suit, desperate to have her skin free of the encasing rubber. What she wouldn't give for a shower in her parents' house, but she'd have to submerge herself again in water in the tub.

The plane, the regulators. The words swirled around her head as she waited for the water to heat. Her body began to ache as she shivered in her dressing gown. She couldn't wait for the tub to fill, nor did she want that much liquid on her skin. She scrubbed and washed the salt out of her hair. The sudden pouring of water from Victor's mouth across her hands. Max closed her eyes.

Jane and Adam, and the vague Russian words. Her plane crashing. The knife, its Cyrillic lettering. The failure of both regulators. The military base that had been on the island for most of the war.

Even if the Russians were doing something on the island, why on earth would they target her? Max levered her sore body out of the tub. Mechanically she dressed, putting on the warmest clothes she'd brought. She pinned her hair up rather than try to dry it.

Max paced the living room. She went to her bedroom and lifted the mattress. No blade rested on the wooden slats. Who knew about it? Victor, John, Emma. John Knox had not been in her bedroom, that much she knew. Victor? He was here alone with it. But she couldn't think that Victor would—he would mean it well. Probably see it as protecting her from herself. She opened the door to their room. She half expected a riot of colours and clothes, but of course Emma would keep it tidy. Emma would want some clothes at the hospital anyway, so it wasn't a betrayal

166

of her friend. It was assistance. And if she also looked for a missing knife, well, so be it.

She packed a small bag for Emma, noting that while Victor's clothes were trendy, Emma's petticoats were patched. Her outer clothes measured up to Victor's, but the state of their finances had never occurred to her. She revised her view on Victor's tailor. Did Emma make them? Did Victor? How did Victor live, going from one piecemeal archaeology job to another? Maybe it came down to Emma's thriftiness, and they didn't worry about money that much. She would pay Victor more. She fought down the bubble of fear that he might not recover. He would be fine.

Finally, she approached their mattress and looked under each corner. No knife. She looked in the toilet cistern, and eventually, noticed faint lines in the screw heads on the box around the bathtub. Her toolbox had everything she needed, and the screws yielded quickly. In the hollow under the rusted tub, she found an envelope. In the envelope, the Russian knife nestled. In the last two days, she'd convinced herself that it might have been a war trophy brought home by some keen local diver. But this knife was crisply sharp, recently used. She needed to tell someone. Angus? Would he be back from driving Emma yet? She swallowed. Her father? John Knox? He'd seen her drawing. Persuading him to listen to her wouldn't include getting him to believe it existed.

She had to get to a telephone.

She searched for Victor's car keys. Not in any of his jacket pockets, not next to his wallet on the dresser top. Not by the front door. Emma's handbag? She found this in the kitchen. The keys rested on the bottom, next to a compact and lipstick. She dropped Emma's handbag on top of the hold all. Her chest expanded freely in the real air, so unlike the darkness in the water, Victor forcing his mouthpiece in her mouth. Her shudder shook the car keys from her hand.

She took the envelope to her room and shrugged her flight jacket on over the cardigan. Her own handbag. The knife wouldn't fit, not angled or straight across the square opening. She couldn't put it in the bag of clothes for Emma. John said to be careful. The police would laugh at her, but if she could show them the knife... Her dive suit lay in a tangle on the floor.

Max swore she would never dive again as she plunged her hands into the puddle of rubber. She ripped her own knife out of the sheath and replaced it with the Russian one. Her fingers fumbled on the cold buckle three times, but managed to lock the damp belt around her thigh between her stocking and her garter belt. The pressure of the knife blade made her stomach lurch, but she dropped her skirt. To a telephone, then to the hospital. She'd figure out whom to call once she reached the phone box. Maybe both her father and John Knox? Victor had been so convinced she should tell John about Jane and Adam. A deep breath filled her lungs, not like the rasping breaths she'd struggled for under the water. She snapped her handbag shut.

The scream curdled in her throat as a man's outline filled the door. Before she could reach for the knife, before she could make any move, he spoke.

'Max! It's me, Richard.'

She focused on his pale brown hair, the tap of his cane as he walked over to her and reached for her arm. 'Sorry to intrude like this, but I heard about your friend. I was worried. You're shaking. Sit down.' He gestured to the bed, but Max pulled her arm away.

'I'm going to the hospital. But I need to make a phone call, so I'm going to the post office first.' She picked Emma's keys up from the chest of drawers. 'I have to go now, Richard. Thank you for checking on me, but...'

'I'll drive you. You're still in shock. You can't possibly drive.' He bundled her outside, although Max picked up

168

Emma's handbag and the bag of clothes on the way, refusing to relinquish them until she placed them in the back of his car. He sat awkwardly in the front and dropped his cane over the seat. It pinged against the metal handle of Emma's handbag.

'I heard about your equipment. How terrifying it must have been.'

Max would not spiral into the darkness and the horror of Victor's pale face. The Aqualung that she let sink into the water to hoist his body into the boat, and then the shallow rise and fall of his chest. She looked up from her clenched fists.

'This isn't the way to the post office.'

'Use my phone. It's closer.'

It took ages for him to turn off the car, creep up to the door and fumble the keys into the lock. Why had she agreed to come with him? She could have made the call by now and be on the way to the hospital to hold Emma's hand.

'I'll get you some tea. Or you preferred coffee, right?' Max nodded. 'Oh, but the telephone first. Let me take your handbag.'

Max clenched her fingers around it. It held the second card Mr Knox had given her. 'Just the phone, please. I'd like to get to Emma.'

He opened the door of a study, warmly illuminated by another bloody Tiffany lamp. The burgundy leather desk set shone, completely bare of paper or pen. What did he do at this desk?

'Take as long as you need. I'll just get you that coffee.'

He shut the door behind him, and she listened to his dragging steps away from the door before lifting the receiver. The knife snuggled against her skin as she sank into the chair. Her father? He would insist she come home, and how on earth could she tell him she found a knife with Cyrillic lettering? She opened her handbag and looked at the bold strokes of John Knox's black numbers. She dialled the first one, and got no response. The second similarly had no answer. She tried his secretary's line, but had no response. She hadn't put on her watch. A gold clock filled an entire empty shelf of Richard's bookcase. Nearly six. John was probably travelling home, or to his club, or whatever foreign managers of newspapers did. She'd try his secretary's home number, and then she'd call her father. Or the local police. Angus. What possessed her to think John could do anything, other than Victor's insistence she talk to him? She asked the operator to place the call.

'Hello?' The voice was calmly professional, and clearly also from the South.

'My name is Max. Max Falkland, and I was given your number—I'm so sorry to bother you, this is probably ridiculous, but...'

'Would you like me to pass along a message, Dr Falkland?'

His secretary knew who she was. 'Could you tell him—could you tell him that Victor Westfield's in the hospital? That our diving equipment...' She paused. 'That it failed. And we checked it.'

'Are you all right, dear?'

The voice gentled, and Max's shoulders relaxed infinitesimally. 'It's probably nothing. You don't need to tell him. It's silly.'

'If he wants to contact you?' The door opened, and Richard moved more quickly than she expected to place a coffee cup beside her.

'County Hospital in Oban.' She repeated the name and slid John's card into her cardigan pocket. The helicopter medic said all acute cases went to County. She hadn't told Emma that. She shuddered.

'Very well. Thank you for ringing.' She paused. 'Take care, Dr Falkland.'

'Thank you.' Max replaced the receiver. They'd had the entire call without mentioning John's name once. Was that normal for foreign managers of newspapers? She picked up the mug. 'Thanks, Richard.' She should ring her father. She sipped the coffee, expecting the thickness of lots of sugar, but the hot vapour of alcohol hit the back of her throat. 'What's in this?'

'Rum. I thought it might settle you.'

'I need to make one more call, and then if you wouldn't mind driving me to the ferry? Or I could ring for a taxi.'

'There's only one taxi on the island. I'll take you. Have some more coffee; you're shaking.'

Max looked at her hand holding the mug. It looked steady to her, although the thought of telling her father did send a tremor across her skin. Would he try to say she couldn't do archaeology anymore? Would he tell her mother?

She could try his club, but on Thursday evening, he was likely to be at home. Maybe she could just tell him about Victor's accident and his overprotectiveness would kick in. But he wouldn't tell anybody official unless she told him about the knife—and that'd she'd had it for three days without telling him. 'Could I have some privacy, please?' Richard rose from his chair as she sipped her coffee. The sweetness of the rum seemed to mask an acridness. Maybe Richard made coffee badly. The cup she had while watching the film had been fine, but—she sipped again, testing the flavour. Nausea suddenly rose from her stomach, swamping her throat.

'Max?' His voice swam towards her, almost visible in the air of the study.

'I, I...' She tried to stand, but her thighs didn't rise at her command.

'It's shock, darling. Just rest for a minute.'

Darling? The room spun, and Max grasped the card in her pocket as everything went dark.

Chapter 16

Max gradually became aware of a softness beneath her. Her head turned into a damp velvet cushion. Emma would be cross she'd fallen asleep with wet hair. But instead of her box room, she saw flickering light. A woman's deep voice spoke, punctuated by a ticker tape whirr. The whirring came to an abrupt stop, but the brightness remained.

'Oh good. I wasn't sure how long you'd sleep.' Richard came to the front of the sofa, and Max focused on the still cinema screen over his shoulder. Katherine Hepburn stood frozen, trapped mid-step, surrounded by trees.

'What—how did...' The coffee, the acrid taste. The weave of her cardigan rubbed against her palm, without John's card in its pocket. The coolness of the knife remained against her thigh. 'What is...?'

'*Bringing up Baby.*'

She shook her head, her cheek brushing the cushion.

'So sorry. I just needed to slow you a bit. Now we can talk properly and make plans for our departure, and our future.'

'Where?' She tried to sit up, but dizziness pressed against her.

'Careful. Moscow, of course. Once I explained you were a sympathiser, they were keen to bring you along. A peer's daughter defecting—what a coup! And I knew you'd want me to come with you, so I asked to escalate the time frame.'

Max closed her eyes. Surely she still slept and this was a dream? 'Richard, I don't understand.' She tried to enunciate carefully, tried to keep any condemnation from her voice.

'I'm afraid they had already gotten to your equipment before we had our conversation in the car—I couldn't stop it in time. But you survived, so that's most important.'

'Ash, stop babbling.'

Max visualised a tall dark man in a black overcoat, possibly leather. The voice didn't carry a strong Russian accent, no stronger than her great-grandmother's when she slipped into childhood memories. Did he own the knife nestled under her skirt? The man who walked around the sofa was no taller than she, and his rounded stomach pushed against his jumper. He had to be nearly fifty. The gun in his hand convinced her to respect him.

'Dr Falkland, you've proved very resourceful. You land a plane well. I heard the ATA training was not very good.'

Max swallowed. The taste remained, and she seemed to lack saliva. 'I flew before I joined up.'

'And your political views have expanded since the war? I understand you do not value your country's—either of your countries'—current roles in Korea?'

Max blinked slowly. He didn't say anything she didn't believe. But a huge gap existed between not approving of the police action and wanting to be a communist. Anyone could see that. Anyone but Richard Ash.

'And I understand from Ash here that you want to defect and be with him?' He motioned with the barrel of the gun towards Richard's smiling face.

How could she dismiss Richard as the fantasist that he was? One kiss, a pity kiss, and Richard saw an entire future? In Moscow? Had the call to her father connected?

'Dr Falkland?'

Max moistened her lips. 'What—' She grasped for anything to say that would lower his gun, give her more time. 'What could I do there? Could I work?'

A small smile crossed his face. 'We encourage work. Archaeology work could probably be arranged. Perhaps some diving, with safer conditions.'

Max shuddered. 'No more diving.'

'Understandable.' He stepped closer. 'Is that an affirmative then?'

Max nodded. Somehow she would escape. She had the knife. But she sat in a basement room and no one knew where she was.

The gun slid into his pocket. 'Excellent.'

Richard flicked *Bringing up Baby* back on.

'It might be relaxing. It's natural to be nervous.' He pressed a kiss to her forehead, and Max resisted pushing him away. 'Our adventure begins.'

Max tried to listen to Richard and the Russian. Katherine Hepburn and Cary Grant crashed through trees and shrubs chasing the leopard, arguing with each other and periodically breaking into song, making it hard to make out words. Moving to the next location. If they were going by sea, where would they go? And how could she get out of a basement room with two men? Richard she possibly could overpower, but not the Russian with his gun.

The toilet. Richard wouldn't have had time to complete the one downstairs. If she asked for the loo, would they want her to pee with the door open? The Russian just might. The acrid taste remained in her mouth. Summoning up the darkness of the water, the rubber awfulness of Victor forcing his mouthpiece in her mouth, the stillness of his body in the water beside her prompted a lurch in her stomach, and this time she didn't fight it. She retched over the side of the sofa, careful to avoid her own skirt. She hadn't eaten anything since lunch, but the stain spreading on the plush carpet satisfied her enormously.

'Max!' shouted Richard. He held her shoulders, and her shivers would be excusable this time. 'You used too much to make her sleep,' he said to the Russian.

'Can I wash up?' Max murmured.

'Down here,' the Russian said.

'There's no water.' Richard helped Max stand, and she wobbled more than she felt. 'I'll help her upstairs. We're leaving shortly anyway.'

'Will you stop this rubbish?' The Russian jerked his hand at the film.

Max moaned.

'I have to help her, Anatoly. Figure it out.'

Richard unlocked the door and ushered Max out. Anatoly. She clung to the bannister, climbing just ahead of him. 'Won't you miss your films once you're there?'

'I'm sure I'll be able to see films still. It's not barbaric.'

'Have they told you where you'll live?'

'*We* will live.' His hand stroked her back, and Max climbed more quickly. 'No, but it will be fine.'

The top of the stairs approached. She could take the crutch, push him down and run. To his car. He had dropped his keys on the table by the front door. Somehow lock this door so the Russian couldn't get back upstairs.

As she mounted the last step, a hand closed around her arm. She stumbled backwards, nearly knocking Richard down anyway. The grip tightened, and a man pulled her through the doorway, saying 'stop' in Russian. This Russian was maybe twenty, easily as tall as John Knox, and equally as broad. The knife no doubt belonged to him. Why had she assumed it would only be the three of them in the house? She had heard two other voices before. How could she possibly hope to escape now?

'I'm taking her to the toilet, Kuznetsov,' Richard said loudly in English. He stumbled over the name.

He didn't even speak Russian. What did he think would happen to him there?

Kuznetsov nodded, and released her arm. It still stung. Max turned towards the toilet downstairs as a banging came from the front door.

'Upstairs,' the Russian said, pointing upwards, although Max understood him. He pushed Richard towards the front door.

Max climbed slowly, straining to hear as Richard's steps dragged and clunked down the hallway. The burr of

175

Angus's voice reached her, and she turned, knocking against the wall. Before she could scream, Kuznetsov's hand closed over her mouth. He held her tightly against his body.

'Just the dog,' Richard said with a laugh. 'Can I help you, Lieutenant?'

'I'm looking for your tenant, Max Falkland. Have you seen her?'

'No, not at all. I assume she's resting after the awful accident. Have you heard how that chap is doing? I saw the helicopter.'

'The doctors are with him. If you see Max, could you let her know I'm looking for her? My name's Angus MacDonald.'

'Of course.' The door closed.

Anatoly appeared at the foot of the stairs, and the two men had a conversation too rapid for Max to follow. By the time Richard had limped back, it was clear the discussion contained nothing positive for Max.

'It seems, Dr Falkland, that you are not as happy to go to our homeland as you say. I should have known, with your Ukrainian grandmother. Ash, you're wrong about her.'

Max pulled at the hand over her mouth. Maybe Angus would still be in earshot. The hand might as well have been made of cement. It constricted even more.

'Max?' Richard's voice went high.

She tried to shake her head, but the man held her steady.

'They were even going to look for your brother. Just to see—I would have done anything for someone to take that chance for me. You're a foolish woman.'

'Foolishness is not limited to her, Ash.' Anatoly jerked his hand. 'Take her in the study. I'll be in shortly.'

'What will you do with her?' Richard asked. Max detected a twinge of concern under the anger.

'A peer's daughter defects tonight. Whether she survives the trip is another question. Make some more coffee, Ash.'

In the study, Kuznetsov released her. Max rubbed the skin around her mouth, the sharp taste of her vomit remaining. She moved towards the desk, and Kuznetsov rushed ahead to clamp a paw on the telephone.

'Okay, okay.' She sat in the visitor chair. Her card rested on the expanse of burgundy. Next to John's numbers were crabbed notes in blue. *Universal Dispatch* was next to the two work numbers, and Mrs P Martin next to the one she'd phoned. He said his secretary was named Joyce. Next to John's home number someone had written Luke Keck. John claimed that his brother's name really was Luke. How many different names did John have?

Angus looked for her only because he'd returned from the hospital. Why would he suspect she'd be inside? Max wouldn't let fear overwhelm her. She had to think.

Richard brought a glass of water in, and Anatoly followed with a glass with half an inch of brown liquid. Two more men the size of Kuznetsov trailed after them. One carried a cardboard box.

'Ash convinced me we could skip the coffee. Please drink this.' The liquid sloshed gently, leaving a sticky film on the side of the glass.

'Why? I can walk to the car, or wherever we're going. However we're going.'

Richard placed the glass in front of her, then unplugged the lamp. The box contained tissue paper, and he carefully began wrapping the lamp. He avoided looking at her.

She'd have to find another mechanic to mend her plane. She fought back a laugh. Her plane could wait until she escaped.

'The drink, please, Dr Falkland.'

'I don't want to be sick again,' Max said slowly. 'Please.'

Anatoly placed the glass on the table with a thud. 'As you wish. But if you make any noise, Kuznetsov will ensure you stay silent. Ash, you have enough lamps. Leave that one.'

Chapter 17

Richard's leg collided with hers repeatedly as the car bumped over tracks and to the main road in the darkness. She squeezed herself as small as possible. Kuznetsov sat on her other side, while Anatoly drove. A second car followed, with two Russians as big as Kuznetsov. No one spoke.

The cars stopped, and Kuznetsov jerked her from the back while Richard still clambered out. The whooshing of the water punctuated the dizziness in her head. Kuznetsov hadn't got any friendlier, despite Max's few words to him in Russian. Maybe her accent was as wrong in Russian as Adam and Jane's were in English. Would they be inside? Had Adam held one of the torches? Had Richard?

Houses dotted the coastline, but no lights shone from windows in the darkness. She stumbled, but recovered before the young Russian could pick her up. She couldn't risk anyone feeling the knife. It was miraculous that no one found it when they carried her to the cinema. Thank goodness for the thick skirt that her mother loathed. Was it only a little more than a week since she'd flown up and changed into the skirt in that terrible pub? She could have been in Denmark, digging a quarter of a trench with Edward. Victor would have been safe there.

'Take her inside,' said Anatoly as the two other young Russians opened the boot to the second car.

'Anatoly, what are you going to do...' Richard started.

'She will be dealt with. Go inside, Ash.'

Richard limped beside her as Kuznetsov guided her inside. 'You'll be fine, Max. They want a peer's daughter in Moscow. Photos, press releases, that sort of thing.'

'You've done this.'

'And it would be better to be dead? They tried twice, do you think they wouldn't have tried again? You're young, healthy, beautiful. We can still be happy together.'

Only the Russian's grip kept her from slapping Richard. 'You're insane. How you construed a pity kiss as anything more...' Kuznetsov's quick trot meant that they far outpaced Richard before he could hear the end of her statement. She was pulled into a darkened building. Gusts of wind came through the broken windows and skylights, and Max skidded on the damp leaves and mud inside. Kuznetsov's small penlight glinted off a row of copper stills. A distillery, long empty. John's bottle of Oban still sat in the cottage. Would he ring the hospital? Would Emma worry when she didn't appear, or would Victor's condition consume her?

'Come,' the Russian said. He quickstepped her down a corridor, and the tap drag, tap drag of Richard's progress followed them.

'Kuznetsov,' Anatoly called. 'Half an hour. Be quick.'

Max swallowed, fighting the vile taste of the medicine and her sick. Before she could reach under her skirt with her free hand, Kuznetsov shoved her into a dark opening. A lingering scent of wood remained, but she fell against a bare wall, not barrels. The penlight ignited again, this time between his teeth. He held rope.

'That's not necessary,' Richard said. 'Dr Falkland and I are going to become better acquainted.' The light glittering in her eyes didn't prevent her from hearing the rage in Richard's voice. Would Kuznetsov help?

'Kuznetsov, lock them in. Both of them,' Anatoly called.

The penlight dropped from his mouth as he smiled. Richard clearly didn't understand, as he stood in place while the Russian backed away. Richard scuffled around awkwardly as the metal bars clanged shut.

'What the hell are you doing? Anatoly! Anatoly!' Richard shouted, beating the bars with his cane. Max reached under her skirt to draw the knife and held it behind her back.

'Where are we?'

Max scuffed her feet against the smooth floor. The leaf fall hadn't reached this far. 'Barrel storage. Seems you aren't as popular as you thought.'

'Anatoly just wants me to look after you.' His cane tapped around.

'Sounds to me like you're a prisoner.' How much could she do with a knife? Her outstretched hand met a wall to her left, so she slid right, keeping a tight grip on the hilt. No wall. How many barrels would they have stored here? She could outrun Richard, but it depended on how much space she had to cover. No light penetrated the blackness.

'You know nothing about it.' He sounded as grumpy as George when Max proved a point.

'I know we're both in here, and all the Russians are out there.'

'They need me. I've helped their cause, enormously. You're only alive because I want you.' His footsteps dragged. Max shifted further to the right, but before she could calculate distances, his coffee breath fanned across her face. 'You can call it a pity kiss to protect yourself, but I know what you meant. Modesty is fine, up to a point, Max, but we should be honest with each other.' His hand brushed her cheek, and Max gritted her teeth.

'Have you been here before?' She kept her tone as practical as possible.

'Why?'

'Because I'd like to have options if they've decided that neither of us need to make whatever their next form of transport is.'

'A sub. But we will. I've been promised.' His finger traced her ear. A shudder raced down her back. 'I'll make it up with Anatoly for you. They can find your brother, if he survived. And we can all live together in Moscow. Your brother and I will understand each other, and you'll be happy. No more questions, just certainty.'

'Richard.' *Fantasist* formed in her mind, but before she could speak it his lips touched hers. Max steeled herself, but as his free hand went around her waist towards the knife, she stepped back.

'Max. This is not the time to be coy.'

'It was a pity kiss.' She licked her lips to rid herself of the taste of his mouth. 'I'm not going to Russia, and even if George is alive, he'd rather stay there than see me defect. It's a fantasy. They aren't taking us anywhere. Do you honestly think they have space for your lamps on a sub? They're going to kill us. Help me find a way to escape.'

Richard pushed Max until the stone wall pricked against her back. She remembered the muscles in his shoulders from his swim.

'You're wrong.' His cane held her legs immobile, and he gripped her left bicep hard. 'And you'll see. You're what, twenty-five? You don't know what levels of misery the world can hold. You don't have to stay in a nice house with me as my bride. I'm sure they have other facilities for you.'

The Cyrillic letter in the handle was rough against Max's palm as she squeezed it. She wouldn't think. She reached forward and drove it down, past the resistance of wool and skin, into Richard's leg. He groaned. Max shrieked, trying to cover his shout of 'bitch'. She pushed him, but he grabbed her as he fell backwards. She landed on top of him.

'Do what you want, Ash, but keep her quiet,' Anatoly called.

Max struggled to rise as Richard rolled. She couldn't get trapped under him. She tried to knee him, and kicked the knife. She covered his mouth as he groaned again, and his hands went around her throat. The pressure increased, and she kicked the knife again, fighting for breath. He bit her palm. Her fingers were slippery with blood when she grabbed his hair and banged his head twice against the concrete just as dizziness set in. He went limp beneath her. Max choked back a sob and scrambled to her feet.

181

No dampness on his head. She fumbled lower and felt his exhalation, uneven but there. Max forced her hand into his pockets and retrieved a square lighter. Thank God he smoked.

She flicked the lighter on, but nothing happened. A deep breath. She tried again, her fingers sliding against the metal. This time it caught, and she looked around the floor for the rope. Just outside the bars. She extended her fingers and brushed the trailing edge.

She tilted the lighter upwards towards the entrance. The rope held the bars together. Kuznetsov had tied them in? The knot hung on the outside of the gate, but she wrested it around. The lighter burned her hands before she managed to complete her inspection. Richard. If she removed the knife, he'd bleed more quickly. Who would rescue him anyway?

Nevertheless, she found the loose tail and began picking at it. She'd been on enough boats on holidays in the States to deconstruct it. It wasn't tight, but all her nails had broken before it opened. She picked up his cane and retied the lock after her.

Had the Russians stayed in the front of the building? Max turned the other direction, but after only ten paces met a dead end. The lighter revealed nothing but a solid wall. She'd have to go back. Her shoes tapped far too loudly, so she unlaced them. The wool skirt's pockets were tiny, so she left the shoes just inside the metal bars. She shuddered as the chill of the floor penetrated her stocking feet.

A new voice rang out. Russian. Max couldn't process the words over the thudding of her pulse in her ears. She tried to still herself, but she didn't know the words Anatoly replied with. His inflection suggested it was a question.

The corridor remained silent. She crept to the end, and saw faint starlight flicker against the stills. Her foot squished into mud, or worse, but she didn't move.

The other man replied, and Max focused on the sound, not his words. He was obviously fluent, probably another man to do the heavy work like Kuznetsov and the other men. But the voice sounded familiar, and Anatoly listened too long for the man to be another subordinate.

'Lies!' The shout came from Kuznetsov, a word in Russian she could understand.

'Stop,' Anatoly said, but a single gunshot rang out. Liquid trickled. The stills must be empty so what could it be? The trickle magnified into a solid pouring sound. The Russian submarine breaking the surface?

In a split second lights bounced into the building and gunfire erupted, sparking crazily from the stills. Max dropped the cane and ran, skidding across the back of the room. She reached the far corner, praying she'd find a door. The lights doused and she hunkered down, fumbling along the base of the wall. Gunfire continued, along with shouts. Her fingers touched the cold metal of a hinge. A bullet skipped along the floor a foot behind her. She found the doorknob and twisted, but it took four times with damp fingers to get it to turn, and she had to stand to force the water-logged door open.

A submarine descended rapidly into the bay. Lights flooded the area again, and Max pressed against the building as bullets pinged against the sub's surface. The thumping of a helicopter sounded overhead.

Someone grabbed her, and she kicked and punched.

'Max. It's me.' The Scottish burr pierced her panic. 'It's Angus. Stop. Come with me. Now.'

'Angus.' The deep breath she took burned her lungs.

'Come on.'

'But the submarine and the, Richard...'

'Are you hurt? There's blood, God, everywhere. Can you walk?'

She nodded. Nothing lasting, nothing permanent. 'Not mine.'

'Come on.' He half dragged her behind the building into the tree line, pine needles pricking her feet. Soon she was installed in the jeep again, and he shucked off his black jacket and threw it to her.

'Did he, were you hurt?' Angus demanded.

She shook her head, then said 'no' when he asked again. Angus started the jeep and drove rapidly away from sirens and further gunfire.

'How did you know? That I was at Rich... that house?' She slid the jacket over her cardigan, shoving her hands in its pockets, away from the sticky surface of her skirt. Richard's blood. Her left fist clenched, and the jolt of pain startled her. She fingered the gash in her palm.

'I didn't. I met—well, I met someone else who was looking for you. We followed the cars because there seemed no other place you could be.' He sniffed. 'When Emma said you didn't turn up at hospital. By the time we saw you being taken into the distillery, I knew it was something more. I radioed for help.'

Max turned towards Angus. He drove with one hand, with the other pressed against his face.

'Were you shot? Are you okay?'

'Just a bump. My nose.' He gave a muffled laugh. 'There should be a handkerchief in my jacket.'

Max fumbled through the pockets, and found one in a chest pocket. He dropped his hand long enough to grab it. 'What happened?' Her own handkerchief was still in her skirt pocket, so she wrapped it around her palm.

'You hit me.'

'With the door?'

'No, you just hit me. You should have, I could have been anybody.'

'I'm sorry. I can't believe I...' She took another deep breath. The Cyrillic letter against her skin. 'I stabbed him. Richard Ash. He was, he would have...'

'Good.' He turned the jeep down a road she could barely see. 'We—I heard you scream. And then the Russian... I was on my way in to find you. But he said you might—well, you managed on your own.'

Aches settled into every part of her body. The familiar tone, speaking Russian fluently. Who else could it be but John Knox? Or did he just turn up at the cottage and let Angus handle it all? 'John Knox?' Hard to imagine John handing over control of anything.

Angus didn't confirm or deny the name. John, back there with the gunfire and the four Russians.

'Where are you taking me?'

'Away, mostly.'

'I need to go to the cottage. For shoes, if nothing else.' She felt Richard's lips against hers again and trembled. 'Can you take me to the hospital?'

The jeep fishtailed to a stop, and his warm hands clenched over her shoulders. She shivered, realising the depth of her chill.

'You said you weren't hurt. What happened?' The burr increased with his fierceness.

'To see Victor. I'm fine.'

'Nothing happened?'

'No. They drugged me, but nothing—no one hurt me. Well, Richard Ash bit me. But I'm okay. Please, go to the cottage.' The helicopter still thudded, although the gunfire dimmed the further they drove. Was John okay?

Angus insisted on inspecting her hand and throat at the cottage, and wanted to leave immediately to have her seen by the medic. She brushed her teeth and washed her feet, despite his urging to hurry. She packed a bag with clothes and essentials and shoved in the bottle of Oban last.

'My jacket's at Richard's,' she said as she climbed back in the jeep. 'Do you think I'll ever see it again? And Emma's stuff is in his car too.'

'You've been throttled and bitten, and you care about a jacket?'

'It's my flight jacket. I've had it since the war.'

Soon Max was installed in the medic's tent. He cleaned the bite and bandaged it, and prescribed rest for her throat. The bruises would come out tomorrow, he said. Angus relaxed enough to leave her alone. Max sat on the cot but wouldn't let herself recline. She dealt a game of solitaire on the blanket and played despite the grittiness in her eyes and the ache in her palm from shuffling the cards. She hefted the bottle of whiskey and then replaced it in her bag. It would only push her towards sleep and dreams.

The camp remained active across the night. She heard men speaking in low voices, and rapid footsteps passed the tent walls. No mentions of her name, or Richard's. She didn't hear John's voice. Had he survived?

Her torn nails scraped against the back of the cards, and she shuddered. She dug in the bag until she found a small manicure case. When the metal file had abraded her nails down to the quick, she made herself stop. What would her mother say? The cards felt slippery when she lifted them again.

A couple of hours later she distinguished Angus's voice from the rest. '...says nothing. Hand's a bit nasty, and a sore throat. Chapman, the medic, agrees. Drug wasn't pleasant but no lasting ill effects. Do you want to see her?'

She listened for the reply, but it never came. Angus's superiors would see her if they wanted. Was John skulking around outside? Had he survived? She peered out of the opening, but saw no one.

Max planned to go to the hospital at dawn, but Angus's colonel insisted on seeing her first. Last time she met the colonel she'd been in her manure and mud-daubed flight clothes, and now, after the hurried packing, she wore a red cardigan and a green sweater. He showed no reaction to her rumpled state. Angus stood at ease at the door of the tent, his nose faintly purple.

She explained about her plane, and finally told someone about the lights. Clearly it had been the sub, she realised now. 'And someone robbed my compartment on the train back to Oban, but that may have been random chance.' Did she honestly think that?

'Why would they target you? Could it be because of your father's position in the government?'

How on earth did he know about that? 'Have you called my father?' He would never let her do any archaeology again.

'I suspect he'll find out. And perhaps you should tell him yourself.' The colonel folded his hands. 'You were very efficient in getting away from Richard Ash.'

'I grew up fighting with a little brother.'

'Did you often slam his head into a concrete floor?' A trace of a smile crossed his face.

'No, sir. Is Mr Ash alive?' She struggled with the word.

'He'll go to trial for treason. He has a very bad headache and...' He looked at the file in front of him. 'Fourteen stitches in his leg.' He snapped the file shut.

'Were there other injuries?'

'None that need concern you. Now, why did you decide to come up here?'

'Honestly, I picked it two days before I flew up. Just from a map. As for why they targeted me, Mrs Fentiman went through my notebook, but I doubt she knows who my father is. She does have my fountain pen.'

'The Fentimans run the Hare and Hound pub, sir,' Angus added.

'I don't think the theft of a fountain pen need concern us, Miss Falkland.'

'Doctor,' Max said. 'I left it in my plane. And it appeared in her hand the next day. So someone at the pub had to be

187

carrying one of the torches. What were they doing? What's so important up here?'

'That's sufficient, Dr Falkland, thank you. We can also return your personal items now. I suggest you do tell your father, but please keep this to yourself otherwise. The Westfields don't need to know about it. Lieutenant, take Dr Falkland to see her friend. And send in my corporal, please.'

Angus held the tent flap, and Max emerged into the horribly bright sunlight. It should be as grey as she felt.

'Why didn't you tell me about the lights that night?'

'You wouldn't have believed me.' The camp looked so tidy, with no indication that a battle with foreign nationals on British soil had happened only ten miles away.

'Why the hell do you think we're up…' He shook his head. 'My apologies. Hopefully there won't be a next time, but tell somebody.'

'Was anybody hurt?' Max asked again. Had John survived?

He tapped his nose. 'This is the worst our troops sustained.'

'Sorry. Thank you, for everything.'

Angus laughed. 'All I did was drive. I'm sure you would have found your way across the island without me. Let's get your stuff.'

She followed him towards another tent, but another officer met them halfway to hand over her jacket, the bags and her shoes. They'd even been polished. She thanked him, and Angus carried her bags to the jeep.

'Listen, when I next have leave, can I look you up in London?'

Max didn't want a husband with sturdy knees any more. 'I'd like that. It's lovely to meet up with old friends.'

Angus grinned. 'Understood. I might look you up anyway.'

Chapter 18

Angus drove her back to the cottage, although he checked the interior before he let her out of the jeep.

'Your colonel seemed certain they had everyone.' She set her feet on the dirt path, walked past the rickety table. The paper Victor had wedged was still there, a sodden lump since yesterday's rain. They'd fed Richard here. She definitely needed a new mechanic.

'How much more can you carry? You are going to London, right?'

'I can at least get travelling clothes.' She looked at the mismatched sweater set. 'My mother will know something is wrong if I turn up like this.' She turned back to him at her room door. 'Who did you think might be here?'

'I'm just being cautious.'

He stood so stiffly he was nearly at attention, and looked out the window. 'You're a bad liar, Angus.'

He smiled. 'I'll feel better when you're off the island.'

Max closed her room door. Her dive kit still lay on the floor. She stepped over it to reach the wardrobe. Nothing had been moved. She'd had a makeshift shower at the camp, with questionable water flow, but at least she didn't smell like vomit anymore. She pulled out her suit and the long line brassiere she'd worn on the journey down, but her skin ached at the thought of the constriction. Had it only been five days since Emma picked her up at the ferry? What if Emma was pregnant already and lost another baby? Max grimly picked up her makeup, smoothing it down over the bruises starting to purple her neck. She ripped off her clothes. The mirror showed another bruise on her left bicep, printed with his fingerprints. It overlay the faint marks from the man on the train. She wiggled into her undergarments and dressed in the suit.

*

They reached the port in plenty of time for the ferry, but instead of getting into the queue, Angus carried her bags towards George, the fisherman who had taken her before.

'Can you take us to Oban? And bring me back?' Angus asked.

'Wasn't that other chap your husband?' George asked. 'You running away with this 'un?'

Max's cheeks flushed. 'A friend. Angus, I can take…'

'We'll go with him. How quickly can we leave?'

Max stared at the waves, ignoring the stench of fish. The helicopter had hovered over their boat, and the other one over the distillery. Was John all right? She closed her eyes against the sunshine. Maybe she could make the 9:12 train.

Angus had talked to George by the boat's wheel for most of the journey, but now he walked towards her.

'You seem keen to get me off the island,' Max said.

Angus rested his arms on the boat's railing. 'Only a few more minutes. You seem eager to see your friend.'

'I am.' And before last night, Angus would have let her get on this boat alone. He would have waved her onto the ferry by herself. The Oban coast grew closer and closer. George didn't bring his wife this time—apparently, Angus was enough of a chaperone.

'How's it look?' she asked, pointing to her neck.

Angus reached towards her, but dropped his hand before making contact. 'Still visible.'

'I'll buy a scarf in Oban.'

'You're extraordinary, Max.'

Max swallowed. It hurt. 'Thanks. For everything.' She leaned over and kissed his cheek. 'Sorry again.'

He laughed. 'I've never had an injury from such a pretty source. I will ring you when I'm next in London.'

'Do.' She brushed the bridge of his nose gently. 'Then I can see if you're healing.' What would her neck look like by the time she saw him again?

*

Max found an open shop near the hospital and purchased three scarves. Would the newsagent sell papers with details of the attack? How much would be released? She didn't turn in.

In the hospital lavatory, she chose the red scarf. Tying it tightly enough to avoid slippage and loosely enough to avoid discomfort presented a challenge, but it provided some colour against her pallid skin. How long could she keep her mother from seeing her neck?

She asked the receptionist to direct her to Victor's ward, and after some debate and Max explaining she was Emma's sister, they gave her the location.

Max climbed the stairs, her leg muscles grinding. How could it have been less than twenty-four hours since she and Victor had walked down to the shore, with him laughing about her love life?

She opened the door, the faint screech cutting across the silent ward. She saw a line of shirred curtains on frames separating the beds. Her shoes seemed unbearably loud, and she swallowed, feeling again that squish of mud under her toes. She tiptoed past the first three empty beds, and then past four other men, three sleeping, and one staring out dully. Victor lay in the fifth, his blue eyes closed. No Emma. Max covered her face.

'I'm sorry, Victor,' she whispered.

'Why?'

She jumped, dropping her hands. He grinned at her.

'You saved my life.'

Max took a deep breath. 'You did that on purpose.'

Victor laughed. 'I recognised your footsteps, but you took so long getting here I was nearly asleep again. I'm sleeping a lot.'

'Where's Emma?'

'Getting food, I hope. I begged her to get some fresh air.' He pointed to a straight-backed chair. 'Have a seat.'

Max sat, resisting adjusting the scarf with an effort.

'You look terrible. What happened after I made my dramatic exit?'

Max shook her head. 'Nothing.' She willed the sound of Richard's head striking the concrete away.

'Nothing.' His fingers twitched on the bedclothes.

'Are they letting you smoke?'

He pointed at the oxygen tank beside him. 'I'm fine, though. They're being cautious. We weren't at great depth; you got me out and breathing. I came to in the helicopter.' He reached for her hand. 'Thank you.'

'You gave me your last air.' Tears pricked behind her eyes. They felt swollen and scratchy.

'Yeah, and look how well it all worked out. You look so glum. What happened afterwards?'

'Nothing.' Her smile was too tight.

Footsteps sounded behind them, and she flinched.

'It's just Emma,' Victor said gently. 'Tell me some other time.' He squeezed her hand, and the bite throbbed.

'Max.' Emma hugged her hard, crying.

'You two,' Victor said. 'You'd think I wasn't lying here the picture of health.'

Emma sniffed, and Max handed her a handkerchief. 'You scared us.'

'I brought you some stuff.'

She buried her face in Max's shoulder. 'Thank you.'

'I didn't do anything.' She led Emma to the chair. 'Here, sit.'

'I've been sitting all day and all night. I can't.' She pushed Max into the chair. 'I thought you might get here sooner. Are you okay? Did the medic look at you?'

'Um, yes. I'm fine.' She kept her gloves on. 'Sorry. There was a… it just took me a while.'

Emma nodded.

'So what's next?' Victor asked. 'When they let me out…'

'We aren't…' Max started.

'Diving again,' Emma said. 'Not for at least a month.'

'Ever,' Max said. 'I think we should head back to London. Give up on this season.'

Victor looked at her closely, but she didn't drop her gaze.

'With my plane still broken and no diving, let's just go home.'

Victor nodded slowly. 'We'll go back and get our stuff.'

'I'll collect the rest when my plane is mended.' She did look down at that weave of the blanket covering his legs. 'The Aqualungs are gone. Sorry, I had to take them off to get you in the boat. I'll see if I can find a way to import two more.'

Victor patted her hand. 'I'd rather be here than have my Aqualungs. Don't worry.'

'I wonder if Richard will want us to pay for the entire summer?' Emma asked.

Max's fingers clenched around a dive knife that wasn't there. 'I doubt it.'

'I'm sure you can convince him otherwise,' Victor said, grinning.

Max stood and paced. She would not be sick in front of them. 'I'm heading back today. I've checked, and there's a train just past nine.'

'Oh, sweetheart, stay. You look exhausted. Have you eaten?'

'I'll get something on the train.' She hugged them both. 'I need to talk to a garage, so I might go now.'

'What about that mechanic Richard recommended?'

'He can't do it after all.' And she would never get in a plane he'd mended. How did the colonel think she was supposed to not tell Victor and Emma? 'I'll ring. I hope you feel better.' She walked the length of the ward, refusing to let herself run.

Chapter 19

At lunchtime, Max made her way to the dining car, her tired body swaying with the motion of the train. She sat at the table with the crisp tablecloth and accepted the menu. The train moved too quickly for her to focus on the blades of grass. She could only see the sweep of green. The bright sunshine on the island had been overcome by grey clouds in the hour she'd walked aimlessly around the train station.

A presence beside the table prompted her back to the menu. 'I need another moment, I'm afraid.'

'I hoped I might be able to join you.'

Max didn't have to look up. 'Mr Knox.' He had survived. Relief trickled down her spine.

'John,' he corrected.

She waited just a beat too long. 'May I help, ma'am?' asked the waiter.

'My—Mr Knox was just joining me.' Friend didn't seem quite the right word.

He sat opposite her, and the waiter returned with another menu. John wore the same grey suit he'd worn at the Society. Not the blue jumper he'd worn on her boat. Had he been dressed in black at distillery like Angus?

Why had she tied the red scarf around her throat? At least it hid the growing purple bruises. Her short nails worried the edge of her bandage. Her hands trembled, so she dropped the menu. Would he lie if she asked?

'I saw Victor at the hospital.' His fingers covered hers again, the warmth shocking against her cold skin. 'They said I just missed you. Again. I'm really sorry I wasn't there to get your calls. It must have been terrible.' He withdrew his hand. 'I didn't realise we were on the same train.'

Max nodded.

'Emma said you swore you wouldn't dive again.'

The diving was the least of her worries now. How could he say nothing about the distillery? She practiced saying the words aloud: I heard you. Talking to the Russians. The gunfire.

John had to have been with Angus last night.

'Max, are you going to say anything at all?' The waiter reappeared and John glanced at the menu. 'Wine?' He ordered something, something she barely paid attention to. 'My county is dry, back home. I didn't learn how—or what —to drink until I went to college.'

Max knew what her mother would expect, a polite quip, a social nicety. She remained silent.

'My mother doesn't know, of course.' His laugh sounded forced. 'Max, you could talk to me, you know. I'll listen.'

'What do you do?' Max risked looking up into his steady eyes.

'I'm a newspaper man. You know that.'

'Yes.' She took a deep breath. 'Is it cold in Korea this time of year?'

'Do you think your brother wasn't shot down?'

'Rich–' Richard Ash sat in custody somewhere. Fourteen stitches. Why had she shared her concerns with him? Why had he put new ones in her mind? 'I met someone who'd been shot down in the Pacific. I'd never let myself think about it before.' She cleared her throat.

'It's warming up. Like here.'

Max nodded. Not like here.

The wine arrived, and John sipped his seriously before nodding. The waiter poured a glass for them both and took their orders. John let her order for herself, but this wasn't a date. The dinner at Richard's had not been a date.

'So have you seen any movies lately?'

The image of Katherine Hepburn blazed across her eyes, as nausea rose in her throat. 'No films.'

'A sore subject?'

'Mourning. I couldn't go and...' She paused. Would she ever look at Katherine Hepburn in the same way? 'John, I know you...' Should she invite a denial?

'I saw George in a bar. Talking about his amazing sister.'

Max forced a smile. 'Then you're definitely lying.'

John sipped his wine. 'I try not to.'

'He didn't want me to get a PhD. He didn't want me to be embarrassing.'

'You were all he talked about.' The waiter brought bread and Max stayed silent till he left.

'The last thing George said to me was to just get fucking married.' She'd told no one, not even Vivian. Vivian would have agreed with George anyway.

'Is that a proposal?' John's face creased into a smile.

Max lifted her glass and returned it to the table. 'You were there.'

John shook his head, still smiling. 'So I decided when I came to London I needed to look up this paragon of brains, beauty and aviation skills.'

'Last night.' Max kept her hands flat against the smooth tablecloth. 'At the distillery.'

'We covered the story. I was closest. Sometimes even managers get to do some reporting.' He pulled a folded newspaper from his coat pocket and tossed it on the table. A photo of Richard in his RAF uniform looked up at Max and she closed her eyes. 'You weren't there, were you? Not that near to your side of the island.'

'No.' What would Emma and Victor say? They'd have seen a paper by now.

John pocketed the paper and pointed at her bandage. 'Looks painful.'

'It's fine,' Max said. 'Do you speak Russian?'

'I have to confess something.'

Max held her breath.

'I haven't made it to the British Library. What is your PhD about?'

The laugh that emerged surprised her. Fine. She could do social chitchat. It would keep her awake. 'The short version—Viking archaeology in Northern Europe. Did you study journalism at university? Where did you go?'

'Carolina. And Languages.'

Max sipped her wine. 'Does that include Russian?'

'I'm fluent in seven, and can get by in a couple more.'

After the meal, John insisted on walking her back to her compartment. A dark-haired woman bumped into him as they headed out of the dining car.

'Excuse me, ma'am.' His accent dripped over the word.

The woman looked up. 'Oh, Mr Carter. And Maxine!'

'Jane?' Surely they had been rounded up with everyone else. Jane's quick smile suggested her cheek didn't hurt, although her make up stayed just as thick.

'I finally convinced Adam to leave that godforsaken island. We're opening a bookshop in London.'

Adam came into view behind Jane. Max saw the flicker on his face before he shook John's hand and then hers. She tried not to flinch. At least Richard had bitten her left hand.

'Terrible business on the island. Decided it was time to cut the honeymoon short. We're heading home.'

'Not to Bar Harbor, surely?' Max asked. 'Jane says you're opening a bookshop in London. Where? I'd love to come see it. Marjorie spoke so highly of you.'

'Yes.' The quick set of his jaw wasn't in her imagination. Had she just ensured Jane would get another beating? 'We haven't found the location yet. We'll let you know. Come along, Jane.' His hand looked too tight on Jane's arm as he pulled her into the dining car.

'I didn't expect they would be… here,' Max finished. She bit back 'free'.

John followed her along the swaying train. 'Neither did I. Maybe we'll see them in their new bookstore.'

Max paused next to the door of her first-class compartment. Even without a bunk, sleep waited inside and the dreams that would come with it. 'Do you play cards? Besides solitaire?' she asked.

'I do.'

'Would you... join me?' What if he said no? How would she stay awake?

'Very well.'

Max slid the door open, ignoring her mother's voice shrilling in her ears. The compartment had windows onto the corridor. And she would not sleep.

Max drew out her cards, although she left the Oban in the bag. Wine with lunch was one thing, but whiskey in a train compartment at just past noon? She tried to forget the numerous solitaire games she'd spread across the medic's cot. Angus's voice telling someone—John?—about her injuries.

'Shall I deal?' John asked, taking the cards from her hands.

'Sorry.'

The train slowed and sighed to a stop. Stirling. Black specks floated in front of her cards. The door of the carriage opened.

'May we join you?' a woman with a strong Scottish accent asked. John rose immediately and offered to help with bags. The two women perched opposite them as John lifted his cards again.

'I'm Mrs Threble, and this is my sister Miss Carr.'

'Maxine Falkland,' Max said. 'And John Knox.' The woman's gaze lingered on her bare hands. Her nails looked dreadful and...

'We're cousins,' John said smoothly.

No ring. Alone together in a compartment. Max sighed.

Mrs Threble took out sewing from her handbag. She threaded a needle and then lined a pink patch up with a purple square.

John called gin, and Max swept the cards up as he added up the points.

'Would you mind if my sister reads aloud? I find it very soothing as I sew.' Mrs Threble stabbed the needle into the corner.

Max shook her head, but it made her throat ache more. She shuffled the cards while Miss Carr fumbled in her own bag. A Dickens novel, no doubt. It'd send her to sleep. Instead, Miss Carr pulled out the newspaper. Max took a deep breath. It'd be the social pages or the...

'Ooh, this is excellent. The mess on Mull. Look at that face, you can tell he's a bad'un.'

Two cards floated from her second shuffle. John scooped them up.

'Sorry,' Max said, stacking the cards again.

'Were you on Mull?'

'Just in Oban,' said John. 'Maxine, I might go have a cigarette. Do you want to join me?'

How odd her full name sounded from his lips. 'Sure.' She half rose.

'Oh we don't mind smoke, do we, sister?'

John eased back into the seat. 'Do you want to do a crossword instead?' He reached in his pocket, but it wasn't *The Times* that emerged but a *Universal Dispatch*. 'I'm better at this one. The setter lives in America, so I don't have to worry about adding a u to colour or juggling pavement and sidewalk.'

Max nodded and tucked the cards back into their box.

Miss Carr started reading, but John rustled his newspaper loudly in search of the crossword. Max still heard snatches 'arrested by Mull constabulary at his home. Ash, a Flight Lieutenant in the RAF, was a POW in the Pacific theatre between...'

'First clue.'

Max looked back at John's right hand, holding the fountain pen he'd used to tally points for the card game. 'You're even more arrogant that I thought.'

'Excuse me?' A frown flickered across his face.

'Who does a crossword in ink?'

'You've obviously never had the joy of completing the crossword in my esteemed paper. First clue. Capitol of North Dakota.'

'You're kidding.' She took the paper away and read the words. 'All right. I see why you use ink.'

John laughed and lit a cigarette. She handed back the paper.

Was Miss Carr still reading? For that half moment, joking with John made the world feel normal.

'In an unrelated matter, some unexploded war ordnance detonated at the Tobermory distillery, but no one was injured.'

Except Angus's nose. And her... She took a deep breath. John didn't move like a man whose suit covered an injury.

He wrote in the capital in black ink. 'Okay, sixteenth president.'

'Lincoln. Are they always so easy?'

'Our market is homesick Americans. World Series winners, 1949.'

'The Yankees.'

John smiled. 'Watch out or I will propose.'

Max laughed. Mrs Threble studied them attentively. When had they shifted closer together, separated only by an armrest? She eased herself back toward the wall of the train. 'Eight down,' she said, pointing to a random spot on the page. 'Cousins.'

'Right,' John said. He filled in six across with Atlantic for the eastern seaboard.

Neither of them knew the state bird for Maine. They bandied about different bird names, till John pointed out they needed nine letters.

Max leaned closer to read the next clue when Miss Carr said, '... Falkland, 14th Viscount Bartlemas...'

She flinched. What had happened? God, had...

'His son died in Korea...'

Another newspaper rested next to John. *The Times.* He handed it to her. She ignored Richard Ash's face and read the headline on the article below. Cabinet reshuffle. Dad's name appeared only a couple lines down. Home Secretary. She exhaled. Thank God. What would Mother have to say about it? He'd be home even less and... The colonel. Had he known? Dad presumably would have been told about the distillery anyway, but now surely he would have been briefed. Was it his first task as Home Secretary to hear that his daughter had been... She closed her eyes.

'I should have told you,' John said, his voice low. 'Sorry.'

'Mortimer Wheeler found out his first wife Tessa died from an old copy of *The Times* on the Orient Express, coming back from a dig,' she murmured.

'Better news, surely.'

Max nodded. She dropped the newspaper on the seat between them. 'Now, this crossword...'

'Didn't you say your name was Falkland?' Mrs Threble asked. 'You his daughter?'

'I beg your pardon?'

'You must be. You went white as a sheet when my sister read his name.'

Max glanced down.

'Are you not related to him too, Mr Knox?'

'Mother's side,' he said.

'I'm sorry about your brother, Miss Falkland. My son died there last year too.'

I'm sorry,' Max said. 'It's a dreadful thing, to lose someone so far away.' She didn't look up at John's face. He'd seen George more recently than any of the family.

Mrs Threble returned to her sewing as Miss Carr flipped her newspaper to the second page. Max relaxed as the simple clues lead to quick answers and Miss Carr read from the depths of *The Times*.

'Want *The Times* next?' John asked. 'I do use a pencil for it.' He patted his coat pockets. 'Except I don't have one.'

Max reached in her handbag, the bag the army had retrieved for her. She fumbled past lipsticks and keys for a pencil. 'It's broken, I'm afraid.'

John took a brown handled penknife from his trouser pocket. Six strokes of the knife, and the pencil had a sharp point. Max watched him push the blade closed and tip the shavings from the newspaper into the ashtray. She remembered his hands replacing the sherry glass at the Antiquaries, the feel of his lips against hers. She wanted to kiss him again, but instead she said, 'I'm sure that's a fire hazard.' John had been the last person she personally knew to share conversation, a drink, with George. That must explain her interest in him. Except she'd never wanted to kiss any of George's friends before.

'I'd chop my finger off if I tried that,' Mrs Threble said.

John brushed flecks of lead off the newspaper. 'Crossword?' he asked.

They settled into the clues and answers, while Mrs Threeble stitched a new pink square to the opposite side of the purple patch and Miss Carr read. Once the excitement of Mull faded, she subsided to a dull monotone. Waves of exhaustion washed over Max, and she dug her ruined nails into her palms and gritted her teeth to stay awake. She couldn't manage witty quips with John anymore.

She jerked, fighting the hands holding hers.

'Max, you're all right.'

Max took a deep breath, and looked down at her hands hooked into claws, John's fingers pulling hers away from her body.

'You're okay,' he said softly. 'You dozed off.' He let go of her.

'Oh.' Her mouth felt dry. 'Did I snore?' she asked, trying for a laugh. It didn't succeed.

'You screamed,' Miss Carr said. 'And scrabbled at your neck.'

Max resisted pulling her scarf. At least she'd cut her nails, or she'd have scratches to go with the bruises. 'A bad dream. My apologies.' She rose. 'Excuse me.'

John stood when she had, and he followed her to the corridor.

'I'm just going to find a WC,' Max said. Her hands shook, and she clasped them behind her back.

'I'll wait.'

'You don't have to take care of me, John.' A flush heated her cheeks. 'But thank you.'

Her scarf had slipped. The lavatory mirror reflected the lilac band, already turning darker. Max rinsed her fingertips in the warm water, trying to keep the bandage dry. When would the journey end? But then what? A summer in her parents' house? More dreams? Richard's hands had closed around her and... She took a deep breath again.

John stood outside the door when she emerged. 'Are you okay?'

Max nodded, and John held the door for her to go back in the compartment.

As the train approached Edinburgh, the sisters fluttered around with their knitting and papers. John lifted the sisters' suitcases from the luggage rack. Max flinched as Mrs Threble gripped her forearm.

'It isn't done, I know, but is he hurting you?' she whispered.

'I—no. No. Not at all.' She hadn't asked Jane; she'd twittered around the edges. How brave this woman Max had dismissed as foolish was. 'Thank you. It was some... Mr Knox has helped.' She kept her voice as low. What had he done at the distillery? Did the Russians survive?

'Good.' Mrs Threble squeezed her arm and then turned to John. 'Thank you, young man.'

John glanced at Max, but he smiled. Had he heard them? John opened the compartment door, and the sisters went out chattering. 'Cards again?'

Max nodded.

They played for ages, John winning far more often than she. By five, she could barely read the card faces anymore.

'Coffee?'

Max tasted again the acridness underlying the alcohol in the cup Richard had brought her, but she managed to nod.

They spoke little over their cups of coffee and sandwiches, but it suited Max. Maybe the caffeine would keep her awake a bit longer. John paid, ignoring her protests. They walked back towards the compartment.

'Hang on a second.' John opened the compartment door next to hers and disappeared inside. He returned with a black hold all.

'You didn't realise we were on the same train.' And he was in the compartment adjacent to hers.

'What are the odds?' He slid open her compartment door this time, and she preceded him in. He had glanced around quickly before he let her in. Like Angus at the cottage. After two weeks of considering her theories mad, did she now have to believe them all?

John slid his case beneath the seat.

'You can fit a fishing rod in there?'

He laughed. 'Mine's in North Carolina. I rented that one. Do you have all your archaeology kit in there?' He nodded at her bag.

'I left most of it.' She shrugged. 'I have to go back once my plane is mended, and I'll fly it back to London.' Another train to Oban, another sleeping compartment. Would she dare leave to go to the WC? 'Your colleague. Mr Fuller.'

'Yes?' He sat opposite her.

'Has he been to Scotland lately?'

'I doubt it. But I've been on leave, and well, the paper is fairly large. We don't see each other all that often. Why?'

'I just thought I saw him on the train to Oban the other day.' Stopping her from being pushed. She still bore faint marks on her arms from the man in the brown suit.

'Frankly, I'm astonished you remember his name, much less what he looks like.'

'Brushes.'

John shook his head.

'The Fuller brush man.' Why was she joking with him? Max looked at him, his blue steady eyes, slightly shadowed with tiredness. He knew. He had to know. Why didn't she just ask him directly? 'I must have been mistaken.' Why hadn't she travelled in something more comfortable than a suit? 'Do you want some whiskey?' It'd make her sleep.

'I'm okay, thanks.'

The silence stretched. Why didn't she just ask him? But would he sidestep the question, like he had about speaking Russian? 'Have you ever been shot?' Max asked.

John tapped his right shoulder. 'Battle of the Bulge. Try to avoid it. It hurts.'

'Not recently?'

'Never as a civilian. Like I said, try to avoid it.' He smiled. 'Think you could get some sleep?'

'I'm a little scared to try.' The words came slowly, and heat rushed upwards from the damned scarf.

'I'll wake you up again.'

'And how long has it been since you slept?'

'Newspaper managers don't have their nights disrupted all that often.' He smiled. 'I'm fine.' He shrugged out of his jacket. He took his silver cigarette case from his breast pocket, and then folded the jacket neatly wrong side out, so the darker grey lining faced upwards. He passed it to her. 'Here—have a pillow.'

Max smiled. 'Thanks.' She nestled it against the wall of the train and rested her cheek against it. It smelled like smoke, faintly of aftershave and... John. What she'd smelled when she kissed him. She closed her eyes, trying to remember that moment rather than Richard, the distillery. The tangle of their tongues, the softness of his hair.

'Hang on,' John said.

Her eyes flew open, her cheeks flushing again. 'What?'

'Put your gloves on. If anyone comes in, I'm saying we're engaged.'

'If I'm asleep on your jacket, I'd go with married or cousins. I don't think anybody would buy us as siblings.' She tugged her gloves on.

John laughed. 'Nope. Sleep well, honey.'

A voice murmured her name, and she woke slowly. Her cheek rested against something smooth, and... her hand was warm. She glanced down, and John's hand curled over hers. As she shifted, he smiled.

'We'll be in London soon.' He withdrew his touch.

'Did I...'

'At first.' He dropped a book on the seat between them. 'I hope you don't mind. It seemed to help.'

'Of course not.' Why did she keep blushing? 'I'm sorry to be a bother.' She unfolded his jacket, the warmth now from her skin.

'No trouble at all.' He slipped into it.

Would it smell like her now? Max lifted his book as he lit a cigarette. 'Do you always read Agatha Christie in Italian?'

John pocketed his lighter. 'I like detective stories. And sometimes I read them in French.'

Had Christie been translated into Russian? 'How long did I sleep?' Max started to scoop her hair up, but remembered the marks at the back of her neck.

'A couple hours. Not too many dreams, I don't think. Is someone collecting you?'

'My parents don't know I'm coming back today.' Max swallowed. What on earth was she going to say to them? The Colonel had said to tell her father, but how did she start that conversation? Dad, remember when I said there wouldn't be Communists in Scotland? I was wrong.

'Are you all right?'

Max nodded. Her mouth felt sticky, and her voice sounded even hoarser than before. 'Did you sleep at all?'

'I'll sleep tonight.' Shadows lurked around his eyes.

'Thanks. It was nice of you to... thanks.'

'Happy to. Excuse me just a moment.' He slid out of the compartment.

As soon as the compartment door closed, Max drew out her pocket mirror. The scarf had slipped again, so she tugged it higher over the purple bruise. John surely had noticed. Her fingers lingered over the bandage, but she couldn't face looking at the wound. It burned. How—his teeth—his... she shuddered. Her fingernails. Mother would despair, but at least she'd trimmed the worst of the raw edges in the medic's tent. Mother had a total ban on applying makeup in front of any male, and Max couldn't imagine what depths of hell she would class doing nail care in front of a man. She reapplied lipstick, finishing the curve of her bottom lip as John opened the door again. 'Sorry,' she said, capping her lipstick and returning it to her handbag.

'Why?' He looked genuinely puzzled.

'Nothing.' Every muscle ached when she stood. 'Excuse me.' She eased past him into the corridor. This time he didn't follow her.

In the light of the toilet, Max couldn't avoid the dark circles under her eyes. What on earth could she say to her parents? She dabbed on powder and ran cold water over her wrists. A rivulet ran down to her bandage, and she tried unsuccessfully to dry it with her handkerchief. The burn spread to throbbing pain. She opened the toilet door. John stood in the corridor.

'There you are.' His shoulders visibly relaxed.

'Did you think I'd been magicked away?' She forced a smile. What did he and Angus fear? If everyone had been arrested… except Jane and Adam were on the train.

'Like you said, I'm just a bit tired.' He held the compartment door for her.

The train pulled into Euston and sighed to a stop. John carried both of their bags, and he stayed close to her as they disembarked. He walked rapidly along the platform, and Max had to hustle to keep up with him. He'd never walked this fast around her before. Of course, her entire body didn't normally feel this tender. They reached the grand hall, and Max looked down at the heads of milling people, the statue with its hand planted on his hip.

John gestured towards the stairs with her bag, so Max headed down. John followed behind her. Max saw no sign of Adam or Jane. Were they the only ones that worried John? What had Angus been looking for at the cottage? She took a deep breath. The hand rail felt cool through her gloves. Would Jane and Adam even show up in a crowded space like this?

They reached the ticket hall, and Max relaxed her shoulders. No one would care or notice her in busy London. She wouldn't be the odd American-accented woman on Mull, faffing about with planes and boats. Here, she was just another Londoner in a mass of people. She turned back towards John, and he nearly collided with her.

'Would you like a drink?' She glanced at her watch. Five past ten.

'I'm afraid I'm expected at the office. I'll likely be there for a while.' He shifted her bag to carry it with his, and his free hand rested on her lower back.

'This late?'

'Unfortunately. Newspapers don't really stop.'

The warmth from his palm seeped into the aches, and she wanted to stop, but she kept walking. She'd have to face her parents eventually.

John steered her towards the taxi rank, where only one couple waited ahead of them. John set down the bags. Max wished he'd kept his hand on her spine.

'If you want to talk though, call me.' He sighed. 'I have a feeling the next few days will be pretty busy.'

'I suppose that happens when you come back off holiday.'

John's eyes stayed steady. 'Yes. But do call. I'm a good listener.'

Two taxis drew up, and the couple chatted to the first driver through the window. Max forced her feet towards the second. John opened the door and lifted in her bag. He stood by the taxi and extended his hand to help her in. Max held it but didn't climb into the car.

'Thank you.'

John scanned over her head, and then smiled at her. 'Actually, could I share your taxi?'

'Sure.' She glanced behind the taxi. Adam and Jane walked towards the taxi rank. She sat on the backseat, pivoted her knees in and then slid across the seat. John climbed in after her. 'Pelham Crescent, please,' she said, as John pulled the door closed.

She leaned back against the seat, her head starting to ache along with her body.

'You want the scenic route, miss?'

'I'm sorry?'

'Americans sometimes like me to take in the sights on the way.'

Max closed her eyes.

'See, I could take you by Hyde Park, or down the Mall and...'

'Whatever is easiest.' Normally, she'd say the fastest, and possibly explain she wasn't American. The taxi driver lit his pipe, and the smoke reached the backseat. 'Actually, the fastest, please,' Max said, rolling down the window. Nausea gripped her throat, but she wouldn't take off the scarf.

John lowered his head to hers. 'Perhaps this is a little late to ask, but does smoke bother you?'

'Pipe smoke, yes.' Max turned and his face was so close. She could kiss him again. 'How late will you be at the paper?'

John shrugged and leaned back against the seat. 'No idea.'

She closed her eyes. Victor's accident. She'd tell her parents about that, and then logically she decided to come home. The water closed around her again, the weight of Victor as she dragged him into the boat. Her foot bumped her bag and she focused on the round shape of Great Portland Street station.

The taxi swept towards the lights of the Langham Hotel. Her parents didn't know she was in London. She could book a room, wait until the bruises faded. But it took ages last time... And what would she tell John? Ask him to come in with her, to climb the stairs to a bedroom? She stifled a giggle and forced the thought away. 'Sorry, I'm being dreadful company,' Max said.

'Hardly. We're both tired.'

Rain started, a few droplets splattering in through the open window onto her skirt. The shops of Regent Street were shadowed.

'Do you mind, miss? The window, please?'

Max rolled up the window, but left a crack for a bit of fresh air to creep in. She traced a trickle down the window. All too soon, the taxi turned from Fulham Road into the corner of Pelham Crescent. 'Here's fine, thanks,' she said. Lights glowed in the windows of the house, and tears pricked at Max's eyes, but she drew her wallet from her handbag.

'I'll get this,' John said.

'Thanks. No time for a drink I suppose?'

'Not really.' He leaned forward. 'Could you wait please? I'm going on to Fleet Street.'

John came around to open her door, and lifted out her bag.

'Best if you stay here then,' Max said. 'It'd only raise questions.' The rain had slowed to a drizzle, barely misting her face. 'Thank you. For everything.' For whatever he'd done at the distillery. Had he fired one of the guns she'd heard? Had the Russians survived?

'I just read for a while.' He held out her bag, but didn't release it into her grip. He'd offered it to her right hand. He rested his other hand on the shoulder of her suit. 'You'll be okay.'

Max felt again the grinding pressure of Richard's mouth against hers. She rose on her toes and brushed a kiss over John's cheek, praying the light abrasion of his stubble would replace the memory. His grip on her shoulder tightened, and they shifted closer. Before their lips met, the taxi driver opened his door.

'You staying, mate?'

'Just a second.' John let go of her and her bag. 'Do call me.'

Max nodded. 'Good night, John.' She turned back to the house and waited for the taxi door to close. It didn't. 'I think I'm pretty safe here,' she called back. She hoped he'd laugh, but he didn't.

'Just making sure. Sleep well, honey.'

As she approached the door, it swung open.

'Good evening, Miss Max,' Harris said, as calm if she had just been out to a lecture. A man she didn't know stood behind him, and he examined her closely.

'Good evening, Harris. Are my parents home?'

'In the drawing room, miss. The Hays are with them as well. Would you like a meal? Or your friend?'

Out the open door, she just spied the taxi door closing. 'No. Thank you.' The Hays. Her godfather Gerald and his wife Matilda. She could creep upstairs. 'I ate on the train. Maybe I should...'

Her father's heavy tread sounded, and then his figure blocked the light spilling from the drawing room door. 'Harris... Darling. We didn't expect you back so soon.'

She pushed a smile onto her face. 'I didn't have a chance to ring, sorry.'

'Don't be silly. Max, put your bag down. Come in.'

She dropped the heavy bag and put one foot in front of the other until her father's arms closed around her. He squeezed more tightly than she anticipated, and she bit back a yelp as her muscles protested. Did he already know? Would a report from a colonel on the Isle of Mull work its way up that quickly to the government? Richard's arrest had made the front page. Of course he'd know.

'Max?' Mother called. 'What on earth are you doing here?'

Her father's arms relaxed. Did his eyes look damp behind his glasses? 'Bit of a surprise inside.' His voice wavered but he smiled.

'Darling.' Her mother hugged her too, but not as tightly. 'Sit down. When did you leave?'

'This morn... Charlie?' Her cousin sat on the sofa, his leg extended in a white cast on the footstool in front of it. 'What on earth are you doing here?'

'Broke my leg—in two places—playing football at school. It was spectacular, I...'

'Gerald and Matilda have already heard the story, Charlie. Maybe you can tell Max later,' Mother said. 'Darling, sit down.'

Max sat beside Charlie. How could she be dropped so quickly back into normality? 'Does it hurt?' Did his body ache as much as hers?

'Yeah. It was three days ago now. I can't go back to school—too many stairs.'

Their house was full of stairs.

'We saw the stuff about Mull in the papers,' Uncle Gerald said. 'But Bartlemas insisted that was nowhere near where you were staying.'

And they believed him? How big did they think Mull was? 'No, of course not. Victor had a diving accident...'

Her mother and Matilda gasped.

'He's fine.' She mentally crossed her fingers. 'I wasn't diving then.'

'Thank goodness.'

How on earth did Mother think Victor would get back to the surface? 'Anyway, so we couldn't do any more diving survey, and with my plane out of commission, we decided to call a day on this season.' The lies fell smoothly from her lips. Lips that Richard Ash had... she forced herself to remember instead the prickle of John's cheek. She shivered all the same. Charlie patted her hand.

'Did you travel back alone?' Mother asked.

'I'm sorry?'

'Did the Westfields come with you?'

'Victor's in the hospital. Just for observation,' Max added quickly. 'He's fine.'

'It seemed there was quite a brouhaha on the island,' Matilda said. 'Imagine the police finding a traitor, just there in Scotland? At least it was all resolved peacefully.'

'Yes.' The thudding of the helicopter sounded in her ears. 'I saw the headlines, but I haven't read a paper yet.'

Mother lifted a paper. 'Have you heard your father's news?'

'Later, Nancy,' Dad said. 'You look exhausted, Max. Would you like some dinner?'

'I had something on the train.' She forced her mouth to curl into a smile. 'I did hear. Congratulations, I think.'

Her father laughed. 'The "I think" may be the most important part of that statement. Let me get you a drink, at least.' He crossed to the drinks cabinet. 'What would you like?'

She'd have to take off her gloves, show the bandage and her short nails. Max looked down at her suit, with travel creases. The men wore dinner jackets, and Matilda's pale pink dinner dress exposed everything from modest cleavage to her hairline. Mother's blue dress did the same. What on earth could she wear? Roll necks didn't pass muster for dinner. 'I don't really feel like dressing, if I'm honest. So I'll just…'

'You wouldn't have to change,' Dad said. 'The Hays are family. Here, have a whiskey.' He put a glass on the table in front of her.

'Is the scarf a new fashion trend in the wilds of Scotland?' Matilda asked.

Max would not lift her fingers to her neck. 'Just a bit chilly travelling.'

'You could take it off now,' Mother said. 'Aren't you too warm?'

'It's fine.' How could she hide her throat for weeks? She should have stayed, although it seemed Angus would have carried her physically off the island if she hadn't gone willingly. The Langham would have been a welcome respite.

'I'll just go wash up a bit,' Max said. 'It's a long journey.'

'Put on something more comfortable than a suit,' Mother said. 'I could help…'

'No,' Max said sharply. Mother blinked. 'Sorry. I slept very badly after Victor's accident.'

'Perfectly understandable,' Dad said. 'Take your time.'

Max climbed the stairs. She resolutely avoided looking in the mirror in the bathroom, and then went to her room. Her bag had been left at the foot of the bed unopened. Lucy had learned the hard way that it was best to let Max unpack from a dig herself, after spilling dirt and debris across the cream carpet. Max had no idea what she'd packed in Scotland. Did any of it match? She unzipped the case and lifted out the Oban. What was John doing at his office? It would be so easy for a man to hide an injury. She poked around in the bag, finding she'd mostly collected matching shoes and all her underwear.

Her notebook. She dug deeper, but it wasn't there. That meant she had no numbers at all for John, never mind his card that presumably either still rested on Richard's desk or sat in police evidence somewhere. Luke Keck. How many names did he have?

A tap sounded at the door.

'Come in.' It couldn't be her mother; she would have already barged through the door. And Charlie couldn't make it up the stairs.

Lucy looked in. 'Do you want some help, miss? I could do your hair, or…'

'I'll leave it down, thanks. I don't know what to wear.' She sighed. 'They're waiting, aren't they?' Lucy normally dressed Mother, and she only helped Max for big parties or balls. Never for dinner. Had Mother sent her up? Dad?

Lucy crossed to her wardrobe. 'There's this, or this…' She drew out two dresses, both sleeveless and with low necklines.

'I can't. Lucy, will you swear not to tell anyone—I mean anyone? Including my mother?'

Lucy nodded. 'I promise, miss, but…'

Max unbuttoned her suit jacket and eased it off. The fingerprints marking her upper arm had grown much darker. His fingerprints. She fumbled beneath her hair to unknot the scarf. 'I had a, a mishap in Scotland.' She drew the scarf away. The band was nearly indigo now.

'Oh my God.' Lucy coloured. 'Excuse me, miss.'

'No, it's dreadful. But you see…'

215

'Yes.' Lucy clicked through the hangers in the wardrobe quickly. 'Here. And we'll figure something out.' She drew out a grey dress, with four small shoestring bows lacing up the bodice and elbow length sleeves.

Max heaved a breath. She'd worn that the night she met John. And she had no way to contact him, unless she rang *Universal Dispatch* direct, and look how far that'd gotten her last time.

'Miss?'

'It's perfect. Maybe a different scarf? Oh, it's ridiculous. My mother's going to know, isn't she?'

'Do you want to keep it from her?'

Max nodded, although her throat ached.

'Give me a minute.' Lucy disappeared, and Max undressed slowly. She pulled on the dress, grateful for the full skirt.

Lucy tapped again, and came in carrying a black choker. It belonged to Mother, but she'd never worn it much. She didn't like costume jewellery. 'I think this might be wide enough, especially if I touch up with some makeup.' She lifted Max's hair to clasp the necklace, and Max winced. 'Is it too tight?'

'It's fine. You're a lifesaver. Thank you.'

Lucy lowered her hair gently. 'You do need to leave this down. The bruise is wider at the back. Did someone...'

'I'd rather not talk about it, Lucy, if that's okay.' If she started talking, the next step would be tears and...

Lucy pushed Max into the vanity chair, and then found her makeup case in the suitcase. Max closed her eyes as Lucy puttered around with brushes and light finger touches. Colours whirled behind her eyes, voices in Russian and English. It had to have been John.

'There.'

Max looked in the mirror. She still looked exhausted, but the darkness around the necklace now looked like shadows rather than an injury.

216

'What we do when it gets darker, I don't know.'

Max hugged Lucy impulsively. 'Thank you. I can't say how much this means to me.' She glanced at the clock. It'd only taken fifteen minutes.

Max rose unsteadily.

'I could tell them you're just too tired.'

'After all your hard work? I'm fine.' She glanced down at her nails. 'I'd forgotten about these.'

'I don't think nail varnish would help.' She flipped Max's hands over and pointed at the bandage, frayed and slightly grey now. 'Are you all right?'

'I'm happy to be home. Please don't mention this to anyone.'

'I won't.' Her face stayed worried. 'Can I change this?'

'It's fine, really.' Max imagined her mother's face when she saw it. 'I suppose I should really.'

'Was it… who did this?' Lucy motioned to the chair. 'I'll get a new bandage.'

'Nobody. I mean, nobody who can bother me anymore.' Max sat down again.

'Did you call the police?'

Did the military count as the police? Max nodded.

'Okay.' Lucy slipped out of the door and returned quickly with a first aid box. 'Lucky for you I was a nurse. Just don't look if it makes you squeamish.' She efficiently ripped away the tape. 'What am I going to see?'

The deep breath filled her lungs. Home. Her perfume, warmth, safety. Not mould and leaf debris. Not the awful taste of the coffee and drug, not Richard's breath against her face. 'A bite.'

'Animal? Do you need…'

'No.'

'Max.'

Lucy never called her Max. 'It was a fight. But I'm—I'll be okay.'

Lucy's smile didn't seem all that sincere. 'Look at the ceiling.'

Max obeyed, trying to keep still as the gauze ripped away from the wound.

'Sorry.'

'How bad is it?'

'Well, I didn't see many bites in the War, if I'm honest, but we'll just keep it clean. Who did this bandage?'

'An army medic.'

'What on earth happened?'

'A huge misunderstanding.'

'On Mull?' Max glanced down and saw a red gash before Lucy pressed new gauze to it. 'I read the papers too, you know.'

'I can't say.' The colonel had been so definite. 'Were my parents worried?'

'No more than usual for Lady Bartlemas.'

'Dad?'

'He's been pacing.'

So he did know. Lucy crisscrossed the gauze with tape.

'There. I'll change it again in the morning.'

'Thanks, Lucy. I can't tell you how much I appreciate this.' Max stepped into a pair of heels and headed downstairs. She would not tug at her necklace, nor would she worry her bandage.

'There you are, darling. I was about to send someone after you. I thought maybe you'd fallen asleep,' Mother said.

Max sat back down next to Charlie. The whiskey glass still rested on the table and she reached out for it.

'What'd you do to your hand?' Charlie asked.

'I just caught it on something.'

'What? Was it when you crashed…'

'No. A bit of firewood.' She found a smile. 'It's much cooler in Scotland.'

'You make your own fires?' her mother asked.

'We've been through this before, Mother. Life is different on a site.'

'And Max is quite good at it, despite her injury,' her father murmured.

'Well, have Lucy look at it.'

So her mother hadn't sent Lucy upstairs. Her father's face remained perfectly bland.

'Will there be any articles from your trip?' Uncle Gerald asked.

Besides the ones in *The Times*?

'I do like to read your writing, Max. Then I get to boast about my clever goddaughter.'

Articles. Her articles. 'Not likely. We didn't get through nearly as much work as we hoped. But I'm still working on converting my thesis, hopefully into a book.'

'Before we disappear entirely down the rabbit hole of academia,' Matilda said. 'That's a lovely necklace, Max.'

Did it bother Matilda to have Uncle Gerald call Max clever? She'd dropped out of Vassar to marry him. 'It's Mother's, actually. Thanks.' She wouldn't touch it. 'Do we have a new servant?' Please God, let them stop talking about Mull.

'Oh, you mean Mr Rawls. He's your father's guard. There's three of them—they rotate. Apparently, there's no way around having them here,' Mother said.

'He's quite unobtrusive,' Dad said.

Her mother's eyebrows rose, but she said nothing. What did unobtrusive look like in daily life? Did he lurk at the door whenever anyone came in?

'What's it like when ordnance explodes? Could you feel it all the way to where you were staying? Was it like an earthquake?' Charlie asked.

'I've never been in an earthquake.' Max forced herself to sip the whiskey.

'Charlie, that's enough. How long have you been travelling, Max?'

'Ten hours, give or take.'

'That's madness,' Matilda said.

'We should be going, anyway,' Uncle Gerald said. 'Come along, pet.'

Max's skin rippled as always when he called her that. Matilda seemed happy, Uncle Gerald seemed happy, but how could she marry someone so old? John's voice whispered in her ear, calling her 'honey'. He couldn't be more than two, three years older than she was. And they hadn't even been on a date, much less... She stood and swayed. Charlie grabbed her elbow.

She glanced down at Charlie. 'How are you getting around?'

He grimaced. 'Footmen are carrying me, at the moment. I'm hoping eventually I can hop.' He thumped his crutches. 'At least I can get around a bit on a level floor, so I can go to the WC by myself.'

'Charlie, we have guests,' Mother said.

Matilda brushed air kisses on Max's cheeks. 'You have such an exciting life, Max. I don't think I do anything that makes me look so tired!'

No one seemed to notice that Max's laugh didn't resonate properly.

'I've spent months doing boring writing,' Max said when everyone else's laughter had subsided. 'This is unusual for me now.'

Uncle Gerald hugged her. 'So proud of you, Max.'

Proud she'd stabbed someone? Proud she'd bashed Angus's nose? Proud she'd dismissed all her fears as conspiracy theories and didn't report them to anyone? 'Thanks, Uncle Gerald.'

She followed them out to the hallway, where she eyed Mr Rawls. He was as big as Kuznetsov. Who might be dead.

'Darling.' Dad touched her arm as the door closed behind the Hays.

'You haven't finished your drink, Max,' Mother said. 'Come tell us about your trip.'

'It was pretty uneventful.' How many more lies would she have to tell?

'Why don't you just go to bed?' Dad asked.

She'd dream. 'Tell me about your new role.' They walked back into the drawing room. 'Besides the large guards.'

'He's away even more than before,' Mother said. 'And it's been thirty-two hours.'

'That's perhaps a bit of an exaggeration.' Dad smiled. 'I'd call it forty-eight since I found out. Did you manage to find any archaeology there?'

'Some sword fragments, mostly.' And a Russian submarine. But he hadn't asked if she'd found anything.

'Did you ever meet this traitor chap?' Charlie asked. 'How big is Mull?'

'Not that big. Tell me about your football match.'

Twenty minutes later, even Mother called exhaustion, so they all went upstairs together.

Max sat on the edge of the bed before undressing. Her bed, her house. London. And a guard downstairs. She rose at the tap on the door.

Her father already wore his dressing gown. 'Are you all right, darling?'

'Fine. Thanks.' She hugged him though, tightly, burying her face in the softness of his shoulder. She would not cry.

'Let me know if you need anything.' Dad rubbed her back. 'I'm always ready to listen.'

Max's laugh sounded better. 'I know your love of obscure Viking archaeology.'

Chapter 20

Max stayed in her room. She didn't call *Universal Dispatch*. She tried to write cogent archaeological arguments that didn't mention Russians and guns and submarines. She typed with her right hand, pecking out the letters. She didn't have her fountain pen anyway. Surely she'd dreamt it all, she thought, but the bruises remained on her skin, blossoming into indigo before changing to a heavy grey and yellow. She wore her winter dressing gown, which she kept tight around her neck each time her mother or Charlie ventured up to her room. She sneezed whenever they did, keeping up her pretence that it was a bad cold. She managed it so convincingly that Vivian didn't risk coming to visit her, although she rang Max daily.

Her father came up twice to play chess with her. He eyed her bandage, but he said nothing. Max couldn't bring herself to talk about the distillery, although she dreamt about it every time she closed her eyes.

Four days later, Mother touched her forehead with cool fingers. Max wanted to twitch away, but she closed her eyes, comfort seeping into her skin.

'You have a fever. And it's not this ridiculous insistence on wearing winter clothes in May. Go back to bed. I'm ringing Dr Goodman.'

'I'm fine.' Lucy had refused to let Max look at her own hand when she'd changed the bandage this morning, and she'd suggested ringing the doctor too.

'No arguments. Come on.' Mother stood by the chair until Max stood.

Max wavered and had to hold on to her desk.

'See? Get to bed.'

She'd have to take off her dressing gown. And her mother couldn't see the bruises. 'I need to go to the WC first,' she said. 'You go call.'

Mother smiled. 'I thought I'd have to argue a lot more. Do you need any help?'

'I'm not that bad, Mother!' She found a smile. 'But thank you.'

Max stared up at the canopy of her bed, the one she'd had since she was thirteen. It cast a shadow over the mattress, but with the curtains open, it wouldn't obscure the bruise on her throat. Dr Goodman had been the family's doctor for years. He'd seen her through childhood illnesses and broken bones. Max had no idea what story to spin as the doorbell chimed through the house. He'd see that she didn't have a cold. And never mind that she was an adult—he would report to Mother as he had when Max was twelve.

A tap sounded at the door, and her mother opened it.

'This is Dr Adams, Max. Dr Goodman was busy, but...'

'Thanks, Mother. Hello, Dr Adams.' He was young, by comparison, anyway. Maybe forty, with small glasses and brown hair. Mother stood by. She might have left her alone with Dr Goodman, but with a young man?

'Thank you, Lady Bartlemas. It would be best if I could examine Dr Falkland alone.'

Mother's hands tightened, but she left the room.

'So you have a cold and a fever?' He perched on the side of the bed and opened his bag. He took out a tongue depressor and a small torch. 'Open wide.'

Max knew what he would see as he peered at her throat, but he said nothing. A thermometer appeared and was placed under her tongue. 'May I?' He motioned to her scarf.

Max shook her head.

'I need to check your glands. I could feel through the material, but...'

And it would hurt.

Another tap sounded at the door, and Lucy eased into the room. 'Miss Max, please show him your hand.'

'And you are?'

'Lucy Anderson, sir. I was a nurse in the war, and...'

He removed the thermometer. 'Dr Falkland, you definitely have a fever. How am I supposed to help if I can't examine you?'

Max lifted her hand from under the bedclothes and extended it. 'This.'

He pried off the bandage, but not as gently as Lucy. 'Right. It's infected. Who has been treating it?'

'Me, sir,' said Lucy.

'Keep it clean. I'll give you antibiotics.' He swabbed it with something that burned. 'And your throat?'

'I don't have a cold,' Max said.

'Obviously. And it's too warm for that scarf.'

Max exhaled. 'Fine.' She pulled it open, and he prodded the bruise.

'Four days along?'

'More or less.'

'It'll fade. Is that all?'

'Yes.'

He glanced at Lucy, who nodded. Did he doubt Max's veracity? He wrote on a pad. 'Is this likely to happen again?'

'Definitely not.' Whatever happened to Richard, Max wouldn't see him again.

He snapped his bag shut. 'Good. Call me again if it gets worse. You know the drill? No alcohol.' He stood up.

He hadn't asked who did it. 'Thank you, Dr Adams. My mother thinks...'

'It's none of her business.' He smiled. 'You're an adult.' He nodded at Lucy. 'And I assume you trust her, or your father wouldn't have rung me about a cold.'

Why had her father rung the doctor at all? Had Dr Goodman even been contacted? She rubbed her forehead. 'Thank you again.'

Chapter 21

Max stood at the crosswalk, waiting for the light to change. Two more stops, and then she'd take her haul to Emma and Victor. Victor had sounded grumpy on the phone last night when he rang to say they were home. Emma had banned him from alcohol, and had curtailed his cigarettes. And she'd insisted on driving home from Scotland. His litany went on and on, and Max hadn't had to lie about what she'd been doing for the last week. A scarf still hid her throat, but the antibiotics meant that her palm didn't throb anymore.

Her car held two bottles of Mrs Brooks's elderflower cordial, and now she had a bag of books and magazines and a bouquet of flowers. Coffee next, and then the bank... a profile in the restaurant window opposite caught her attention. John. He wore a blue suit she'd never seen before. His companion faced away from the window, but Max saw pale hair pinned up in a bun. A flush rose in her cheeks. What did it matter? It seemed unlikely they would see each other again, anyway.

The light changed, and she crossed the street. It would take her far out of her way to go to the next traffic signal. If he saw her, did it matter? Why, oh why was she carrying the bright blooms? Couple that with her red dress, and she certainly stood out.

She reached the other side and pivoted quickly towards her car, which was parked just around the corner. The click of her heels was lost in the roar of a bus.

'Max.'

No sleep, and now she could add in auditory hallucinations. She kept walking. Victor would ask her how she felt and... Someone grabbed her upper arm, and she gasped and jerked free. It was only a few feet to her car and...

'Max.' John's voice.

She took a deep breath and turned.

'Sorry. You didn't seem to hear me.'

No hat. His hair as perfect as when she'd met him, surely trimmed since they last saw each other. And his face bore none of the tiredness of the train. If only hers didn't. 'Hello, John. How's work?'

'Calming down.' He sidestepped to avoid a child holding their mother's hand. 'You didn't call, and I wasn't sure.' He stopped and slid his hands in his trouser pockets. 'I wasn't sure if I should.'

'Sorry. I've been... a bit unwell.' Did he mind that she hadn't?

'Better now?'

At least he didn't mention her terror on a London street in the middle of the day. Had her cheeks cooled at all? Her pulse still beat too fast. 'I'm fine.'

'I was at a restaurant just around...'

'I know.' His shoes had as high a sheen as they did the first time they met. 'I mean, I saw you through the window.' She forced herself to look back up at him.

'It's Joyce's birthday. My secretary. Come join us?'

His secretary. 'You can't abandon someone during their birthday lunch.'

'We just arrived—I'm sure Joyce would love to meet you.'

After her panicked phone call? 'I can't, I'm afraid. Emma and Victor returned yesterday. I'm taking them some bits and bobs.'

'So he's recovered?'

'The hospital says so. Emma is being very strict. Well, I should...'

'Are you free tonight?'

Max hesitated only a fraction of a second and nodded.

'Dinner?' He shoved a hand through his hair. 'I did promise I'd graduate to buying you food eventually.'

How would she explain she wasn't drinking? 'That would be lovely.'

'I'll collect you at seven-thirty? Pelham Crescent, right?'

Max nodded. 'You have a good memory. Number twenty-eight.'

'Give Victor and Emma my best wishes.'

'Okay.' She smiled, trying to ignore the sudden lightness in her chest. 'Go.' She waved her hand. 'Whatever will Joyce think?'

John laughed. 'Yes, ma'am. It's nice to see you.'

'And you.' She wanted to kiss his cheek again, but she turned back towards her car.

Max looked in her rear-view mirror and practiced a smile. Breezy, happy. She could manage it. She opened the door and started gathering bags, but before she'd pulled them all out, Victor was beside her.

'Thank God you're here.' He took parcels from her. 'Please tell me you have booze in here.'

'Nope. Orders from Emma.'

'The doctors didn't say I couldn't drink. She's just decided it's a bad idea.' He pushed the passenger door shut with his hip. 'I'm amazed she's let me out here.'

'You look pale.'

'Because I've been inside solidly for a week.' He looked over the top of the car at her. 'You're the one who looks washed out. What's up with this scarf thing?'

'I've had a cold. I'm just a bit chilly.'

'Hmm.'

They crossed the street together, and Emma hugged her once they were inside. Soon they sat around the kitchen table as Emma made tea.

'You certainly left in a hurry,' Emma said. 'We brought back as much of your stuff as we could fit.'

'Thanks. It was a rush to make the ferry.' Wouldn't they wonder what she'd done all that night? 'I'll head back up as

227

soon as my plane is ready to be collected.' Had they picked up the dive suit from the floor of her room? At least her blood-spattered skirt had been disposed of at the army camp. 'Did you see my notebook?'

'I don't think so. Victor?'

Victor looked up from slicing a cake from Mrs Brooks. 'I can't remember. What the hell happened about Richard Ash? Weird, yes, but a traitor? I wouldn't have thought it.'

'No.' Max refused to touch her bandage.

'I'm not sure how we pay the rest of our rent, if he's in jail.'

'I don't think we bloody do,' Victor said.

'I'll tell the agent we're vacated as soon as your stuff is out.' Emma placed a cup and saucer in front of Max.

Max pulled off her gloves and tried to keep her palm flat on the table.

'What'd you do?' Victor asked. He carried plates to the table.

'Oh, this? I scraped my hand in the garden. Charlie's home. He broke his leg playing football.'

'You were gardening? I thought you left that to your mother,' Emma said.

Victor watched her too closely. 'What have you done this week? Besides pampering Charlie.'

'I've been a bit ill, but I'm better now.'

'So the rest of the summer. Shall we go join Edward?'

'No,' Emma said. 'Not for at least a month. I want you home eating properly.'

Max smiled. She curled her hands around the cup, but an ache started in the bi... wound as the heat hit it. She pulled her hand away. 'I'm not sure my parents would let me go anywhere now. By the way, when you next see them, you were diving alone.'

'They bought that?'

Max shrugged.

'You're an accomplished liar, Dr Falkland.'

She flushed. 'It kept them happy.'

Victor walked her to the door. 'We'll have a party when Emma says I can drink again.'

Max opened her handbag and handed him a thick envelope.

'What this?'

'Your pay.'

'For two weeks?'

'You turned down other work for my vanity project. It's the least I can do.'

Victor tapped the envelope against his palm. 'I won't say no, honestly. But it wasn't a vanity project. We could have done some serious work there. We could still go back. Wait a month, find a new place to stay...'

'No.'

Victor dropped the envelope on the hall table. He moved close and she expected a hug, but he grabbed her hand and ripped off her glove. 'What really happened to your hand?'

'I scraped it.' On Richard Ash's teeth. 'I'm fine, honestly.'

'Yeah. Clearly.' He dropped her hand and gave her back her glove. 'You really would be more than welcome to stay for dinner.'

'I have plans already.' Her pulse thrummed. 'Thanks, Victor. I'm awfully glad you're okay.' She kissed his cheek.

'Thanks to you.' He held onto her shoulders. 'You don't seem yourself.'

'I'm fine. It's just been a bit of a cold. Probably from diving in frigid water and not drying my hair properly. You heard Emma.' Her laugh sounded a little congested. 'Now, you should rest. I'll carry these things to the car.'

'Nonsense. I can carry these.'

Max looked at the box with the tins, the sugar. 'Why don't you just keep these?'

'Max, we're not a bloody charity case. You've paid me. We can buy our own food.' He cocked his head to the side. 'You do realise, of course, that it wasn't your fault? That you saved me? You don't have to make up for it or anything. Diving equipment fails.'

If they weren't at the bottom of the sea, would Victor be able to prove they had been tampered with, as Richard Ash said? 'I'll replace the Aqualungs.'

'For God's sake, Max, listen to me. Get over it. You're alive, I'm alive, we're all doing really well, hale and hearty and back home in London.'

Emma came into the hallway. 'He's right. You look so pinched.'

'And don't say it's a cold. Of course you've been upset about the stuff in Mull. I mean, hell, I've never met a traitor before, much less been on a date with one. Or whatever you called that dinner.'

Max nodded.

'Have you talked to anybody?'

'Such as?'

'Well, me for one. Or your friend John Knox. And yes, I know he's a journalist, but he was in the army for a long time. Your father. Good news on his promotion, by the way.'

'We have a guard at home now. It's all strange and new.'

Emma walked closer and patted her back. 'Lots of changes. And you're still coming out of mourning.'

'What are you doing tonight?'

'Just dinner.' She could talk to John. Would he admit that he had been there? He at least knew about her injuries, although he hadn't asked where they had come from and…

'You're away again,' Victor said. He tapped the side of her head gently. 'Try to focus on what's here, kiddo. Anybody exciting?'

'I'm sorry?'

230

'Your dinner date? Or is it just a dinner party with your parents?'

She flushed. 'It's with John, actually. I ran into him in town.'

'Good. Somebody to talk to.' He lifted a box with the groceries, and Emma picked up two bags, which left Max to grab a bag with shoes and a hairdryer. They piled it in the passenger seat.

Emma hugged Max. 'Don't worry about talking to John too much. Just enjoy yourself.'

Max looked in her wardrobe. She'd stopped by Vivian's on the way home to borrow a choker, but what dress went with five strands of pearl beads? She had the Dior dinner suit, with its full black skirt. The short sleeved silk top had four buttons below a low neckline, but could she bring herself to wear red? Would he remember telling her to wear red?

She flicked along through the hangers. Maybe green...

A half knock at the door, and her mother came in before she could speak. 'Darling, Mrs Brooks said you won't be in for dinner. Are you planning on coming with us? There should be space in the box, so we could...'

'I have dinner plans.' She could keep her mouth shut, but what if they arrived back before she did? She wasn't sixteen, yet her cheeks flushed.

'With whom?'

'John Knox. I ran into him in town. You remember, I met him at the Antiquaries.' It'd only been a few weeks, but it felt like months.

'The American who kept calling, and who left your party?'

Max nodded and crossed to her vanity. Her mother's reflection remained perfectly bland. Max tugged her dressing gown higher. She loathed the bloody thing now.

'I thought perhaps you were avoiding him deliberately.'

'No.'

'You might have said you were busy, since he asked for the same evening.'

'But I wasn't.' Max pulled a comb through her wet hair. 'He... it wasn't the first time he's asked.'

'Very well.'

'Mother.'

She turned back. 'Yes, darling?'

'You don't have to hide upstairs tonight so Dad can interrogate me.'

She smiled. 'I didn't plan to. He didn't ask the right questions, anyway.'

Max laughed.

Max came downstairs at a quarter to seven. Thank God her parents had to leave early for the curtain. Mr Rawls stood by the door. She still couldn't get used to the presence of a guard. Dad could call him a driver all he wanted, but Mr Rawls couldn't be anything but a guard.

'Hello, Miss Max.'

'Hello, Mr Rawls.' Her father came into the entryway before she could come up with anything to say. How did Mr Rawls feel about the theatre? Would he get to watch it at all, or would he scan for threats?

'What's this about a date? Your mother tried to even get out of going to the theatre so she could inspect him. But you know how we like *The Merry Widow.*'

'It was last minute,' Max said. 'I'm not sure...' She stopped. It was a date. And last time she'd said that... she swallowed.

'You look splendid.' Her father held her hands, and she realised how cold her own were. 'I've always liked Americans, as you know.'

Her mother came in after him. 'That's a lovely dress. Will you be warm enough?'

A reasonable question, given the way she'd been bundled up for the last week. The honeydew green chiffon jacket matched the pleated bodice of the dress. The chiffon was just opaque enough to obscure the faded marks on her upper arm. And it meant she wasn't wearing red. 'I'll take a coat.'

Mother touched Vivian's necklace and Max kept her face composed with effort. 'Is this new?'

'It's from Vivian.' No one asked. Everyone acted as if covering her throat was normal.

With air kisses by cheeks, they bustled out the door, Mr Rawls preceding her father. Max walked into the drawing room, where Charlie sat with a book, his leg propped up.

'Do you mind me going out?' she asked.

'I'd mind it worse if I had to go to the theatre with them. I'm going to go watch television as soon as you're gone. See if I can convince Mrs Brooks to make me a tray.'

'I'm sure she will.' Max looked in the mirror. Crimson lipstick, loose hair to hide the back of her neck. Small pearl earrings. Vivian's necklace was far gaudier than anything she would normally wear. She fussed with the ties of the jacket, which trailed to the hem of the white skirt.

'When are you going?'

The mantle clock said 7:03. 'Twenty-seven minutes.'

'Wanna play cards?'

'Sure.' She fetched a pack of cards and stepped out of her heels. She dealt gin rummy on the sofa cushion between them.

The doorbell rang precisely at seven thirty. She shifted, but Charlie grabbed her arm.

'I have absolutely nothing this evening. Finish this hand, at least. Besides, Harris is going to get the door.'

She heard it opening, and the rumble of John's voice. Footfalls came towards the room, and she suddenly remembered her shoes rested on the floor. Her mother would be horrified. She uncurled her legs, but hadn't reached her heels before Harris announced Mr Knox.

'Hello,' she said, rising.

John waved her back. 'Finish the hand.'

She sank back into her seat. 'John, this is my cousin Charlie Falkland. Charlie, John Knox.'

'Hiya,' Charlie said. He frowned at his cards.

'Charlie is clearly known for his poker face,' Max said.

'Who's winning?'

Charlie pointed at Max.

'Want some help?' John asked.

'Please.'

John leaned over Charlie's shoulder and tapped a card. 'Discard that one.'

'Hey,' said Max.

John laughed. 'That's an impressive cast.'

Max studied her own cards and drew one.

'I broke it playing football. I guess you'd say soccer? In two places.'

'Ouch.'

Max discarded the ace of diamonds.

'Take that one,' John said.

Max shifted a card in her own hand. She'd never had a date around Charlie before. Charlie's face glowed. He discarded a spade, and it was exactly what she needed. But for that sparkle of joy in Charlie's face... she scooped up the card and laid down her melds. 'Gin.'

'Damn,' Charlie said.

Max frowned. Mother would tell him off, but she didn't. Charlie totted up the points.

'Max has seventy-six,' Charlie said. 'I have rather less.'

'We should probably go,' Max said.

'Come on, one more hand,' Charlie said. 'Then you can properly beat me.'

Max looked at John, and he smiled. 'I don't mind if you don't.'

'But he helps me,' Charlie added.

'Okay.'

'How are you feeling?' John asked. He brought a straight-backed chair from the card table, and set it beside Charlie.

'It itches, but Aunt Nancy says I can't scratch it.' He turned to look at John. 'Oh, did you mean Max? She had the doctor around more recently than me.'

'I'm fine,' Max said. 'Sorry, do you want a drink?'

'No, thanks.'

Max dealt. Thank God her hand didn't hurt so much now. She'd still have to explain not drinking to John. Max watched as John pointed to cards and murmured to Charlie. The train ride she'd been so exhausted, but how much better was she now? She curled her legs back up under her full skirt.

Charlie won that hand, with serious coaching from John.

'Again,' he said.

'Nope. I've played with John; he'll just keep winning.'

'When?' Charlie asked, but he didn't wait for an answer. 'You're still ahead. Come on, please.'

He was as bad as George. Max took a deep breath, but John shrugged.

'Oh, for God's sake. Did you have a reservation?'

'It would be okay.'

'Excellent.' Charlie shuffled the cards quickly.

Max closed her eyes. Her first date—if she didn't count Angus—in four years and she was playing cards with her sixteen-year-old cousin.

John pointed out fewer cards to Charlie this time, and the hand progressed.

Harris appeared in the doorway. 'Are you staying for dinner, Miss Max?'

'No. Thank you. We're going as soon as this is over. Aren't you hungry, Charlie?'

Charlie showed his hand to John, who pointed again. He discarded a heart. Thank God.

Max picked it up, and had gin. She set her cards down. 'That's it.' She uncurled her legs and slid on her shoes. John rose.

'Thanks for playing, Mr Knox,' Charlie said.

'Anytime.'

Max gathered her handbag and gloves. 'Bye, Charlie.' In the hallway, John held her coat as she slipped her arms in. Harris handed John his hat and closed the door behind them.

'Sorry about that,' John said. 'I get too competitive.'

Max smiled. 'You cheered him up no end. Thanks.' She sighed. 'I was just worried he'd ask to come along. I would have said no, by the way.'

'Thank goodness.' His hand touched her back briefly and steered her to the left. 'What will he do?' He opened the door to his car, and Max climbed in.

'Watch television, I assume,' Max said when he closed his own door. 'My parents are at the theatre. I should have said, sorry.' He'd left *South Pacific* before the second act. Had he had a ticket at all?

'I assumed as much.' He started the engine.

The last time he'd driven her, she'd kissed him. This time she wouldn't have the excuse of whiskey. 'Where are we going?'

He pulled out of the parking space. 'I thought we might go to a Chinese restaurant, but then I wondered if you'd mind?'

She swallowed. 'Not at all. George and I used to… well, before he shipped out of course. I haven't had Chinese food in a while.' She paused. 'You don't—it seems odd that you'd want Chinese food after Korea.'

'I suppose. I really liked Japanese food, but that's nearly impossible to find, even in London.' He laughed a little. 'I left it rather late to get a reservation on a Friday night.'

Max lifted the menu. At least her nails weren't so painfully short, even after seven days. And she'd varnished them crimson again in the long days in her room. The restaurant's scarlet and gold motif nearly matched her polish.

'Wine?' John asked.

'No, thank you. You should though.'

'Anything?'

'Just water.' Her wound lay quiet under the neat bandage. 'Like Charlie said, I've been a bit ill.' And the memory of the coffee and the drug had been overwhelmed by the metallic taste of antibiotics.

'Are you better now?'

'Yes.' She smiled. 'And not contagious.'

John laughed. 'Good to know.'

Max read the menu, waiting for John to ask what she wanted. He didn't. The waiter approached, and looked at John expectantly. He gestured to Max, and she ordered herself, and then John ordered.

The waiter took away the menus, and Max shook her head. 'That was unexpected.'

He smiled. 'You strike me as someone who might prefer to ask for what she wants herself. I didn't mean to scandalise you.'

She'd never been on a date like this. 'Did George tell you how much I hate handing over my order?'

'No. I'm glad I guessed right though.'

So what did she want to ask? Was he at the distillery? 'Your suits are English,' she said instead.

'I came here, via Japan, after...'

'After Korea.'

He nodded. 'I'd been in the army since '43. I didn't have much in the way of civvies.' He smiled. 'And you? American music, American hair...'

Max laughed. Did she ever think she'd be able to laugh so soon after hearing the word Korea? 'A mix. My grandmother posts us a lot of things. From records to dresses to whole hams. Do you get sent much?'

'Some. Particularly when I got an apartment here.' He straightened the chopsticks resting by his plate. 'I've moved around a lot. They were happy for me to have a base.'

He didn't call it home. What would his flat look like? Rented, no doubt. Would he have bookcases? Could she be attracted to someone without bookcases?

'Would you ever move back?' he asked.

'I don't know. I like London.'

'Me too.' John smiled. 'I still haven't gotten to the British Library. Tell me about your PhD, please.'

Max laughed. 'Most people don't ask for a reason. You can tell me to shut up when it gets boring.' But he didn't. He asked questions and she talked more about it than she had since her viva. The food came, and they progressed on to general talk about living in London.

'How are you sleeping?' John asked after they'd finished eating.

Max shrugged. 'Same as usual.' She forced her lips up into a smile. 'Do I look tired?'

'Actually, yes,' John said.

'Gee, thanks.'

'Beautiful, but tired.' He reached across the table, but Max moved her hand to her lap quickly. 'I know the dive was difficult. Victor told me a little about it at the hospital.'

She'd worried about it, and now he'd brought it up. 'It's not the dive.' She fought the rush of nausea, the taste of rubber. 'I hurt someone. When I close my eyes there's blood and…' She swallowed. 'Noise.' The crash of his head on the concrete. 'And…' She stopped. The pressure of Richard's grip around her throat. She refused to touch her choker. She closed her eyes. John had called her beautiful. The silence stretched.

'He's also still alive. As are you.'

'That's not been in the papers.'

'I hear things.' He lifted his glass of water. 'Things we can't print.'

He didn't have to drink water just because she was. 'You're lying, John Knox. I know you were there. I recognised your voice. And Angus wasn't that good at dissembling.' He started to speak, but she wrapped her hand around his. 'Don't say anything. Thank you. If I'm right.'

'No need to thank me. I didn't do anything.'

When John climbed into the car and shut the door, he turned to her. Max couldn't be sure who initiated the kiss. These kisses were slow and exploratory, not the reckless rush of the kisses in Scotland. Max's hands closed over his shoulders. He traced the shell of her ear and she shivered. Their breathing was ragged when they stopped.

'You changed your perfume,' John said, his lips against her hair.

'No.' She tried to clear her fogged mind. 'It's my friend Vivian's. I borrowed her necklace.' John touched a bead and she winced. 'She wears rather more than I do.'

'It still hurts?'

'I told Vivian I was mugged. She's now convinced Scotland's the most dangerous place in the world.' She forced a smile. 'It's a fashion conundrum to cover your throat in summer in a dinner dress.'

'Is that why the doctor came?' His arms stayed around her. She didn't want to move.

'My hand. It got infected. The doctor didn't ask. God knows what he thought. My mother thinks I've had a cold.'

John lifted her hand. 'May I?' She nodded and he tugged gently at each fingertip until the glove came free. Victor had ripped it off. John's thumb brushed over the bandage, then circled her palm. Tingles danced across her skin.

'It's better. I'm fine.'

'You're amazing.'

'I'm sorry?' Max said. How did having injuries make her amazing?

'Most people would be a wreck after—well, what I assumed happened. You've handled it with aplomb.'

'I'll remember that at three in the morning.'

'You could always call me.' His even teeth shone in the streetlights.

'I doubt you'd be this cheerful.'

John kissed her again and her ungloved hand slid into his hair. 'I would be happy to talk to you at any time of the day or night, Max Falkland,' he murmured, before his mouth covered hers again.

Had she really thought once that John had no romantic interest in her? They only stopped when someone outside the car whistled. Max withdrew to her side of the car. 'I guess we're being less than discreet.'

John laughed. 'It's Soho. I can't think we're that shocking.' He turned on the car. They chatted about music as John drove towards her parents' house. He parked down the street, between streetlights.

'Are you free tomorrow?' he asked.

'No.' How she wished she could cancel. 'I'm going to a dinner party with my parents. My mother has been horrified I've stayed in for the last week.'

'You'd better keep Vivian's necklace then.'

Max nodded. She pulled her glove back on, aware she should have done that on the drive over. 'Thank you. I've had a lovely evening.'

'Thank you.'

How could she feel shy after the kisses they'd just shared?

John opened his door, and she gathered her bag as he came to her side. He helped her from the car, his hand warm even through her glove.

She rested her fingers on the sleeve of his coat. At the front door, John held onto her elbow.

'Max, I meant what I said about calling me. I know what it's like to wake in the middle of the night after an... experience.' He smiled. 'Do you still have my card?'

'I lost it.' In Richard's house, with the Russian's scrawl marking it. Luke written next to his home number. 'What name is your phone listed under?'

John paused just long enough to make her wonder. 'Mine, but it isn't.' He reached in his inside coat pocket and pulled out a folded sheet of paper. 'Here. All my numbers.'

Max slid it into her bag without looking at it. 'You knew I'd lost your card. John Knox, what is it that you do? And why do you wake up in the middle of the night?'

'I've been through two wars, honey. I wake up for a lot of reasons.'

'I'm sorry.' She looked down, at the creases of his trousers, the shininess of his shoes.

'Don't be. I'm not unusual.' He lifted her chin. 'Tonight has been wonderful.' His lips found hers and she leaned into his chest. The kiss ended, although he still held her. 'A curtain just twitched.'

Max laughed. 'I'm not surprised. Good night, John.'

'Good night.'

She closed the door behind her, realising they hadn't set another date. She sighed.

'Max?' Her mother didn't waste any time. She stood in the doorway of the drawing room. 'A nice time, darling?'

Max followed her in. Her father now played cards with Charlie at the table. Max sat on the sofa and took off her shoes. 'How was *The Merry Widow*? Who's winning?'

Mother examined her closely. 'How was your date?'

'I am, of course,' said her father. 'The production was dreadful.'

Had her lipstick smudged? 'Why?'

'Don't ask,' Charlie said.

'The adaptor went mad, I think,' Dad said. 'Different structure, changes to the plot—even the characters' names were different! Outrageous. I predict an early closure.' He smiled, and Max laughed.

'Please, no more musicals! Anyway, I like Mr Knox. More than any other bloke you've had around,' Charlie said. 'Come help me, Max?'

'You haven't met anybody except Daniel,' Mother said. 'Not that there have been many to meet.'

'Nancy.' Her father's voice lost its teasing edge. 'Leave her alone.'

'It's fine, Dad. He's very nice, and we went to a Chinese restaurant in Soho.' And he kissed really well, if she could bring herself to trust him.

'Chinese?'

Did her horror relate to George's death or the idea of Chinese for a first date? Max crossed to the table and sat beside Charlie. They kept their conversation strictly to the cards, and Mother retreated into one of her magazines.

That night, Max woke from a vivid dream of kissing John as she unbuttoned his shirt. Two am. She laughed. If she called him now... Still, it made a welcome change from the dreams of Scotland. She rolled over and went back to sleep.

For the dinner party, she wore the red Dior with Vivian's necklace. She was seated next to the Sterlings' younger son Harold, who had just finished his PhD at Cambridge. He prattled on about chemistry and his research for ages.

'It's great when they call you doctor for the first time,' Max said when he paused to gulp wine.

'Oh, Max, don't be silly. My viva was last week. You wouldn't be the first.' He laughed. 'You can still call me Harold, of course.'

'Perhaps I'd prefer it if you called me Dr Falkland instead,' Max said. Horrid Harold, George would have said.

'It's in archaeology, isn't it? The arts.' Harold puffed out a bit of air. 'That's not a real scientific discipline.'

Max flicked her eyes down to her plate. Could she tip it over his head? What would her mother say?

'Then I suppose you're suggesting my PhD isn't real either,' Dad said.

Harold apologised, but he still didn't ask about her PhD. She doubted she'd have gotten an apology if her father hadn't interrupted.

John had asked about her research. She tried to focus on the article she wanted to finish writing rather than thinking about John. Beautiful, he'd said.

'Max, darling,' Mother said, perhaps for the second time. 'Mrs Sterling was asking about the weather in Scotland.'

'Fine. A bit chilly, but that's to be expected in April.' She forced a smile.

'And did you know this traitor they arrested?' Harold asked.

Now he asked her questions? 'No.' She felt again the pressure of Richard's lips against hers, and she wiped her mouth with her napkin. She lifted her water glass. She'd kill for a tumbler of Oban. Hell, any whiskey would do.

'Such an amazing story. You don't think of that happening just there in Scotland.'

Would she face this all summer?

That night, Max woke again with the same dream of Richard's fingers closing around her throat, only this time she couldn't fight him. She gasped. She'd escaped, and he was in jail. Surely. Her father would know, but she couldn't ask him. Would John? Would he brush that question aside too?

But he'd said to call him. Anytime.

Max opened her bedside table drawer. John's sheet of paper crinkled as she withdrew it. He'd written H next to one, W to another. Joyce was the only word he'd written in full. Printed in black ink, and her home and work numbers also noted with a W and H. The paper fluttered in her fingers, the tremor in them not abating. She threw on her robe and walked through the open door to her study. She would read. Work. All the things she'd done for the last two weeks. And yet she opened the door to the hallway and brought the extension into the study. It only reached two feet into the room once she'd closed the door, so she sat on the floor next to it. Her fingers were too cold for May as she dialled. It rang and rang, but no one answered. Max slammed the receiver down and put the phone gently on the hall table. She pulled out an old archaeology journal and curled up on the sofa. She didn't need anyone to talk to. She needed to deal with it on her own.